A Fatal
Overture

Books by Kathleen Marple Kalb

A FATAL FINALE

A FATAL FIRST NIGHT

A FATAL OVERTURE

Published by Kensington Publishing Corp.

A Fatal Overture

Kathleen Marple Kalb

KENSINGTON
PUBLISHING CORP.

www.kensingtonbooks.com

KENSINGTON BOOKS are published by

Kensington Publishing Corp.
119 West 40th Street
New York, NY 10018

All Kensington titles, imprints and distributed lines are available at special quantity discounts for bulk purchases for sales promotion, premiums, fund-raising, educational or institutional use. Special book excerpts or customized printings can also be created to fit specific needs. For details, write or phone the office of the Kensington Special Sales Manager: Kensington Publishing Corp., 119 West 40th Street, New York, NY, 10018. Attn. Special Sales Department. Phone: 1-800-221-2647.

The K with book logo Reg. US Pat & TM Off.

Library of Congress Control Number: 2021949550

ISBN: 978-1-4967-2725-1

First Kensington Hardcover Edition: April 2022

ISBN: 978-1-4967-2731-2 (ebook)

10 9 8 7 6 5 4 3 2 1

Printed in the United States of America

Acknowledgments

First thanks, as always, go to my agent Eric Myers and my editor John Scognamiglio for giving Ella, and me, the chance to take this journey.

At the end of the day, these stories are all about family, the families we're born to, and the ones we create through work and love. So, I want to give special thanks and love to mine this time.

To my "work family," my colleagues at 1010 WINS Radio, much appreciation for understanding, support, and "book talk" when you'd really rather have been laughing about the latest stupid criminal story.

To my family of affection, my beloved writer, and non-writer, friends, thank you for beta reads, plot discussions, and encouragement. You've kept me going through more rough patches than you can ever know.

To my immediate family, endless gratitude. My mother listened to hours of story ideas and reassured me that someday, someone would indeed buy my books. My husband thought he married a sensible journalist but still backed me all the way when I jumped the line into fiction. And then there's my son. He didn't ask for his mom to be an author, but he stood by me every way he could. He's my hero.

Safe and well until next time,
Kathleen Marple Kalb

A Fatal Overture

Chapter 1

The Highland Ladies Step In

One would think that a day that ends in a marriage proposal, never mind unexpected visitors and violent death, would begin with some hint of the drama to come. But one would be sadly wrong. That Wednesday in late January 1900 started simply enough. A charity board meeting in the morning, followed by a good vocalization session and a fencing lesson in the early afternoon, the normal stuff of my life between productions and tours. And, at times, between murders.

"I surrender," the Comte du Bois said, ending our match with a grin that made him look even more than usual like an amiable gargoyle. "Well done, Mademoiselle Ella."

We bowed. It was the first time I had ever defeated my fencing master.

"Surrender!" Montezuma, my Amazon parrot, crowed from the rafters, bursting into a raucous drinking song that our sports writer friends had seen fit to teach him.

I foolishly thought this was the extraordinary moment of the day. Little did I know that all manner of complications awaited me before my head would touch the pillow again.

Hoping to leave the studio before Montezuma could get to the rather off-color final verse, I smiled and shook hands with my instructor, who was neither French nor a count but did a quite adequate job of convincing most people that he was. As a leading opera singer, I had met enough genuine aristocrats to know the difference, but since the good Mr. Mark Woods of the Bronx kept me in top form for my heroic trouser roles, he could call himself *Louis Quatorze* if it pleased him.

"Miss!" Sophia, our young housemaid, called, barreling through the door, out of breath and nearly frantic. "You have visitors!"

That wasn't especially unusual, though Sophia's level of upset certainly was. I put my foil in the cabinet and gave her a soothing pat on the arm. "What sort of visitors?"

"Um, three older ladies."

"Older ladies?" I sighed. Probably a committee from the latest benefit. While I usually sang whenever asked for such things, because neighborhood charities had often been the only thing standing between my late mother and me and the poorhouse, I would hopefully be in London this time. "Likely some charity or another. I hate to disappoint them."

"I don't think so, miss." From the terror in her hazel eyes, the ladies might have been a delegation from the Devil himself, which I somewhat doubted.

Although, considering the unusual things that happen here in Washington Square, I could not entirely discount the possibility.

"Well, let's find out." I shepherded our little ensemble downstairs, thinking about London, which was where I should have been at that exact moment.

The original plan had been to take our new opera, *The*

Princes in the Tower, for a winter engagement, but the two oldest children and husband of my leading lady, Marie de l'Artois, contracted scarlet fever. While everyone recovered, thank God, Marie did not want to pack up the family and cross the sea for the run until she, and they, had time to build themselves back up. So it was now a spring premiere.

The theater owner was annoyed at first, but with rapturous reviews pouring in from New York, and the clamor after the announcement of the delay, he realized the value of added anticipation and scheduled more dates. So he was now happily looking forward to a longer stand, which of course meant more money and acclaim for all.

Much less easily mollified was my . . . I'm not entirely certain what to call him. Beau is far too light a term, but there is not, to my knowledge, a formal designation for the man with whom one has an "understanding" but has not yet officially agreed to marry. Particularly in the wake of an amazing and unsettling farewell kiss followed by an utterly shocking, and mutual, declaration of love.

Simple enough to call him Gil. To give him his full dignity, Gilbert Saint Aubyn, Duke of Leith. Trained as a barrister (trial lawyer), modern enough to accept the idea of a wife who sings, but not enough to want her to vote. Good company, and awfully good to look at. Without a doubt the man I want to marry and father my children. The husband and children I did not think I wanted or needed a year ago.

But we had yet to resolve how we would manage a family life around an ocean, a singing career, a duchy, and heaven only knew what else. And I saw no reason for haste in upending my very happy and comfortable existence until we had a good answer for that. My guilty secret: I was not at all sorry to have been kept on this side of the Atlantic for a couple of extra months.

Gil had understood entirely about Marie's children and had sent telegrams of concern. But the letters between us had first become more passionate and then, in the last exchange, noticeably more tense.

I loved him. I wanted him. But I did not think it was fair to expect me to give up everything I am to become his wife. I knew he did not really expect me to give up *everything*, but I did not yet know how much he *did* expect. The answer to that question would tell the story . . . and I was more than a little afraid of what it might be.

Not to mention afraid he hadn't really meant what he said just before he left, since he'd never written it. If he had, how difficult, even for a British aristocrat, would it be to replace "Yours with much esteem" with "Love" at the end of a letter?

I had reached the foyer, the very scene of that disconcerting declaration. Resolutely, I brushed off the memory and shook hands with the *comte*, then bowed him out. After a chuckle at the glimpse of myself in fencing breeches in the hall mirror, I smoothed my reddish-blond hair and walked into the drawing room. My visitors would simply have to tolerate it.

Three older ladies had taken over the room. They seemed respectable and harmless enough, with no hint of evil intent or provenance.

No scent of brimstone, either, though perhaps a tiny trace of Hungary water.

The two sitting on the settee were tall and spare, the third, in the big wing chair normally occupied by my sizeable cousin Tommy, small and plump. All were dressed with elegance and care in traveling suits, the tall silver-haired ones in stark black, the smaller lady in dark gray that set off the pale copper color that remained in her hair, the outfits topped with sensible yet stylish hats. On first glance, I guessed Society matrons of some description, though more elegant and reserved than most.

As I drew closer, I realized something more was in play. From their features and coloring, I suspected they were sisters; all had similar high cheekbones, sharply straight noses and wide-set eyes, and the eyes were a distinctive ice blue.

A very distinctive ice blue. I had only seen that eye color once before. Which almost certainly meant I was in far bigger trouble than I'd thought. I might in fact have been safer with the Old Scratch.

"Good afternoon," I said in my most carefully polite tone. "Shall I ring for some tea?"

"Well, aren't you a pretty and nice one, even in your silly breeches?" the small lady replied in a crisp London accent faintly flavored with Scotland. "I understand why Gil is so taken with you."

"I'm sorry?"

"Oh, there'll be plenty of time for niceties later," she replied, those familiar eyes burning into mine. "So when are you going to put my son out of his misery and marry him?"

"Flora!" chided one of the taller ladies.

"You really should . . ." began the other.

She gave what I assumed were her siblings an irritated glance and let out a little sigh. "I suppose I should at least take care of introductions."

"Yes, please," I managed.

"As you've no doubt deduced, I am Flora Saint Aubyn, Dowager Countess of Blyth, mother of the incorrigible Gilbert."

"Delighted." I bowed, knowing that it would be bad form to shake hands.

"As are we. These are my sisters, Caledonia, Lady Mac-Quarrie and Charlotte, Dowager Lady Byewell."

"And I'm sure you know I am Ella Shane." I would actually have been quite surprised if they did not know I was born Ellen O'Shaughnessy to an Irish father and Jewish mother on the Lower East Side, but I saw no need for lengthy explanations at the moment. I bowed again. "A privilege to meet you all. Allow me to offer you tea."

"That would be lovely. The hotel staff apparently does not know how to make a proper cup." Caledonia appeared truly anguished.

"And the less said about the luncheon the better," added Charlotte.

I moved to sit in the other chair. "I apologize for my attire. I was taking a fencing lesson."

Countess Flora laughed, transforming her face, just as Gil's laugh did his. "My dear son told me you have to dress appropriately for your work. I'm not troubled by it."

"Neither are we."

It was unclear if Charlotte or Caledonia said it, but it clearly didn't matter.

Mrs. Grazich, our cook, appeared just then with the tea tray, no doubt having been tipped off to be at the ready. I poured, and the ladies busied themselves investigating the various dainties on offer. Mrs. G was definitely in the mood to impress, having scrambled an exceedingly elegant display of little tea cakes decorated with icing flowers, cucumber sandwiches in various shapes and tiny apple tarts.

This had far less to do with our august visitors and far more to do with Mrs. G's impending nuptials. She was spending her last weeks before marrying our dear friend and informal uncle, the noted sports editor and essayist Preston Dare, by expressing her happiness in elaborate cooking and confectionery. Tommy, I and our friends were more than pleased to share the joy, on all counts.

At any rate, once everyone was appropriately refreshed, I accepted praise for the well-brewed tea and delicious and decorative accompaniments, and allowed the ladies to get to their business. I returned to my chair with my simple cup, skipping sweets for the moment with the thought that I might enjoy them more later—and the faint hope that I'd somehow misunderstood the earlier discussion.

"Right, then," Countess Flora said, exactly as her son does when he's set to begin a serious conversation. "We have come to urge you to come to London with due speed and, hopefully, to welcome you to the family."

I had not misunderstood, nor would I ever have expected this. If I'd given any thought at all to Gil's mother, I would have expected at least mild disapproval, considering my profession and parentage. I took a sip of tea and offered a careful reply. "Thank you most kindly."

"I am certain you will be a positive addition to the clan. But why have you not come to London?" As blunt as her son could be when provoked to it.

"You do understand that there was sickness in my singing partner's family?"

"I do." Her eyes held mine for a full measure. "You understand that you could easily have come to London on the original schedule and waited for her to join you for the run?"

"Does he think that?"

"I make it a practice never to guess what my son thinks." She sipped her tea. "I only know that he's quite unhappy over the delay and appears to think more is involved than the health of Madame de l'Artois's wee ones."

I looked into my own cup.

"Surely you do not have another suitor."

"Of course not. I—" I broke off before the damning admission. I could not in any propriety tell her that I love her son. I wondered if he had told her that he said he loved me.

"Then what?" From the gentle note in her voice, and

her searching gaze, she certainly knew enough, if not the exact details.

"I am not just a woman, Dowager Countess. I am a singer, the leading artist in my own company. However much I may want to marry a man, I cannot just leave the career and life I have built."

"He hasn't been fool enough to ask you to give up everything for him."

"No."

"Well, that's a relief." She smiled. "You are worried that he's going to turn into some old-fashioned Bluebeard and lock you away for himself the minute he gets his ring on your hand."

When she put it like that, I had to laugh. So did the other ladies.

"Not exactly, but there's a grain of truth there, Dowager Countess."

She sighed and shook her head. "You have an excuse, having grown up a poor orphan girl."

I bristled.

The dowager countess patted my hand. "I mean no insult, my dear. Our family needs an infusion of fine, hard-working, American stock, and good Jewish common sense besides. But you would not know that marriage contracts are quite common in some social circles, or what to demand."

"Marriage . . . contract?" I was not sure what part of that incredible statement shocked me most.

"Of course." She smiled. "My poor silly son should have thought of it. You'll simply agree on terms. A tour every other year, or a New York run each winter, or whatever you two find appropriate. You make an agreement, sign it, and all done."

"But women have no legal rights once married."

"Except those granted in their marriage settlements, of course."

I stared at her. It could not really be that simple.

"Of course it's that simple." All that and she read my mind, too? "When two people from families with great holdings marry, they have a contract setting out who has control of what, and often where they live and all. You two will be no different."

The other sisters were smiling.

"Quite so." Countess Flora beamed at me. "Now, may I telegraph my son that you will be coming to London ahead of schedule?"

"I'm not sure, I have engagements, I . . ." I realized I was blushing and stammering like a silly maiden half my age. Silly maiden was right at the moment, for certain.

"You've put a great deal on the poor dear girl, Flora."

"Only right." Charlotte shushed Caledonia. "She's strung poor Gil along quite long enough."

"Well, I think we can all agree on that." Countess Flora gave a decided nod. "We've taken quite enough of your time for now. Why don't you meet us for luncheon tomorrow?"

"Please," I said, clinging to graceful manners in hopes that it might restore my control of the situation, "it would be my pleasure to host you."

"We'd be guaranteed a good meal at least," muttered Caledonia.

"Anything but turtle soup," sighed Charlotte. "Or what they *claimed* was turtle soup."

"Very well," the dowager countess pronounced, shooting her sisters a sidelong glance. "We'll look forward to it."

They rose and swept to the foyer like a procession of full-rigged ships.

I bowed to each and when I reached Countess Flora, she pulled me down and planted a very deliberate kiss on my cheek.

"Welcome to the family, my dear."

"Thank you, Dowager Countess." I decided it would be very undiplomatic to point out that we were still a rather long way from that. Or that one other person might have an important say in the matter.

She sniffed. "I'd far prefer you to call me Mother, but I suppose I shall have to tolerate that until the banns are posted. Be quick about it, will you?"

And there the matter might have rested for the night, if Charlotte (or possibly Caledonia) had not found a dead man in her bathtub when they returned to the hotel.

Chapter 2

Family Dramas

Tommy was home, and I had neatened myself up into a very sweet lavender sprig-print merino afternoon dress by the time the messenger from the dowager countess's hotel arrived, the calm words of the note's few sentences entirely undermined by the hurry and flamboyance of her hand:

> *An unfortunately dead man has appeared in the bathtub in our suite. We have called the police, but please do come if you can.*

We grabbed our coats and hats and set out to walk the short distance to the Waverly Place Hotel, the same place Gil stayed when in the City.

"His mother and aunts are here?" Tommy asked as bits of leftover snow from the storm earlier in the week crunched under our boots.

"Yes, heaven help us."

His bluish-green eyes narrowed and his jaw tightened. I recognized the protective scowl, the same expression that was the last thing more than one man who'd insulted me saw before stars from a justly famous right cross. Plenty of people still know the name Tommy Hurley for his boxing championships, not for managing the Ella Shane Opera Company.

We've been looking out for each other since I was an eight-year-old orphan and he was a twelve-year-old boy who didn't quite fit in with the other brutes in our Lower East Side neighborhood. He was kind to me when his mother, my aunt Ellen, took me in, and I returned the favor by jumping in on his side anytime he felt the need to respond to bullies yelling things like "sissy."

While we in the family know Tommy isn't the marrying kind, no one's got the right to insult him, and I was happy to do my worst to anyone who tried. And after Tommy grew half a foot and became the star of his boxing gym, people amazingly enough stopped assuming that there was something wrong with a fellow who loves music, books and his family, and didn't join in the other boys' rough talk.

There is, of course, not one thing in the world wrong with Tommy, or the brother who doesn't marry in general. Plenty of Irish, and other, families have a brother or sister who isn't the marrying kind, and many, like us, see it as a blessing to have a relative who can care for an elderly parent or give special attention to a godchild who might otherwise be lost in the family shuffle. Or, like Tommy's mother and me, just rather selfishly rejoice that we will never have to share our beloved boy with another woman.

These days, we don't have to worry about scrapping in the street, but we do run into any number of complications with the company and friends. Some friends are better than others.

"Are they here to break up the match?" he asked.

"No, no. To encourage it."

Tommy burst out laughing. "His mother sailed across the ocean to urge you to marry him?"

"With her sisters in tow."

"Good heavens, Heller, now you're really done for."

"Probably. She tells me we could make a marriage contract that grants me the right to continue my career."

He nodded, considering. "That would solve the issue, if true."

"We'll have to work out the details."

"In which no doubt lurks the Devil," he agreed. "But that would surely settle matters."

"Quite possibly."

His serious expression gave way to a grin. "Then congratulations."

"What?"

"On your impending engagement, of course. If it's that simple, you'll be married by summer."

I shook my head. "Has anything in our lives ever been so simple?"

"We can hope, can't we?"

We were at the hotel. Tommy held the door for me, and we were immediately welcomed by a very young Black-Irish copper who recognized him.

"Champ. Dan McNeely. My brother Joe boxed at the same gym as you."

Tommy gave him a warm handshake. "Glad to meet you, officer. This is my cousin, Miss Ella Shane."

The officer smiled. "I've heard of her. A pleasure, miss."

We exchanged a friendly shake as well, and he nodded to the stairs. "You'll be wanting to see the ladies upstairs. Detective Riley is already there. Suite on the top floor, all three of them sharing. Guess English ladies don't like to be alone."

"They're Scots, officer," I corrected.

"More like us Irish?"

"A bit," I agreed.

"Then they definitely like to travel in packs."

We all laughed, but then the officer remembered his demeanor.

"Sorry. It is a very serious matter."

"Has the coroner come?"

"Not yet, but he will. Of course, Miss Shane will wish to gather up the ladies before that happens."

I nodded and didn't bother to correct his old-fashioned assumption that ladies should be kept from serious or gory matters. In this particular case, it was probably a good idea.

As we crossed the first landing, I saw a maid slinking through a hall. The red hair straggling out from her cap looked familiar, but surely not. Her amber eyes met mine. Surely yes. Miss Hetty MacNaughten, crack investigative reporter of the *Beacon*, and my good friend, was going to owe me some answers.

I urged Tommy along so he didn't notice her, and we kept going.

Up in the suite, Countess Flora was standing in the center of the sitting room with Cousin Andrew the Detective, a relative of Tommy's best friend, Father Michael, and a family friend in his own right. The detective appeared to be attempting to interrogate the dowager countess, who was upbraiding him.

Ladies Charlotte and Caledonia were on the settee, one in a blanket over a wrapper, holding what appeared to be a generous whisky, the other still in a traveling ensemble, tending to her sister, patting her arm and murmuring reassurances that the afflicted did not seem to find soothing or necessary. Both seemed more annoyed than upset, actually.

"Ella, darling!" Countess Flora spotted me first and walked over, holding out her hands. "This nice young man is attempting to convince us that we must find other accommodations."

Cousin Andrew met my eyes over her head as she took my hands and kissed my cheek. I'd seen that expression of utter exasperation on our copper more than once; he was certainly wishing that someone, anyone, else at his precinct had caught this case. "Perhaps you would acquaint Her—Grace?—with American police procedure?"

"I am only a countess, dear boy. Ma'am is quite sufficient."

"All right."

"Now, when dear Ella here marries my son, you *will* have to call her Your Grace. Do you know each other?"

"Yes, Dowager Countess," I said quickly. "Detective Riley is a friend of our family. Have you met my cousin, Thomas Hurley?"

Tommy stepped up with a bow, holding back both a handshake and a laugh. "Honored to meet you."

She gave him an approving look-over. "Ah, you're the manager and protector."

"Essentially." He smiled. "Ella doesn't require a great deal of managing or protection, but we do well together."

The countess returned the smile. "I imagine you do."

For a moment, they just stood there, amiably taking each other's measure and pleased with what they saw. Only a fool would not like and respect Tommy, but I was happy to see that she passed muster with him.

"Well," she said finally, "I am glad you two are here. Perhaps we can sort all of this now."

Cousin Andrew made a sound that was clearly the biting back of a sigh of relief. "Why don't we start with what happened?"

The countess nodded. "We were preparing for dinner, planning a quiet meal en suite in hopes that the room service might be less wretched than what we suffered in the dining room at luncheon. Caledonia decided she wanted a bit of a soak first, even though really, one doesn't generally do that at this time of day—"

"The body?" Cousin Andrew asked.

"Well, she went to run the bath. We heard a shriek—"

"I did not shriek, sister," Caledonia cut in coldly.

"She never shrieks," Charlotte agreed. "It was more of a shout."

"No, not a shout." Caledonia turned on her, and they started bickering. Of course, the countess joined in. It was hard to be sure, because some of the conversation appeared to be in Gaelic, but from the sound of things, it seemed they were returning to lingering grievances dating from their long-ago girlhood.

Cousin Andrew looked to me. I held up my hands. Tommy shook his head.

We might have been standing there for the next year if not for a sharp voice behind us.

"Mother, what have you done now?"

The voice was quickly followed by my first sight of Gilbert Saint Aubyn in months, his tall form in a heavy overcoat, blowing right past all of us to loom over his mother, who was a good foot shorter than him.

"Gil! What a delightful surprise." She got on tiptoe and kissed him on the cheek as if he were visiting her at teatime. "And of course you'll want to greet your lovely bride and her cousin."

"My . . . bride?" He stared down at his mother, still not looking at me.

"Of course, *mo laochain.* I've explained everything to dear Ella, and all that's left is for you two to work out the marriage contract. When do you want to announce the engagement?"

"Perhaps I should talk to Miss Shane first?"

"Well, silly, she's right here."

"Oh, of course." He turned to me.

Our eyes met, and my months of doubts and worries and recriminations vanished in an almost audible snap. Everything that had been in his aspect when he looked at me before was still there, and the current that crackled between us, too, stronger than ever. For a moment, I could hardly breathe, and I knew he felt the same.

We stood there silently for a full measure or more. I wanted to fly into his arms, and I had the distinct impression he wanted to pull me to him, but that, of course, was not an option. Even if we had an actual engagement rather than an "understanding," no unmarried couple would embrace in public. Most married couples would not.

"Shane," he said finally, his voice soft and low.

I held out my hand. "Good to see you again."

He laced fingers with mine, a much more intimate gesture than propriety would encourage, but no real transgression. "Good, indeed."

"Oh, yes." It came out as a sigh.

"See? Of course she wants to marry you!" crowed the countess.

We broke apart then, suddenly embarrassed and shy, both clasping our hands behind our backs.

"The murder?" Cousin Andrew cut in.

The entire cast turned to him.

"Are you quite sure it's a murder?" Gil asked.

"Well, he surely didn't stab himself in the eye," observed the detective.

Chapter 3

A Quiet Evening at Washington Square

By dinnertime, the ladies were properly settled in the guest rooms on my floor of the town house, exclaiming over the comfort and coziness of our establishment. Coziness for certain, since we would all be living cheek-by-jowl for the duration of the visit.

I was afraid to ask for an estimate on that.

I was also not entirely sure how I had ended up hosting the entire ensemble.

After talking to each of the ladies in turn, Cousin Andrew had once again gently informed them that they could not stay in the suite. Somewhere in that conversation, I offered to host them for dinner while arrangements could be sorted out, which they understood for an invitation to stay with us.

Too stunned to correct them, and afraid of offending the family of a man I did, after all, hope to marry one day, I merely shepherded them back to the house and asked them to have their things sent on.

We do, as it happens, have a good number of spare rooms, since Tommy and I each have a floor essentially to ourselves. Normally, this is a luxury that we greatly enjoy, having grown up in a tight little tenement on the Lower East Side.

Over the years, we'd entertained a guest or two, usually visiting family, singers who were playing a benefit, or sports writer friends of Tommy's in town for some event or other. We had never, though, been blessed with three at once.

Sophia and Rosa turned a little pale at the sight of the ladies, and I resolved to diplomatically remind our guests that American household workers are rather different from British domestics. And to pay the young ladies extra for the duration.

In any case, Mrs. G rose admirably to the occasion with a simple but elegant meal, finished with a truly lovely meringue torte filled with luscious chocolate mousse and trimmed with candied orange peel. While our guests merely appreciated the torte as a pretty and tasty dessert, I smiled at its true significance.

Preston, Mrs. G's fiancé and our beloved informal uncle, is exceedingly fond of lemon curd tarts, which means a great deal of excess egg whites. Fortunately, many others in the household, not least me, adore good meringue in all its forms. Victory for all.

And most certainly victory for true love, since I had no doubt Preston would be slipping by to see his lady and partake of the said tarts before proceeding to a late night at the *Beacon*. Preston had always been fond of Mrs. G, and she of him, but it was only in recent months that their acquaintanceship had become more. It was a joyful surprise to us all, since Mrs. G had been widowed for a decade, and Preston had shown no interest in anything other than light and respectful flirtation with barmaids and shopgirls since a cholera outbreak claimed his wife and child some thirty years ago.

Now, though, they were as blooming with happiness as any young couple. More so, because they had earned it.

May we all be so happily matched if we are the marrying kind.

After dinner, we adjourned to the drawing room for a convivial family scene.

I had poured coffee for all and was preparing to settle onto my chair when Sophia appeared in the doorway, frantically yet quietly trying to catch my eye. Tommy and Gil were parsing the differences between snow-removal methods in New York and London, with the occasional mournful exclamation from the ladies, and I had no trouble slipping out unnoticed.

In a corner of the foyer crouched a smallish figure in an immaculate but worn black coat and an equally carefully kept but probably secondhand hat. I recognized the red knot under the brim before she turned, but otherwise, I would never have known it was Hetty.

"Yardley isn't here, is he?"

"You lucked out. He has a big boxing tourney tonight." Yardley Stern, Tommy's sports writer friend, not to mention Hetty's colleague and perhaps someday more, was at some large bout in the outer boroughs.

She let out a sigh of relief. "Good. I don't need another lecture on the potential danger to my virtue on this one."

That certainly piqued my concern. "What?"

"I'll tell you when we go for a walk the day after tomorrow. In the meantime, don't say anything to anybody."

"All right," I said slowly, catching something odd in her aspect.

"*Anybody*, Ella. I know your man's in town again."

"And I don't tell him everything." I left the 'your man' comment for the moment. Gil and I have an agreement:

we never lie, but we have each given the other permission to leave out information we cannot share at a particular moment.

"Good. Keep it that way."

"Does this have anything to do with the dead man in the ladies' tub?"

Hetty winced as if I'd slapped her. "No more than anything else does."

I gave her a hard look. "Really?"

"The murder is definitely not my story."

It was an odd response—I could not really call it an answer. "What does that mean?"

"It means I'm not telling you anything else right now."

"Just tell me you're safe." I had to at least press her on that.

"As safe as I need to be."

Once again, I caught something strange, but I wasn't sure what, and I knew she would give me no more right now. "All right, then."

"See you in the park Friday morning—it's my half day off."

"Fair enough. Home safe."

"Thanks."

She scurried out the door. I picked up a recent copy of the *Beacon* with a banner article (sadly not Hetty's) on the record-setting cold of a day or so before.

"See, it simply never gets this cold in London," I said, walking back in and neatly covering my absence.

Weather is always a useful topic of conversation; everyone has an opinion and is happy to express it at length, no matter what the elements may bring. Certainly, it set up a lively discussion to carry us through most of that evening.

It entertained us, in fact, until the fire was low, and the younger members of the company were starting to become rather fatigued. Our august guests, however, like other matriarchs of our acquaintance, seemed to be quite inexhaustible.

Finally, in a minor act of desperation, Tommy offered to guide the aunts up to the studio to greet Montezuma, with the hope that he could then take them to their accommodations. I suspected he was diplomatically leaving the countess, Gil and me to any private discussion, but for yet a while longer, we talked only of the care, feeding and personality of Amazon parrots.

The countess regaled us with a few colorful tales of the misdeeds of her own companion, Robert Burns, who shared the poet's gift of language, but also a less exalted facility for drinking songs. Much like a certain avian of my acquaintance.

During all of this, Gil seemed to be merely tolerating the conversation, and as she warmed to her topic, I noticed a muscle flicking in his jaw, which usually meant he was at the limits of his patience. I was not wrong.

When she paused for a breath, during a tale of Robert Burns's shocking comments at a ladies' tea, Gil turned to her.

"Mother, please go."

"Gil, darling." She blinked a little at his bluntness. "I planned to stay up and read this fascinating new book from dear Ella's collection."

"Read upstairs. I'm certain Shane has lamps in her spare rooms."

The countess looked from Gil to me, and smiled brightly. "Ah. You want some time to spark with your sweetheart."

"Spark?" I repeated slowly. I knew what it meant, but I was stunned to hear the slang from her.

"I have two rather fast grandnieces, Ella dear. The younger set is entirely too liberal, but really, once one's engaged, there's no harm in enjoying the privileges . . ."

"*Mother.*"

Her smile turned to a wicked grin, hinting of the spirited young Highland lady she'd once been, and she rose, picking up her book. We both stood to bid her farewell, and she patted my arm with a knowing nod before turning to her boy.

"Good night." She gave another musical chuckle as she got on tiptoe and kissed his cheek, then shot me a last smile and swept out of the room. "I hope it's a very good night, *mo laochain.*"

Chapter 4

Sparking by the Fire

"What did she just call you?" I asked as the countess's footsteps trailed up the stairs.

Gil blushed. "Oh, just something Scots mothers call their boys."

"Translate, please." I wanted to know, and I was really amused by his discomfiture.

" 'My little hero.' "

I managed to keep my reaction to a smile. "Sweet."

"I suppose. She's incorrigible. So are they all."

"They're delightful." I sat down on the settee by the fire. "If she calls you her little hero, what do you call me?"

"Mo chridhe?" He'd used the endearment once when comforting me after a painful memory and just before our last kiss. "Ah, a rather more serious thing."

He joined me on the settee, perhaps a little closer than was proper for a courting couple, even with an "understanding," and very carefully and deliberately picked up my hand, slowly lacing his fingers with mine.

"It means 'my heart.' Which is about right, I think, Shane."

"Yes." The syllable was all I could manage, sitting so close to him, with the warmth of his hand in mine and the intensity of his eyes on my face. Inevitably, I found myself remembering our farewell kiss, a really rather small transgression followed by the far larger matter of the words we'd exchanged.

One can walk away from a connection, a friendship, even a kiss, after all. Not so easy to forget that declaration.

So what do we do now?

We sat silently, watching each other, for what seemed like an eternity, enjoying each other's presence, while anticipating—perhaps dreading—what could come next.

Finally, Gil spoke.

"I meant what I said before I left." He held my gaze.

"So did I."

Bashert. My mother's word. I could almost hear it in her soft, accented voice: Hebrew for "meant" or "fated." She always described meeting and falling in love with my father at Immigration that way. Frank O'Shaughnessy and Malka—Molly—Steinmetz never had much of a chance at a happy life, but they made the best of what they had, until typhoid took him, just over a year after their marriage. She survived till I was eight, scraping together a living for us with the piecework that was all she could manage with her limited education and the consumption that would kill her.

But though the marriage brought her little but poverty and pain, she never regretted it because she had that brief time with the only man for her.

As I am here now with the only man for me. But I'm not my mother. I have so much more to lose.

"I know it's not that simple," Gil admitted, looking down at my hand in his. "But although she's taken entirely the wrong tack, my mother has supplied a reasonable so-lution. We can negotiate a resolution and put it into a mar-riage contract."

"Is that really legal?" I was a bit dubious, but he should know. My beloved had trained as a barrister, a trial lawyer, before several serious outbreaks and minor Imper-ial skirmishes cleared his path to the coronet.

"Perfectly. We agree on terms, and you maintain your career and your rights."

"It could be the answer."

"But that does rather beg the question," he continued, taking my other hand.

"What question is that?"

"The only one that matters." He took a breath, as if steadying himself, then fixed me with a direct and serious gaze. "Miss Ella Shane, Ellen O'Shaughnessy, *Meira bat Malka*, will you do me the great honor of becoming my wife?"

My eyes filled at the proposal, the careful inclusion of my stage name, my birth name—even my correct Hebrew name, which he would have had to research—and what he meant by it. He wants and loves all of me. For a second, I had to struggle to find my voice, long enough that uncer-tainty crept into his face.

"Yes!" I said quickly. "Oh, yes."

The uncertainty was replaced by a little-boy grin for a moment and then something entirely adult. "I assume you'll want to keep it private until we settle the contract."

"That's wise, I think."

He leaned a fraction closer. "But since we are, in fact, engaged . . ."

"There's no harm in sealing the agreement, in private."

"None at all."

The last syllable died against my lips as he kissed me, very carefully, almost reverently, the official acknowledgment of the engagement rather than any real expression of the passion between us. When he drew back, I admit feeling a bit off balance, perhaps even a little disappointed.

But then he grinned at me with a truly naughty gleam in his eyes. Wicked Duke, indeed. "Spark?"

I blushed. "As you may be aware, some of the more adventuresome young folks sometimes spend evenings together kissing and cuddling."

"They do, do they?"

"Yes, I agree with your mother, it's much too fast for my taste."

"But an engaged couple of years and discretion," Gil said, pulling me closer again, "might reasonably allow themselves a little sparking."

"Perhaps a little." Suddenly, as his arms tightened around me, I felt terribly shy and more than a bit out of my depth. Good Irish girls are taught to protect their virtue and reputation until they marry, and exactly nothing about what they are supposed to do once wed.

Never mind engagement, a weird in-between place where promises have been made, but everything could still fall apart, leaving one as damaged goods or worse if unlucky or reckless. I knew of a few girls in the old neighborhood who had lived to regret celebrating their engagements, even if I had precious little idea how the celebration actually occurred.

Gil, ever good at reading me, backed away and just looked at me for a measure or more, then very gently traced the line of my face. "I love you, Shane."

I nodded. "I love you."

He moved farther toward the other side of the settee, his face serious. "And as much as I would enjoy sparking, I don't want you thinking I would ever take advantage."

"Oh." Now I really was quite disappointed, not least in myself. Was I truly so old-fashioned that I couldn't celebrate my engagement with a kiss or two with my new fi-ancé? And good heavens, didn't the man deserve something for his trouble? What must he think of me, sitting here, coolly talking it all through as if I'm signing a new tenor?

"Kiss me," I said.

Gil stared for a second, no doubt puzzled by my sudden change of mind.

"It *is* a privilege of engagement."

He smiled and took my hands again. "I'm quite fond of enjoying the privileges."

The kiss started slow and careful, but quickly became more passionate, Gil pulling me into his arms as I responded to him. He was the only man I'd ever kissed, and he'd never kissed me like this, holding me so close and tight, his mouth warm on mine.

Sparking, indeed. A silly name for something so amazing.

"Heller, I—"

The sound of Tommy's voice was embarrassing enough. His genuine, happy laugh was worse.

Gil and I instantly pulled apart, neither of us able to summon demeanor or words for that moment.

"Well," Tommy said, trying for sternness, but with a strong note of amusement still in his tone, "I assume I can be the first to congratulate you on your engagement."

"Yes . . . I'm sorry . . . We . . ." Gil tried and failed to manage a cool reply as he returned to his side of the settee and straightened his tie.

"Engaged or no, you're lucky it was me and not Preston." Tommy laughed again. "He'd punch you in the nose."

"Probably deservedly," Gil said with a guilty glance at me.

I smoothed my hair and glared at Tommy. "We *are* privately engaged, Toms. Subject to settlement of the marriage contact."

"And privately celebrating," he teased.

"Well, yes," I admitted, as I realized that there was a trace of rose petal lip salve visible on Gil's lower lip. Good thing I don't rouge.

"Good for you." That to me. To Gil, with a big smile, "Well, it's about time she accepted you. Welcome to the family."

They shook hands. "Thank you, Tom. We'll likely need your help working out terms for opera seasons and whatnot."

"Glad to. In the morning, though? It's well past midnight."

Gil took the meaning and nodded. "I should return to my hotel."

Tommy nodded back, the men agreeing amongst themselves. "We should all get some rest."

"Thank you again, Shane, for accommodating my mother and aunts."

"Of course."

"Why don't you walk your man to the door, Heller?" Toms said, in easy acknowledgment of Gil's new position. "Good night, Barrister."

"Good night, Tom."

In the foyer, I quickly brushed away the bit of pink salve from his lip, and Gil chuckled, then took my hands. "Well, fiancée, what think you?"

"*Bashert.*"

"What?"

"My mother's word for her marriage with my father. Hebrew for 'meant,' or 'fated.' "

He nodded. He knew I almost never speak of my parents. "A good word for us, too."

"I think so."

For a long moment, we were silent. Even a happy milestone like a marriage brings the memory of those who will never see it.

Finally, he squeezed my fingers and looked down at my hands. "At some point, there will be a ring and other jewels."

"I've never cared much for them."

"We won't be gaudy, but I like the idea of my ring on your hand."

"When you put it like that"—I returned his smile—"perhaps I should let you give me something very simple."

"Gilbert! You're still here?"

We both turned to see the countess steaming down the stairs, thankfully still fully dressed, if not in the least ashamed to have interrupted our private moment.

"Mother." He let go of my hands and turned, shaking his head.

"I thought you might come up to the mark tonight. Are congratulations in order?"

"Yes," he said through gritted teeth.

"At the moment," I added, "just privately, until the contract is settled."

She beamed and drew me into a hug I couldn't have resisted if I'd wanted to. I was surprised to find that I didn't mind. "Glorious! I'll be delighted to have you as my new daughter."

"Thank you." I smiled back. "I'm delighted, too."

The countess gave me an assessing look, much like her barrister son's. "I know you lost your mother at a terribly young age, dear, and of course I could never take her place. You don't have to call me Mother if you don't want to."

It was of course far too early to love her, but I was suddenly very glad indeed to have her as my future mother-in-law. I had been willing to call her Mother because my own parent was always Mama . . . but her words warmed me in a way I hadn't expected. "Thank you for understanding, but it's really all right. I will be honored."

"The honor is mine, dear. Now, you will need a ring."

"Mother," Gil cut in with a warning tone.

"Americans care much more about engagement rings than we do, *mo laochain*. She deserves some kind of sign after all." She took a ring from the first joint of her pointer finger, an old Romantic fashion, probably from her no doubt adventuresome youth. Beaming, she handed the delicate gold band of flowers, each with a different colored stone in the center, to him. "It's small, but quite good. Until you can get to a proper jeweler and buy something suitable, it will do nicely."

Gil, squirming and blushing like the misbehaving little boy she was treating him as, took the ring and turned to me. "Shane?"

Of course, neither of us had a choice in the matter. I smiled and held out my hand. He tried to put the ring on the wedding finger, but it was too small, so he settled for the little finger, shaking his head and laughing to himself.

"Better there right now, anyhow, since we aren't making a public announcement yet," I reminded him.

"It will do for the moment." He gave me a wry smile, even as the dowager countess jumped back into the fray.

"More than do." She drew us both into another hug. "Now, children, I am going to return to my book. Go to the hotel, Gil. You don't need to risk any further temptation."

And with that, she swept back up the stairs, leaving my now quite settled, if still private, fiancé and me to stare after her.

"Well, I guess I have been welcomed to the family."

"Thoroughly."

We laughed together, and then, finally, he took my hands again. "I am very, very glad you have agreed to marry me."

"I am very, very glad you asked."

"*Bashert*, yes?"

"Yes."

He smiled. "Now give me a goodnight kiss and get to sleep. Mother and her sisters will lead you a merry dance tomorrow."

"Good night, my love." The endearment felt strange, but good.

"Good night, *mo chridhe*."

This time, it was a very light and proper kiss, followed by equally light and proper kisses on each of my hands, enough to make me well aware that what he was thinking was neither light nor especially proper. Or at least not especially proper until we were actually wed.

After I closed the door, Tommy walked out of the parlor and handed me a sherry, clinking my glass with his own.

"Well done, Heller." He had, of course, heard everything.

"We still have to settle the contract."

"And the murder."

"Oh, yes, that."

Chapter 5

From Romance to Reality

Neither Tommy nor I are normally early risers, but we also tend to find it difficult to sleep the sleep of the angels when murder's afoot. So I was not especially surprised to find Tommy awake when I finally gave up trying to doze just as the late-winter sunrise began. I was, however, quite surprised to see Cousin Andrew at the door a few minutes after I came downstairs.

"Rather presumptuous to just turn up at our door, Andrew," Tommy said with a mild dirty look.

"It was a long night. I would not have knocked if the downstairs lights weren't on."

"Poor you." I offered a soothing tone. "Let me go down to the kitchen and see if there's coffee."

"Thank you."

Mrs. G was just starting her day, but thankfully, the first pot of the morning was ready, and she turned up some raisin bars for "that nice little redheaded detective."

Once we were all settled in the parlor, Cousin Andrew happily devouring raisin bars while Tommy and I gingerly approached the coffee, conversation commenced.

"Oh, much better." Cousin Andrew allowed himself a smile as he finished his first bar. "I've been at the Waverly Place Hotel all night with this mess."

"And what sort of mess is it?"

The detective put down his second bar and took a sip of coffee. "Quite a nasty one. The deceased turns out to be one Darren Eyckhouse, son of the owners of the hotel."

"Never heard of him." Tommy drank a little of his own coffee. "Hadn't really even thought about the hotel much until the Barrister stayed there."

"It's just sort of been there," I agreed.

"The ladies were staying there, too. On the Duke's word?"

"I'd guess . . ." I bent over my own coffee cup, inhaling the strong scent in hopes it might clear my brain a bit. One would not have thought that a few casual mentions of my (unofficial) fiancé would be enough to draw my mind off into silly roseate daydreams. But one would have been very wrong. I managed to drag myself back for a small observation, though I did steal a glance at the ring. "He is still staying at the hotel."

"And you probably know the ladies are here," Tommy added.

"Yes, at some point I'll likely need to talk to them again." The detective took another bar with a sigh. "Hopefully that can wait."

Tommy and I joined in the sigh, as the Irish will.

"At any rate, Eyckhouse appears to have no enemies or gambling debts, though a couple of the younger maids turned very pale at the mention of his name."

"Did they now?" I asked, the ugly meaning behind the maids' reaction slapping me right out of my happy haze. "You know there is a good deal of abuse of young girls in service."

"In general, yes. But I did not get that impression here," the detective said, contemplating his empty cup.

"But you wouldn't necessarily, Andrew," Tommy reminded him.

I refilled the cup and gave him a sharp look. "The girls going pale may be all the sign you'll get. They're likely terrified of losing their jobs."

"Horrible life, service." Cousin Andrew sipped his coffee. "Thank God my sisters were able to avoid it."

"I wouldn't wish it on anyone," I agreed. I had helped Aunt Ellen with cleaning houses and taking in laundry, but my mentor, Madame Lentini, had taken me on before I had to find an outside job to do my part in the house. I'd seen what a few of my older relatives went through before they married, though, and that was quite enough.

"So what is your theory of the crime?" asked Tommy.

"Well, the medical examiner is uncertain of the time of death because the room was cold, so I cannot eliminate anyone. Including your ladies."

"They have no motive," I remonstrated.

"Motive matters to Sherlock Holmes," the detective said with a sharp look at us, "not to real prosecutors. But you're right. Nobody is going to bring a case that would put them afoul of the British Consulate unless they were very sure."

"People don't just wake up one day and start murdering random men." Tommy drank some of his coffee.

"Especially not elderly British ladies," I added.

"Probably not." Cousin Andrew took another bar. "I honestly don't suspect them, but of course we have to eliminate them."

Tommy shot me a glance and then took the last bar. "I suppose. If you made me guess, I'd say he made one unwanted advance too many on those very pale maids and someone made sure he wouldn't do it again."

"Best find out if any of them have brothers," agreed the detective.

"Best find out if any of them have weapons," I said, shaking my head. "I wouldn't just sit around waiting for Tommy to rescue me if some man put his hands on me."

Cousin Andrew laughed. "*You* wouldn't, Miss Ella, but those poor little skivvies are a lot different."

"Maybe not that different." Tommy shook his head. "People are capable of a lot if they're frightened."

"True." The detective drained his cup.

I started to pour again, but he held up his hand.

"No?"

"No, I need to get some sleep when I get home. I've promised to squire Miss McTeer back from a rehearsal for her students' Lincoln's Birthday recital."

Tommy and I smiled.

"All right, all right." Cousin Andrew blushed like the good Irishman he is. "So I'm planning to offer her a ring soon, and I'm reasonably certain she'll take it."

I clapped my hands. Tommy grinned.

"Not a word, you two. She could still say no."

"Have you made it clear that you will not stand in the way of her work?" I asked.

"Not only that, I've found a progressive private school on the West Side that would love to hire her."

"Then all you need is to find a ring she'll like," I observed.

Cousin Andrew's smile froze.

"Oh, stop it, Heller." Tommy smacked my arm. "She'll love any ring that's in your hand, and you know it."

"I hope so."

I gave him a reassuring smile. "She will."

"Good. I don't know for rings . . ."

"Neither do most ladies. We just care about the right man offering them." I got a significant glance from Tommy at that.

"Good to know." He stood.

Tommy patted him on the back. "You'll be fine."

The detective sorted himself out and pocketed his notebook. "In any case, I hope I'll be seeing you to discuss happy matters . . ."

"But we know it'll likely be something a bit less pleasant first." I stood as well.

We walked the little detective to the door as he yawned. Hopefully the coffee and raisin bars would keep him awake enough to find his way home.

After Cousin Andrew left, the ladies appeared for a fashionably late breakfast, apologizing profusely for oversleeping, though none of us was especially bothered. I feared I would find myself forced to amuse them all day, since the calendar offered little in the way of obvious escape; I was singing at a benefit for an orphanage that night, which normally meant a quiet day about the house for me.

Had I not been wise enough to explain that I required some extra vocal practice on my piece (actually an aria from *Xerxes* that I could sing in my sleep and no doubt *had* toward the end of the last exhausting San Francisco stand), I might well have been forced to spend the entire day answering all manner of well-meant and impressively intrusive questions.

But I reckoned without my beloved.

He appeared at midday, guidebook in hand. Apparently there is only one thing British ladies in their golden years enjoy more than matchmaking, and that is sightseeing.

"Delightful." The countess beamed and her sisters chirped agreement. "Let us get our wraps, and we shall leave dear Ella to her work."

"Work?" Gil asked.

"I am singing at a benefit for the Foundling House tonight."

"We are of course attending, Gilbert, and have been promised a backstage visit."

He met my gaze with carefully suppressed amusement. "Of course we are."

"All donations appreciated for the foundlings," I replied with my own very small smile.

"Indeed."

While the ladies trooped upstairs for hats and coats, Gil and I managed to steal a few moments in the foyer.

"Just tell me you are not planning to throw the ring at me and send the lot of us back to Britain after a night and morning with them."

"Not at all."

"Good." He took my hands and looked around the room. "Alone?"

"Tommy and Preston could return at any moment." Despite that, I looked hopefully up at him.

He bent down and kissed me, quickly but not without passion. "Entirely within the privileges."

"Entirely."

I would have happily entertained another kiss, but his face turned troubled. "What?"

"I am not certain, but there is something very strange going on with my mother and aunts."

"How so?"

"They were much too cool about the killing last night."

I gave him a sharp glance. "Come now, they're not delicate flowers. They're ladies of years and discretion who've no doubt seen a good bit of ugliness. Didn't you tell me they all do various kinds of poor relief?"

Gil shrugged, but his face didn't relax. "That's true, as far as it goes, but there is something wrong here."

"There's plenty wrong." I shook my head. "A man was stabbed to death in their tub, and they may be sailing past the unpleasantness as a way of dealing with it."

He gazed down at me. "Sweetheart, I know you sail past all manner of unpleasantness, but in general, my mother and aunts do not."

"No?"

"No, when confronted with unpleasantness, they beat it to death with whatever weapon comes to hand, and restore calm."

"Well, then."

He put a soothing hand on my arm and managed a smile. "They like you. You are entirely safe."

"Perhaps not entirely." I held his gaze as he moved his hand down my arm to lace fingers with mine, no longer a soothing touch but a sensuous one.

"Since we are still alone . . ." He bent down, the last word dying out so close I could feel his breath on my lips.

"Barrister!" Preston's voice rang through the room as the door slammed open, Tommy and Father Michael a half step behind.

We stepped apart quickly, though I was quite sure everyone except possibly the priest knew exactly what we'd been doing.

Gil shook Preston's hand. "Good to see you again. Do I understand that you are very close to the altar?"

"Three weeks." He beamed. "Father Michael here was giving me a little premarital instruction."

"Really?" I asked. I could not imagine what the priest could tell Preston that he did not already know about anything, never mind marriage.

"Yes, and as it happens, he's actually taught me something very important." Preston nodded at the Father.

"It will sound rather silly," the priest said with a blush, "but every happy married couple I know tells me a version of the same thing. There is one sentence you need never be afraid to say. . . ."

"Which is?" Tommy asked.

"I was wrong and I'm sorry."

"Well," I observed, "that only makes sense. It's often the best way to mend an argument with a friend, after all."

"Ah, but people don't always know to treat their spouses as well as their friends," Preston said. "It's a good reminder."

"I would agree." Gil glanced at me then, completely giving away the game.

"Barrister?" Preston asked. "Have you something to tell?"

Gil had joined me, Tommy and the rest of the cast in teasing Preston into revealing his engagement to Mrs. G, so clearly there was revenge in the air.

"No public announcements until the marriage contract is settled," I said briskly, "so not one word outside this house."

"Well," Preston said, taking my hands and kissing me on the forehead, "then just inside this house, all love and happiness, kid."

My eyes were a little damp as he turned to Gil for a handshake. "Very quiet congratulations, Barrister."

"Thank you."

"I don't need to tell you that you'd better be good to

her, do I?" Preston added before letting go of the shake, with just a tiny bit of the hard look.

Gil just nodded, once again the men settling things among themselves. Maddening at times.

"Blessings to you both," Father Michael said rather formally, though his eyes were twinkling. "*Bashert*, then?"

"Just so," Gil said, shaking his hand with only a slightly puzzled expression.

"He mentioned the word first," I told Gil, smiling at the priest. "And he was right."

"Gil! Who have we here?" The Dowager Countess and her sisters were standing on the landing, with friendly smiles, and very curious eyes.

A flurry of introductions followed, and finally, the British contingent took off to see if New York's museums were up to their standard. Tommy and Father Michael adjourned to the parlor for checkers and play-fighting, and Preston slipped downstairs to visit his beloved.

I took my leave for the studio, where I enjoyed a light vocalization session and plenty of extra time chattering with Montezuma. Exactly the sort of relaxation I needed before a demanding night.

Yes, I did spend a few minutes after I finished my work looking at the ring in the light of the piano's music lamp. I may be an artist of some note, and a lady of years and discretion, but like every other engaged girl, I needed a bit of time to moon over the symbol of my new happiness. It truly was a beautiful little piece: daintily worked flowers, each holding a tiny stone, still small enough to be unobtrusive, but sparkly enough to make a statement.

Many singers take off their wedding bands or cover them with a flesh-colored bandage when in costume, but I doubted it would read from the stage. Even if it did, I would not remove it. Gil put it on my hand, and there it would stay.

"Pretty thing." Montezuma said, looking down from my shoulder as I turned my hand this way and that.

"Not as pretty as birdie." I stroked his bright green head.

"Pretty birdie!"

Confidence is not a problem for Montezuma.

Chapter 6

Good Works and Evil Intent

The benefit night began quite uneventfully, as I enjoyed once again being in a theater with other singers. Since I was the top artist of the night, I was last on the bill and spent most of the time after my run-through catching up with some of my acquaintances.

It was a particular pleasure to spend a few minutes with bass-baritone Albert Reuter, who'd been falsely accused of murder during the run of the *Princes*, and who would be coming to London as our Richard III. Albert had spent the late fall and early winter recovering from a few terrible weeks in the Tombs and, once healed, taking a number of good, and lucrative, dates lined up by his (and our) booking agent Henry Gosling.

His understudy, who ended up turning in a brilliant run, basso Ruben Avila, had since received a wonderful offer from a French company, leading him to pack up his mother and their books and steam right over to Paris. Early word was excellent, and while I would miss him sadly, I was delighted to hear that he was settling in so well.

The Avilas are Cuban, or at least said to be, by way of

Birmingham, Alabama, and the French open-mindedness about the background of their artists was likely to be very helpful to Ruben's career and life. Especially after the terrifying ending of the run, which had seen Ruben narrowly escaping death at the hands of the real killer.

With, I admit, a little help from me.

At any rate, I started the night in a very happy frame of mind, and giving a strong performance of one of my favorite arias only improved my humor. It was only after the show, when the social requirements of the evening commenced, that matters became considerably less pleasant.

Tommy and Gil, as my protectors, official and still unofficial, joined Rosa and me in the dressing room right after the final bow, to congratulate me and also to glare at the stage-door Lotharios.

And stage-door Lotharios there were. The first was Teddy Bridgewater, with his mother, but more importantly with Tommy's and my dear friend, his uncle Cabot. The head of the Bridgewater family, an old Knickerbocker (the name was originally de Brede Wege) clan so high in the social firmament that he had no need of pretensions, Cabot was surprisingly good company, as well as committed to using his many resources to improve society.

At the moment, Cabot and Tommy were working on a new plan for reading groups for newsboys and other youngsters who had to quit school to work for their families. Between good works, he often came to the town house for tea, discussing books and baseball and solving the problems of the world.

Cabot's presence was a delight as usual. He'd made a generous donation to the foundlings, of course, then in the dressing room offered me a teasing salute in my ancient general's costume, happily welcomed Gil back to the New World with only a small side glance at Tommy, and gave

Rosa a new lady's fashion journal. It was not just a nice gesture, but encouragement for her voracious reading and dreams of writing.

After that, he joined Tommy and Gil in the gents' corner while I greeted the dregs of the clan.

The men did make quite a nice picture, all tall and graceful in black tie, Tommy a bit sturdier than the others, but each handsome in their own ways: my cousin the perfect example of the auburn-haired Celt, Cabot the high-toned blond Knickerbocker, and Gil, of course, the classic dark hero type. Elegant they were, but anyone with sense would have recognized the gleam in their eyes as the same seen on little boys waiting for their next misadventure.

Other views in the room were far less pleasant. Presenting her usual sunny appearance in sausage-casing black bombazine was Teddy's mother, who follows him everywhere, ostensibly as chaperone but actually as wet blanket. She has never yet graced me with a word, or even a direct gaze. Perhaps she is afraid that I will turn her to stone.

She had no such scruples about gazing at Gil. Gazing is actually the wrong verb. Leering is more to the point. I have no idea how she squared this with her alleged respectability, but there it was.

Oh, was it!

It was the sort of look that from a man to a woman would almost certainly move her protectors to violence, and quite honestly, I wanted to slug her. I am not, and never have been, one of those jealous, possessive females. But if anyone is going to look at Gilbert Saint Aubyn with open, unadorned lust, it's going to be me.

A lady has her rights.

It was probably my reaction to his mother's rudeness that gave us away to Teddy. He had seen Gil in the dressing room during the run of the *Princes*, and there had certainly been gossip, but no one outside the town house could be sure of anything.

Teddy, however, saw me glaring at his mother and drew his own conclusions. His flat face flushed brilliant fuchsia, and his dishwater-colored eyes flicked from Gil to me. "Oh, it's like that."

"What it is or is not like, Edward, is none of your business," Cabot said firmly, giving his nephew a glare that should have flattened him.

"She was mine before any of you got here," Teddy snapped.

Gil and Tommy tensed and exchanged glances, and Tommy nodded to Cabot. Leave it to him if you can.

"It's quite inappropriate to speak of a lady in that fashion, Edward."

Teddy's face took on a nasty, blotchy hue, but he said nothing.

"Edward, we should be going," his mother told him firmly, taking his arm. I was not sure whether to be more stunned by the fact that she'd spoken, even if not actually to me; her unmistakable Southern accent; or the strange stiffening of her son's body as she guided him to the door.

Many years ago, when I tended my little cousins, I'd seen toddlers do that when thwarted and spoiling for a tantrum. Not the worst comparison I've made . . . and nothing I expected from an alleged adult.

Cabot made an apologetic bow to me and the other gentlemen and took charge of his relatives. Teddy was almost growling as his mother guided him out, and I heard him snarl something as they cleared the door, but I did not have time to consider it. The countess and her sisters walked in just then, requiring my full concentration.

Naturally, British aristocrats travel with all appropriate attire, as we'd seen when a procession of porters from the

Waverly Place Hotel arrived with their trunks, but I was still quite impressed to see them in full evening gear. All three were in pearl gray, a soft and subtle color that wore well with their pale skin and icy blue eyes. The countess went in for a good bit more in embellishment, with a lovely net overlay embroidered in sparkly crystal over her crepe gown. The sisters had chosen satin and brocade, more elaborate fabric in simpler cuts. Since they were traveling, none had a tiara, but all three chose impressive hair ornaments that made up for the lack, in plumes (the countess) or beads.

All in all, a rather intimidating delegation, should they have chosen to be.

They did not, however. Instead, the trio was quite delightful, as seemed to be their habit, descending on me with much sincere praise, looking around the dressing room with great curiosity and asking well-considered questions. We had barely settled into conversation, though, when there was another knock.

I am aware that it is probably impossible for a mere knock to sound filthy and repulsive, but I always know when Grover Duquesne, Captain of Industry, as Hetty has christened him, is coming. A man ticking far past his prime in age and appearance, he is a relic of the time when swells kept even serious artists like opera singers as pets. It has always been a matter of considerable frustration for him that he could not add me to his collection.

Unlike any number of other men who come backstage to offer praise on occasion, the Captain of Industry has a faint but unmistakable hint of menace in his demeanor. As if he would have no qualms about acting on his repulsive intentions were he fortunate enough to catch me alone, no matter what I might say about it. I'm quite sturdy enough, with sword or without, to fend him off, but I sometimes find myself wondering what outrages he might have perpetrated on less robust females. Probably better not to know.

The last time I saw him, he and Gil had words in Washington Square Park, ending with Gil suggesting I forbid him to visit the house. He had never been welcome at my home in the first place. As for the dressing room, if I'd thought about it, which I had not, I would have expected that Gil, and the continuing presence of Tommy and frequently Preston, would have been quite enough to scare him away.

Apparently not.

Tommy, who knew about the park incident, not to mention many earlier offenses, opened the door with a scowl. "Mr. Duquesne."

The Captain of Industry ignored Tommy, never a good idea, and marched right over to me, bearing his usual red roses. He and his ilk have spoilt them for me.

"Miss Ella. So lovely to see you again." In his eyes lurked many unlovely things.

"Thank you kindly." I took the roses and offered a neutral smile, carefully not looking at Gil, whose presence Duquesne had not yet marked.

"A magnificent performance as always. It always amazes me that such a beautiful woman can enact a man so well."

There was not one filthy or inappropriate word in those sentences, and yet somehow, it sounded like something Mr. Comstock would not permit to go through the mail.

"How good to see you again, Duquesne."

Duquesne froze at the unmistakable crystalline arctic tones of the London accent. There is very little on earth more menacing than the sound of a powerful British male using politeness as a weapon. It says, in ways that the threats men yell in barrooms on this side of the Atlantic simply cannot: I am capable of causing you untold and exceedingly painful harm, which may not be limited to that which your doctor can fix.

"Well, if it isn't the duke. What brings you here again?" As was usual for him, the Captain of Industry attempted to cover his rudeness with joviality.

Gil waited a full measure before responding, to make it clear that Duquesne had no right to know, even if he chose to answer the question. "Well, my dear mother and aunts are visiting Miss Shane while we settle a family matter."

"Really." Duquesne looked at the ladies, who were gazing upon him with the fondness they'd no doubt shown the giant beetle specimens at the natural history museum. His gaze traveled to Gil and then to me.

Whether it was the presence of the ladies, or the way Gil described the visit, or quite possibly merely the phase of the moon, the dawn came hard upon the Captain of Industry then. It suddenly became clear to him that not only was I not the bit of fluff he'd always assumed I was, but that I might soon be a personage of considerably more consequence. He did not like this realization one bit, and even less did he like the man who'd forced him to it.

Duquesne's piggish little eyes narrowed, and something in his aspect recalled Henry VIII at his ugliest, perhaps when he was ordering someone hanged in chains. More to the point, I was suddenly reminded that he was the man who had ordered his Pinkertons to fire upon miners striking for minor wage increases and a tiny measure of safety.

Dressing rooms are chilly in the winter under the best of circumstances, and the temperature seemed to drop another five degrees as Gil held Duquesne's gaze, the ladies favored him with similarly icy glances, and the Captain of Industry's face turned patchy red.

"Thank you for coming," I said calmly. "It was so kind of you to help the Foundling House."

"Right. You know about foundlings, don't you?"

I had the distinct impression that at least three of the people in the room wanted to punch Duquesne in his roseate nose, and I do not mean Tommy, Gil and Cabot. But this one was mine. "Indeed, I do, Mr. Duquesne, which is why I make sure to help as much as I can. Have a lovely evening."

Tommy opened the door without a word, because any speech he could have managed just then would have been most shocking to the ladies. As the Captain of Industry stomped away, the countess's crisp voice rang out, deliberately pitched so he could hear: "And they wonder why we don't welcome the robber barons in our circles. Swine."

Once the door was closed, the coldness was replaced by a musical laugh multiplied by three.

"Well done, children," the countess proclaimed. "I do not think you will need to worry about that one again."

I did not share her sunny certainty.

Chapter 7

A Morning Constitutional

The countess and her sisters were nowhere in evidence when I rose, only slightly later than usual, bundled up and headed out for the promised walk with Hetty in Washington Square Park. Normally, I would have stayed in bed quite late to recover from the previous night's performance, but it had not been especially taxing, and I was exceedingly eager to see Hetty, who was keeping the schedule of a lowly maid, with a half day off one morning a week.

In any case, my own calendar was rather light at the moment: I had been taking only a few benefits and other minor engagements, a master class here, and a board meeting there, and so on. Despite that, I did have a rather spectacular variety night to raise money for the children's hospital a few weeks hence, my last show before the London run.

None of it was enough to keep me terribly busy, so I had been happily spending my extra time beyond my usual daily vocalization and fencing or dance practice in seeing friends and catching up on my reading. It likely sounds dull, but after the arduous autumn run of *The Princes in the Tower*, marred by murder and much backstage drama, it had been a luxurious treat.

Or at least it had been when the London run was set for early January. By now, the first week of February, it was starting to wear. I will admit to being at least a little grateful for the advent of the Highland ladies, if not the untimely death, for some much-needed excitement.

The situation with Gil, and the possibility of a resolution, was of course not yet to be thought or spoken of outside the house. Even had I been ready to talk about it at any length with anyone other than Tommy, and I truly was not, Hetty clearly had other concerns at the moment. She did not need me burbling about my happiness or vexing about my fears that we would not be able to work out a way for me to keep my career.

It would be more than maddening to a woman who was still fighting for a fair chance in her work, not to mention having no luck whatever finding a helpmeet. I did not count her more or less constant sparring with sports writer Yardley Stern as a romance, though it might yet become one. If he could stop talking about his hopes for an Angel in the House, that is.

Hetty had no desire to be anyone's angel, in the house or elsewhere.

On the way to meet her, I gave a good handful of coins to Mrs. Early, the beggar widow who always staked out a bench near the park, and once again thanked God for my good fortune. Perhaps a bit more at the moment. Gil and I were still far from the altar and the happy ending, whatever that might be, but we surely had a far better chance than many others have in this world.

Hetty saw me taking my leave of Mrs. Early and grinned. She did exactly the same thing with a one-legged Civil War veteran who begged outside the *Beacon*, so she had no room to tease me about my soft heart, but she often did anyway. Friends will.

Today, Hetty looked much more her normal self in a somewhat severe gray wool coat topped by a lovely, if rather reserved, green velvet hat. It was finished with a sweet oversized bow and a shiny pin, but she didn't go in for plumes and most other fripperies. Not appropriate in a serious journalist. Also, Hetty has a deep grudge against hats, having been forced to write about them for years on end.

I'd left the diva wardrobe and airs at home, wrapping up in a very warm midnight-blue coat and matching velvet hat, though my hat did feature a wreath of satin flowers and a nice iridescent beaded pin. The fact that I was also wearing one of my prettiest day dresses, lilac wool with lace-and-ribbon trim, on the assumption of visitors, well, one visitor, later, was again not a matter for discussion.

"I'm looking for a cook and housekeeper to replace Mrs. G. Do you know anyone?" I asked, with a wicked grin.

"Very funny. When are she and Preston going to wed?"

"Two weeks. It had to be before Lent." Mrs. G is a devout Catholic, and while Preston has not darkened the door of a church in decades, he greatly respects her faith. "They're quite adorable at the moment."

Hetty chuckled. "You can say that. If I do, he'll strangle me."

"Probably." I shrugged. "In any case, do I assume you are working on a new exposé?"

"Sure am."

"Does the dead man in the ladies' bathtub play into it?"

"Quite possibly." Her mouth twisted with distaste, and something else. "Eyckhouse."

"What about Eyckhouse?"

"Son of the owners. Looked over the maids like they're his personal harem. Would do a lot more than look if he cornered them."

"Disgusting," I said.

"And if they fought him, or even complained, you know what would happen."

I—and everyone else from my corner of the world—surely did. "The *girls* would be dismissed, probably without a character."

"Exactly. Their lives ruined because of that predator."

I had to ask the next question. "He didn't—"

"He was just one of many evil creatures," she replied with a bitter scowl. It was not an answer, but I suspected it was all the reply I would get for now. "You would not believe the things that the people who run domestic help agencies do to young women."

"Unfortunately, I would. I've seen artistic directors at opera companies, remember?"

"True. You didn't keep that stiletto to cut bread."

Many years ago, an artistic director had cornered me in a rehearsal studio. If my mentor Madame Lentini had not appeared, waving a stiletto and offering to induct him into the ranks of the castrati, I don't know what would have happened. After that, Madame gave me my own stiletto and orders to use it if I had to. It went in my vanity drawer after Tommy and I started our own company, until I gave it to Hetty for her first dangerous investigative assignment. It soothed my mind to know she still had it.

"But I had Madame Lentini behind me, telling me not to be afraid to defend my virtue," I reflected as we turned away from the fountain onto one of the paths spoking out from it. "If I hadn't . . ."

"Exactly. The girls going to those agencies often don't have anyone to turn to. They have to do what they have to do to get work."

"Some of the agencies are run by women, aren't they?"

"Many are, which helps. But even they rarely stand up for their girls if the client is abusive."

"There's always another girl." I shook my head. "There may not be another client."

"One woman actually said that to me in as many words. These girls, she says, should be grateful for the work. And a really good girl could fend off a bad man."

"Only if she's issued a stiletto," I spat. "How is she supposed to do this, with the sheer shining power of her chastity?"

Hetty scowled. "Apparently so."

"I prefer the stiletto."

"Me too." She shrugged, and there was something very hard in her face. "You can tell there is quite a good story here."

"Absolutely." I kept my eyes on hers. "Do you believe the dead man in the bathtub has anything to do with this?"

Her aspect clouded for a second, and I wasn't sure if it was the distressing incident or something else. "He's the owner's son. I suspect he put hands on the wrong young lady and she put him there."

"As good a theory as any."

"I think so. But whose bathtub?"

"The Dowager Countess of Blyth and her sisters." The names were in the register for sure.

"A relative of your duke?"

"His mother. She and the aunts are visiting."

Hetty's eyes gleamed with interest. "Visiting you?"

"Yes, and staying with me now, to boot."

"Keeping them under your own roof?" She scowled, making the same wrong assumption Tommy had. "After they came to town to break up the match, nasty old birds? Really—"

"No, encouraging it."

She gasped. "No."

"Yes."

"So?" Hetty gave me a little mock shake. "What on earth are you waiting for?"

"You know very well what I'm waiting for. I can't just walk away from my work." That much was true. As well as the central issue to be resolved when we stopped sparking and started negotiating that contract.

"Too true. But he, unlike many other men, does not seem to want you to."

"Not entirely, anyhow," I agreed.

"Every once in a while, Yardley walks me home, you know."

"Right." The walks, which had become a bit more frequent this winter, had been the only possible sign that something was actually happening there.

"And almost every time, he makes some damned reference to wanting a wife at home. Or a woman by the hearth or some damn thing."

Two *damns* in two sentences! "Men."

"I'd almost put up with it if he were a little more appealing."

"Oh?"

She shrugged. "He's a good friend. I suppose if he ever gets past the wife and slippers thing . . ."

"Perhaps he just doesn't understand that a woman can do work she loves and still warm his slippers."

"I'm not sure he understands I love my work as much as he does."

"That's a far bigger problem than the occasional foolish comment."

"True. Even your man puts his foot in it occasionally."

"It's the simple state of being male." I shrugged. "Sooner

or later, something foolish will come out of their mouths. The question is—do we tolerate it?"

"There's foolish and foolish." Hetty's face tightened. "You never have to doubt that your man adores you and respects your work."

"I suppose not."

"I'd even settle for just the adoration, Ells. I'm not sure what I'd do for a man who looked at me like that."

"Hopefully you will get to find out one of these days."

"I'm getting a little old for fairy tales."

"It's not a fairy tale. It's just the right man at the right time." I patted her arm. "Wait and see. You never know what life has for you."

Hetty chuckled, her face rueful. "What it has for me this afternoon is scrubbing chamber pots."

"Ugh." I had done my share of that when I cleaned houses with Aunt Ellen before I met Madame Lentini. What an awful job at any time, and now, when Hetty was already feeling low? "Probably not the sort of filth you hoped for on this assignment."

She sighed. "Think you can convince one of your beau's aunts to kill someone? I'd love a good society murder right about now."

"I'll ask. They might find it a pleasant diversion."

We shared a small, wry laugh, and soon Hetty turned for home to change into her wretched maid's uniform and return to her duties.

I hated seeing her so melancholy.

After sending her off, I made a stop at the apothecary. The druggist's daughter, Miss Hermione Chalfont, compounds the most marvelous scented soaps, bath salts and hand creams, in addition to the rose petal lip salve I adore, and she was happy to put together a basket of dainties for Hetty, suggesting that the clean scent of lavender and rosemary would erase the miasma of her day and promising it would be waiting for her when she finished her hours of drudgery.

My happy errand done, I turned for home with a new tin of lip salve, a bottle of my own favorite rose and cinnamon-scented hair oil, and a smile. One of the great advantages of being a lady of some means is the ability to treat my friends on occasion. Not to mention myself as well.

Chapter 8

The *Princes* Reunite

That afternoon saw our august visitors exploring the Ladies' Mile, a much more frivolous expedition than I might have expected of them, but a welcome one, since I had business of my own. Actually, very pleasurable business.

Marie de l'Artois, my favorite singing partner and costar of *The Princes in the Tower*, as well as the composer, Louis Abramovitz, and his wife and lyricist (and our costumer), Anna, were all coming over for a good rehearsal session. Better, since it was Friday and sunset comes early in the winter, we had planned a company-family Sabbath dinner, complete with candle lighting and Mrs. G's famous roast chicken and accoutrements, which would be left warm and ready for Sophia to lay out because our lovebirds had their own plans for the evening.

Marie wasn't quite ready to risk her wee ones outside on a cold day, and Louis and Anna's little boy, the Morsel—born Morris—was with his *bubbe*, so it was not entirely a family night. Still, simply being able to reunite most of the company was wonderful after all that Marie had been through.

We embraced soundly when she arrived, a few minutes before Louis and Anna, and I took a good look at her. More than a month after the worst of the sickness, the sparkle was back in her pale-blue eyes, and her skin and silver-blond hair were once again glowing and smooth. She'd chosen a cornflower cashmere dress with a fluffy lace collar and cuffs, the perfect shade to set off her delicate coloring. "You look amazing."

"Quite nice yourself."

We smiled. I had gone over to her house several times over the last few weeks, bringing soup and baked goods and lip salve and other little treats to help and cheer her, but when one has been through such a terrifying experience, nothing heals like a return to the usual daily activities.

"How is everyone?" Her youngest, who would have been in the gravest peril, did not contract the disease, but the two eldest, and especially her husband, had come frighteningly close to death. Scarlet fever, like so many other illnesses, is still beyond our medical science, and all one can do is nurse the victim and hope for the best. There had been a terrifying night when Paul had reached the crisis, and I just sat with her, holding her hand and praying to Anyone we thought might listen.

Not something one will soon forget.

"Jimmy and Polly started half days at school this week, and Paul has been back to the office since last week. They're still a bit thin and weak, but stronger every day."

"Wonderful."

"Yes. I think London will actually be a good break for us all. They can rest and eat too many cream scones while we're at the theater."

"Ah, cream scones," I sighed. "Not for me."

"You, my dear, will have other compensations." She grinned at me. "Any word from the Mother Country?"

"Not just the Mother Country, the mother and aunts," I said, pulling her over to the settee. We were in the house, after all, and she would see the ladies this evening.

"Oh? Tell."

"His mother and aunts appeared on my doorstep two days ago, demanding I marry him."

Marie's eyes widened. "Oh, heavens."

"And then they found a dead man in their bathtub at the Waverly Place Hotel."

"I saw that in the paper. What happened?"

"Someone stabbed him in the eye."

"One of them?"

"Surely not."

She laughed, and all the music was back in it. "One never knows with those British matriarchs."

"True. There's more. He followed them."

"Did he now?"

Her eyes focused very sharply on me, just as I happened to touch my hair. Really, I did.

"What is that on your little finger, Ella?"

"Not one word outside this house," I said quickly. "Not one word to Louis or Anna. And especially not to Hetty—"

"Oh, get to it already. I'll keep your secret."

"Pending the settlement of the marriage contract," I started.

"Marriage contract!" She grabbed my hand. "It does mean that."

"Informally. Subject to that contract, which may not be easy to settle."

"Oh, pish." She pulled me into a hug. "I'm so happy for you."

"I'm pretty happy, too."

Marie took my hand again as she pulled back. "And what a lovely little ring. Very, very nice, but not fancy. Perfect until you decide to make a public announcement."

"That may be a while."

"Nonsense."

"Really. Please, keep it quiet, all right? We may not be able to agree on terms."

"The hell you won't."

"Marie!"

"I've never seen any two people who belong together more. Except Paul and me, of course." She patted my ringed hand. "Sooner or later, you'll decide that nothing matters as much as each other."

"I can't just walk away from my career."

"And you know full well he would never ask you to." Marie shook her head. "*I* know you. You're still scared."

"Terrified." Not of Gil, of course, but of what he was going to do to my happy, settled life.

"So was I. But true love will take care of that."

"Really?"

"If you let it." She gave me another grin. "Just have enough faith to get out of your own way."

"Madame Marie!"

"Mr. and Mrs. Abramovitz, miss," Sophia called, running into the room after Louis and Anna.

More happy greetings, more approving inspections of Marie, and thankfully, no other observation, or at least acknowledgment, of the new ornament on my hand. We quickly adjourned up to the studio for a very good practice.

Even though she'd been vocalizing daily for the last several weeks, Marie was concerned that she might not be at the top of her form. We were happy to tell her she had no cause to worry. Montezuma had quite enough joy just following her melody line; he absolutely adores her.

Despite our extra performer, the practice went very well. It took us a couple of hours to work through the music, and it was absolutely nothing but pleasure. It's true that we love the packed house, but for true musicians, there is also much joy in simply practicing together. Like many accomplished professionals, we do our work as much for ourselves and one another as for the audience.

A most satisfying afternoon.

Finally, as the daylight began to fade, we bade a friendly farewell to Montezuma and started downstairs to the parlor.

In the foyer, an enormous tawny figure confirmed my expectation that Cabot would be joining us for dinner. Noble, his English mastiff, was happily occupied with a soup bone and, I knew from previous visits, would soon be snoring away. Despite his size and unavoidable resemblance to the Hound of the Baskervilles, Noble is a truly sweet and gentle creature. He is also a beneficiary of Cabot's kindness; some society friend of his had ordered a ferocious guard dog from England and when the giant ball of love that is Noble arrived, had actually planned to destroy him. Fortunately, Cabot stepped in.

They are virtually inseparable, and quite adorable together, though, of course, in the interest of politeness, Cabot does not bring Noble to the table. I gave the dog a pat on his head and scratched behind his ears, and he gave me a couple of friendly licks on the fingers.

I wondered what the British contingent might make of Noble, but no one in the parlor seemed especially concerned.

"Done with your practice, dear?" asked the countess, looking up from her preprandial sherry. Her sisters were sipping the same on the settee next to what had become her chair. Once again, they were dressed in harmonizing tones, this time shades of mauve, more pink for the silver-haired sisters, more gray for the countess with her gracefully fading copper locks. And again, the countess had gone for a touch more embellishment: a border of silver embroidery at the neck, sleeves and skirt gores of her crepe gown.

I wondered if they'd consulted on costume before the trip, or if it just happened naturally.

Neither here nor there at the moment. I greeted them with a smile. "Exactly so."

Gil, Tommy and Cabot were at the checkerboard, apparently not playing, but just talking out of the ladies' earshot. Cabot seemed to be moving a bit gingerly as he stood, and I wondered if there was some problem.

First, though, there were introductions to make.

Marie's eyes sparkled at the sight of the three ladies. Louis and Anna seemed a bit more uncertain, despite their equally extensive experience with Society, but everyone quickly fell into the forms as I handled introductions, and then, with a little encouragement from Tommy and Gil, surprisingly comfortable conversations.

As I went to the whatnot to get a set of Sabbath candles, I was happy to hear Marie and the countess chatting about children and grandchildren, Charlotte and Caledonia engaging Anna in a surprisingly acute discussion of the finer points of fashion and the gentlemen trading opinions on our theater for the upcoming London run.

When we marked the Sabbath in my dressing room, I usually asked Anna to do the blessings and lighting, but I knew she would not be comfortable in this group, so everyone would have to accept my execrable Hebrew. I put out the small pewter candlesticks that were the only memento I had of my mother, and gently placed the candles inside. If the consumption hadn't taken her when it did, they would have been next for the pawn shop.

Mama would not especially care that her daughter was marrying a duke. She would care very much that her daughter was marrying a good man with a kind and loving family.

My father, gone long before I was old enough to know him, was a cipher. I imagined him as being sort of a flame-haired Tommy, loving and protective by my mother's description, and the one certain thing I knew of him: he had ordered her to keep me out of the sickroom when he was dying of typhoid, likely saving my infant life at the cost of a final sight of his daughter. Frank O'Shaughnessy, I thought, would put little weight on Gil's title or means, and very much on his love for me, and his acceptance, and admiration for, my career.

Even before I started the blessings, my eyes were a bit damp. My parents could never have imagined a scene like this, but they would have heartily approved of the love and joy in the room.

Tommy looked to me. "Ready?"

"Yes."

"Mother, ladies?" Gil carefully shepherded his family over to the small side table.

From their curious faces, I knew he'd told them that I light candles, but I could also tell they were very happy to participate. Countess Flora gave me an almost girlish grin. "It's time? Lovely."

"Please forgive my awful Hebrew," I said as I took up the matches. "I've never had time to learn it properly."

Anna leaned over to the ladies and whispered something, probably assuring them it's better than I admit, which is untrue.

"No one will correct your grammar, Shane."

Gil's reassuring smile warmed my heart as I lit the candles, reciting the same simple blessings I'd learned from my mother. Once the candles were lit, we all watched them for a moment in silence, enjoying the warmth of the moment.

Then the countess pulled me into a hug. "Lovely, dear."

It was not traditional, not that anything we do is traditional of course, but the countess's action led everyone else into an exchange of embraces or handshakes, and in the case of Gil and me, a sweet kiss on the cheek, accompanied by a whisper: "Your Hebrew is as good as my Gaelic, *mo chridhe*."

"Now what?" asked the countess.

"Well," Tommy said with a grin joined by Cabot, now a regular visitor at family Sabbaths, "the best part of all. We eat!"

He offered her his arm, as I took Gil's, and the rest of the party moved toward the dining room. Once Toms had settled the countess in her place of honor, I pulled him aside.

"Is Cabot all right?"

"Nasty little fall this afternoon. A slat broke on the ladder in his library."

"Ugh."

"Just bruises, but ugly. He'll be fine."

"Good. You told him to send for Cousin Rafe the Handyman?"

"He's going over tomorrow."

We smiled together and went on with dinner. It wasn't the right time to wonder why the ladder had broken in Cabot's presumably well-maintained manse. In any case, Cousin Rafe, the son of Aunt Ellen's older sister, would find and fix any deficiencies . . . and charge a fair price instead of trying to gouge the rich man.

None of that merited attention now, in the face of a happy Sabbath meal with family and friends.

"A lovely observance, dear." The countess patted my arm as we sat. "You do this every Friday?"

"We don't always manage a good family meal, but I light the candles every week. It reminds me of who I am and where I come from."

"Nothing wrong with that," Charlotte or Caledonia, I'm not sure which, agreed.

"It also gives us all, Jewish or not, a chance to share some love and joy with God in the room." Tommy's serious tone belied the relish with which he was dishing up a serving of Mrs. G's admirable parsley potatoes.

Cabot, who as a Knickerbocker considered himself at least as pedigreed as our Britons, paused in his demolition of a generous portion of roast chicken and raised his glass with a warm smile. Whatever damage the fall from the ladder had done, it was not serious enough to dent his appetite.

"To love and joy."

No better toast.

Chapter 9

The Young Ladies' Book Club

Saturday brought one of my happiest recent projects: an afternoon with Mack McTeer, the twelve-year-old sister of Cousin Andrew's beloved Katie. Mack had been the couple's chaperone to a matinee of the *Princes*, attached herself to the company and engaged in a little minor theft, which led me to take her in hand as a sort of cultural godmother.

Also as a sort of practice for any feisty young female children with whom Gil and I might one day be blessed.

On this particular Saturday, we began with a midday visit to my favorite lending library, followed by a small scientific exhibition in the same vicinity, a rather challenging improving mission but still manageable as long as we bundled up properly. I never braved the cold without doing so.

Rosa tagged along to the library because she needed to get her stock for the week, too. All three of us brought large sturdy bags for our books and paid no heed to the occasional odd glance from a passerby, since an educated lady must have her books, and one is certainly capable of carrying one's own.

Mary Grace McTeer, the name Mack's family chose for her, much the way they choose her aggressively ladylike wardrobe, was just a bit of a hellion. A very smart girl, to gauge from her marks at St. Brigid's, but one who did not take well to authority.

On this particular day, Mack was wearing a very proper gray wool coat over a pink-and-gray plaid dress with a simple gray hat and big pink bows at the end of her dark braids. Her eyes, gray and sparkly, narrowed when I told her she looked quite pretty.

"It was Kitty's. She likes pink."

Kitty, I believed, was two or three years older than Mack, and the sister whose clothes immediately filtered down to her. There was nothing I could do about that; Mrs. McTeer would take it as an insult if I bought Mack a dress she liked better as a present, because it would suggest she could not take proper care of her. So I just changed the subject. "What books are we looking for today?"

"Chemistry," Mack said with a grin. "I'm still studying the elements."

Rosa laughed. "I'll be happy with a new novel or two and maybe an interesting book of poems."

It may sound as if Rosa's sights that day were far lower than Mack's, but I knew, as did everyone else in our house, that Rosa dreams of being a writer and devours the English language in all its forms: several newspapers a day, novels, poetry, anything she can find to study the rhythm of words and how they tell a story. She was a babe in arms when her parents arrived from Italy and still speaks Italian at home, though she has no trace of an accent.

For her part, Mack is still deciding what she wants to be, but she's quite certain it goes well beyond her mother's idea of a good little girl. Hence the minor theft, of an important prop, during the *Princes*. Since then, a broadening reading course and visits to exhibitions had kept her active young mind busy and given her many things to think about other than larceny.

Her interests seem to run to mechanics and science, which admittedly are a bit out of the accepted range for young females. But our new century is bringing many brilliant lady scientists, and I saw no reason why Mack should not follow her fancies.

A visit to the lending library has always been a treat for me, from the time I was a young girl, when my singing teacher, Madame Lentini, explained to me that I could choose a book or two and take them home to read. Even though I was with Madame, the librarian gave me a hard look and a stern, and entirely unnecessary, lecture about keeping the books safe. I'm sure she gave that reminder to all children on the first visit, but I guarded those books with my life. The idea that I could read anything I liked and bring it back for something new felt like a fairy story. Books *were*, to some extent, my fairy godmother.

Books and Madame Lentini, of course. The legendary diva started me on a reading course when I was just a bit younger than Mack. It was a major part of my training, and probably a test of determination as well. At first, Madame was not sure what to make of me, a scruffy little creature with a huge voice, sent to her by her sister, who had heard me singing while Aunt Ellen and I cleaned her house. *"Your instrument is a gift,"* Madame had said, *"and now you must build an accomplished person around it."*

Perhaps I had also taken Mack on as a way to give back some of what Madame gave me.

Inside the elegant library building, a converted mansion kept warm on the chilly day, we took a long, luxurious wander through the stacks. Each of us looked at and touched and read a few pages of many different books, before settling on several we wanted to take home and enjoy. Books are a great joy for me, and sharing that pleasure with my young friends only increased it.

Eventually, well supplied with reading matter, we strolled out of the library. It was Rosa's half afternoon off, and I tucked her into a hansom that would take her to her home, where hopefully her busy family would allow her a few hours of reading time. The Benedict (di Benedetti before Immigration) parents are generally good about giving their working daughters time to rest and study.

I suspected they would be much less tolerant if the young ladies wished to spend their off-hours with boys, but neither Rosa nor Sophia has shown much interest in the male of the species beyond an occasional appreciative glance at Gil or Cabot. Both are still very much at the age where they're more interested in becoming themselves than finding a man, and good for them.

Mack, thankfully, was at least a few years away from any such complications, and once we waved Rosa on her way, we set off to explore one of her current passions: a demonstration of new combustion engines at an exhibition hall a few blocks away from the library. She had seen a notice about the exhibit in one of her father's newspapers and wanted to see how they worked.

We spent what seemed a very long time studying the engines and talking to their inventors, who were quite bemused by having to explain the inner workings of their projects to an adorable young lady. An adorable young lady who clearly understood the science and mechanics involved, I might add.

I had only the vaguest comprehension of any of it, but I was delighted to nod and smile because Mack was so happily fascinated. Mercifully, the mother of one of the inventors was an opera fancier and glad of the opportunity to talk to me.

She was the one doing me a favor, and I made sure she knew that. I always consider it a treat to talk with regular patrons, unlike stage-door Lotharios. Opera fanciers, particularly, are extremely well educated about their hobby and often have intriguing, and useful, insights. We actually looked up *Xerxes*, the piece we revived for the San Francisco tour, on the recommendation of an opera fancier who suggested it would be a good fit for me.

Eventually, Mack had her fill of pistons and sprockets and who knew what else, and it was time to deliver her back to her family. We hopped into a hansom as soon as we left the hall, since it was becoming quite unpleasantly cold, and headed back downtown for the last event of our day.

At the McTeer house, Katie and her mother were awaiting us with tea and excellent soda bread. Mrs. McTeer, like any respectable Irish woman, often expressed her appreciation for my taking Mack on our various cultural adventures with baked goods, and it was my job to accept with thanks. It was Mack's job to regale her mother with whatever we had learned today.

As always on library days, she also brought a book for her mother, today *Our First Ladies*, a collection of short biographies of those famous wives and daughters. With seven children and a baker for a husband, Mrs. McTeer had little reading time during her busy day, but she rose early and stole a few minutes before the young ones awoke and commenced their demands.

I was thrilled to help give her something of her own.

Katie's dark green eyes were more sparkly than usual, though I saw no new ornament on her hand. But when she allowed as how Cousin Andrew was coming over to enjoy family dinner with the clan that night, the only one in the week that her da did not have to rise early to bake, I suspected the game might be on.

Just as Gil had asked Tommy's blessing before speaking to me, Cousin Andrew would have to win Da McTeer's approval. In our case, Gil had actually talked to Tommy months before and obtained not only approval, but advice on how best to proceed.

I doubted Katie's da would be so generous, but one could hope.

My suspicions were confirmed when Cousin Andrew arrived as I was putting on my coat and talking with Mrs. McTeer about Mary Todd Lincoln's unfortunate later life. Like most Irish redheads, Cousin Andrew is very pale, and when nervous, radiates a faint and unmistakable blush.

"Miss Ella!"

"Just returning Miss Mack after a lovely expedition to the library."

"Ah. I'm a bit early for dinner . . ." He saw Katie behind Mrs. McTeer and me, and the blush deepened.

Mrs. McTeer cut her eyes to me, and we both carefully smothered smiles. Clearly, Cousin Andrew had a powerful ally.

"Have a lovely evening." I contented myself with a tiny quirk of the brow as I bowed to him, though I was quite certain now that there was a ring in his waistcoat pocket.

"Um, yes." He took a breath, clearly trying to force his mind to work. "So I'm glad I ran into you."

"Really?" I choked down a giggle at his flustered state. I had seen no sign of this behavior from Gil, though in the last few moments before he proposed, I suppose he had been very quietly tense. Though of course he was quite certain of the answer.

Cousin Andrew should have been as well. And he and Katie would not have to work out a contract, for goodness' sake!

"Yes. I don't want to go into indelicate details here, but

you may be right about the matter at the Waverly Place Hotel."

"How so?"

"The medical examiner believes it was likely a woman."

He would say no more about such grisly matters with his ladylove and her watchful mama on the scene, of course, but the fact that he was changing his theory was quite interesting. "Well, then."

"A surprise to me."

"No doubt." I smiled at him. "Not the time or place now, of course."

"No." His blush deepened again.

"Well," I said, with an encouraging pat on his arm, "have a truly wonderful evening."

I exchanged grins with Katie and a knowing smile with her mother, and took my leave. On the short hansom ride home, I admit I spent more time thinking about the murder than the impending marriage; Katie and Cousin Andrew would do just fine, but somewhere out there was a woman—possibly even a young girl—who was anything but fine.

Chapter 10

In Which the Matriarchs Meet

It was emphatically *not* intended as an engagement announcement tea, but rather as a small Sunday afternoon visit to bring the families together over baked goods. But, of course, there was no hiding anything from Aunt Ellen.

Tommy and I attended the early Mass at Holy Innocents, where Father Michael welcomed us with a smile and the happy news that he would soon be preparing for another family wedding, since Katie (and her da!) had made Cousin Andrew the happiest copper on earth. Which was exactly how he had put it when he ran by the rectory very late Saturday night to tell his cousin.

After sharing in the rejoicing, we returned home to await the whirlwind.

At least it would be a well-catered one.

Mrs. G, with her very current experience in the combining of somewhat divergent families, allowed as how sweets go a long way toward easing matters. So she outdid herself with fairy cakes gilded with orange icing, cucumber sandwiches in the form of little flowers, a platter of cocoa-flavored meringues and a sizeable plate of her renowned penuche fudge.

She laid it all out in the drawing room early, then took off for her own Mass and family dinner, reluctantly leaving the brewing of the tea (our favored Earl Grey) to me, even though she knew I was perfectly capable of managing it.

The ladies busied themselves in the parlor with their books of the moment and what certainly sounded like an argument over who had declined the most proposals before settling on their respective spouses. In other words, a fairly standard morning for them.

I dithered far longer than I should have over what to wear, knowing even as I did that it was nothing more than an expression of my nerves at finally presenting Gil to Aunt Ellen and vice versa. Never mind the ladies.

They were more than a little intimidating to me at times.

Though my aunt is the personification of grace and kindness, she is still just a very nice lady from the Lower East Side. I know, after a couple of decades in more rarefied circles, that the simple good manners taught in a strict Irish home are actually far more useful than any diagram of forks in an etiquette manual, but Aunt Ellen would not, nor believe me when I said so. I hoped a very comfortable, and very delicious, family tea would set everyone at ease.

I reminded myself sternly that my beloved and his family are not snobbish Londoners, but Northerners, not to mention Highlanders. Much less pretentious, much less worried about a person's place in the hierarchy, and far more concerned about their character.

That down-to-earth view of humanity, I knew, was a large part of why he was marrying me—and more importantly, why I was marrying him.

Of course, I was probably not giving Aunt Ellen enough credit. No one intimidates the Irish. The English, after all, have been trying for well over a thousand years without noticeable success.

Pulling my thoughts back from the history lesson, I finally settled on one of my favorite winter dresses: a deep-purple wool-and-silk blend with a slight sheen and extravagant embroidered trim: pansies dancing all over the collar, cuffs and down the front and skirt panels to the hem. Probably a little too pretty-girl, but the flowers gladdened my heart.

Plus, with Rosa and Sophia on their off day, the front buttons were much easier to fasten without help.

By the time I smoothed my hair and dashed down the stairs, Gil had already walked over from the hotel, and he and Tommy were chatting idly about plans for Preston's bachelor night.

I knew this because I heard Preston's name, a reference to the wedding date and absolute silence when they heard my footsteps.

"Heller! About time." Tommy looked me over with a laugh. "I was going to tell you to just come down in your wrapper."

I laughed, too.

"That's rather better than a wrapper, Shane." Gil smiled appreciatively. "Do you like pansies?"

"Only in embroidery." I walked over to him and got on tiptoe to give him a kiss on the cheek, entirely proper among the family. "You know lilacs are my favorite."

"That I do."

We exchanged one of those silly smiles that I used to envy happy couples. Fortunately, that is when the doorbell rang.

Aunt Ellen and the youngest cousins live in a small brownstone a short walk away. Tommy and I set them up when we were both starting to make money, our first priority being to spare Aunt Ellen the backbreaking washing and cleaning she'd had to do to help pay the rent when we were young, and even at that time, since Uncle Fred left only a tiny pension from the bricklayers' union.

These days, Aunt Ellen has just two cousins left to raise, Kat and Suze, ten and twelve, and devotes much of her time and energy to various good works in her parish. For her, it's a way of ensuring that everyone benefits from our good fortune.

Makes sense to me.

With her freedom and leisure, she's also developed a fine sense of style, both for herself and the girls, and I was not surprised to see her in a very elegant light gray wool dress and charcoal coat, with a slightly lighter velvet hat trimmed with a matching satin bow. She never wears color, considering it inappropriate for a widow of a certain age, but it's truly amazing what she accomplishes with black, white and gray.

Those also happen to be shades that suit her pale complexion, now slightly fading dark auburn hair and blue-hazel eyes. She's tall and strong like Tommy and me, and we all look a bit alike. It's a family joke that no one would ever doubt that we belong to one another because we have the same face, but we all really do have very similar brows and cheekbones.

The cousins, both dark haired and green-eyed like Uncle Fred, were in the standard frilly white dresses that young ladies wear for dress-up. I would have expected nothing less from Aunt Ellen's sense of propriety. Fortunately, she allows them latitude in the choice of coat and hat color, so Kat was in red and Suze in blue. They were also completely bored with the idea of tea.

I had anticipated this and set up the dining room with a sizeable tray of treats and milk, and laid out the Parcheesi board so they could amuse themselves. They favored Tommy and me with quick hugs, took a brief, utterly uninterested glance at Gil (truly, there is nothing like young girls to make one feel insignificant!) and sped off for their match.

We adults did not laugh until they were mostly out of earshot, and the moment thoroughly broke the ice.

Aunt Ellen and Gil were still smiling when Tommy made introductions.

"Are you related to the Saint Aubyn who helped his tenants during the Hunger?" she asked as he bowed.

I had not known of this until an Irish acquaintance brought it up a few months ago, and I was surprised that she did.

"My great-uncle."

"You're from good people, then."

"Thank you. I'm honored to know your son and niece."

After his carefully formal statement, they gazed at each other for a moment, and then Aunt Ellen grinned. Not smiled, grinned. So did Gil.

"All right, Mrs. Hurley, you've caught me." He laughed. "We do in fact have a private understanding."

She laughed, too. "I saw the way you look at her."

Gil shrugged. "Never try to put anything past the matriarchs."

"What a thing to say, Gilbert!"

Of course, the rest of the matriarch contingent loomed standing in the parlor doorway, with expectant smiles. They could not, of course, have consulted Aunt Ellen on dress, but they, too, were in varied shades of gray, so all of the senior ladies seemed to be costumed as a chorus. Probably more appropriate than we knew.

"You must be dear Ella's aunt," said the countess, advancing on Aunt Ellen and holding out her hands.

For one instant, Aunt Ellen looked a bit uncertain, but when her eyes met Countess Flora's, there was an almost audible click, as they shared some immediate bond of understanding. Well, they are both excellent ladies who now devote most of their time to good works and meddling in the lives of their families.

And indeed, the meddling commenced immediately.

The pleasantries were barely exchanged, the tea poured and the sweets passed before the countess took it upon herself to bring Aunt Ellen up to date.

". . . and so, Mrs. Hurley, you see, I had to give him my ring because he did not trouble to come prepared, though really he should have."

"It's just as well, Dowager Countess," Aunt Ellen said, shaking her head at me. "Ellen has never been in a hurry to marry, and if he'd given her any indication it was coming, she'd have found a way to run."

"Please, since we are going to be family, do call me Flora. May I call you Ellen?"

"Of course."

"Is dear Ella named for you?"

"Yes, her father was my favorite brother."

And so it went on. Mrs. G did indeed turn out to be our salvation, though. Eventually, they moved on from obliquely upbraiding Gil and me to praising the sweets and discussing beloved family recipes, with the Highland ladies accepting Aunt Ellen's invitation to come to her house and teach her to make real Scottish shortbread . . . and not incidentally exchange several decades' worth of family gossip.

We were most thoroughly done for.

Tommy, Gil and I decided the safest course of action was to join Kat and Suze at the Parcheesi board. They resoundingly defeated us and took quite unseemly glee in doing so, but minor humiliation at the hands of two high-spirited young ladies was far preferable to listening to our august relatives discuss our various faults.

The only consolation was that, other than Kat and Suze, none of us was a winner on this afternoon.

Just before Aunt Ellen and the cousins went on their way with a bag of books, a box of sweets and many hugs, she took me aside for a moment.

"That's your proper man, *acushla*," she assured me. "Just marry him already."

"It's rather more complex than that."

"Only if the two of you make it that way. Don't." Her face tightened a little. "I need to warn you about something."

I suspected what was coming. Another message from the second sight. Aunt Ellen does not actually get messages from the second sight because there is no such thing. But there is also no denying that she occasionally picks up things in the atmosphere. Or that we all love her so much we tolerate this little quirk of hers. "Warn me about what?"

"This is a strange one, I'm afraid. I'm seeing fire, child. No place or explanation. Just fire. And it feels very bad."

"Fire?" I shook my head.

"Yes, fire. Please be careful." Her face was troubled in a way I'd never seen it. "If I get anything else, I will let you know."

"Thank you." I was spooked enough by her demeanor to just take the warning gravely.

"Good." Her smile returned, and she started shepherding the cousins to the door. "Don't wait too long to come over now."

"We won't, Mother." Tommy gave her a hug.

After the door was closed, he turned to me.

"Fire?" he asked.

"Well, it's getting on toward a year since the Windsor Hotel fire. Perhaps one of the papers had an article."

Tommy nodded. "That would do it."

The disaster last St. Patrick's Day had killed dozens, and

given many New Yorkers nightmares for weeks. A mention of it might well have led to Aunt Ellen's vision.

Whatever the truth, as soon as they left, the house settled into quiet again. Gil and I managed a semiprivate conversation as the ladies attempted to teach Tommy one of their favorite card games.

"They're very fond of you and your cousin," he observed. "Mother tells me Tom reminds her of her favorite brother, James."

"Really."

Gil smiled a little. "Uncle James is a don at St. Andrew's. He teaches medieval history, and his church Latin is truly impressive."

"That is quite an accomplishment."

"Truly. He's devoted his life to study and has never married." His eyes held mine. "He was very good to me after my father died."

I nodded. "Many families are blessed when there's a brother who doesn't marry."

"Exactly. Uncle James is not the marrying kind, and that's quite all right."

"I assume he has an active and happy life nonetheless."

"More invitations than he ever has time to accept." Gil smiled. "And, he has lived for the past fifty years next to Sir Ralph Hodges, an expert on John Knox and the Reformation."

"That must make for fascinating dinner table conversation."

"Sometimes in Latin."

"Oh, heavens."

We chuckled together.

"Mr. Bridgewater and Tom are friends, are they not?"

"Not of fifty years' standing yet . . . but they do have much in common."

Gil nodded. "That's very good for Tom, I think."

"I think so, too."

"When you are in London, we will persuade Uncle James to come down for a performance."

"If Sir Ralph wishes to come, too, he is of course welcome."

"Only if you are willing to accept his critique of the Latin blessing before the battle."

I laughed. "We always accept a certain amount of enlightened criticism from family."

"Speaking of family," Gil said, taking my hand with a faint trace of a guilty look toward the card game, "those two young ladies have convinced me that I have missed a great deal."

"What do you mean?"

"My sons were at school for much of their youth, of course, and boys are much different creatures than girls."

I laughed. "Kat and Suze are much different creatures in general."

Gil joined my laugh. "That they are. But rather amazing, too. I think I might enjoy raising a girl or two if we're blessed."

"I warn you, I have not waited this long to be a mother to pack the little stranger off to school."

"It's always been the way for boys, but girls are generally taught at home." His fingers tightened around mine. "May kept the boys at home longer than most, and we were arguing about sending them to school when she, when—"

I squeezed his hand and waited. It was very difficult for him to speak of his late wife, who died of the Russian flu some ten years ago. Millicent, Duchess of Leith, always known to him as May, had left a terrible hole in his heart.

"I think you are right, Shane," he said finally, the rasp

in his voice betraying the emotion he was fighting. "If we are blessed, boys or girls, they'll have tutors at home, or go to day school close by."

"Well, it would be most unfair to inflict any child of ours on boarding school," I started in a light tone.

Gil smiled faintly. "If they're as spirited and determined as you . . ."

"And as intelligent and stubborn as you . . ."

The smile widened. "We'd best hope they still like us when they rule the world."

Chapter 11

A Cookie With Cousin Rafe

If Cousin Rafe the Handyman had not been the son of Aunt Ellen's upright and rather terrifying sister Mary Katherine, he would have been quite dangerous to the ladies. As it was, with the strict code and excellent manners imposed by Aunt MaryKat, Rafe Coyne merely enjoyed light flirtations with the adoring and appreciative crowd of females who gathered whenever he stopped moving for a few minutes.

It's not that he's unusually attractive, though being fairly tall and dark haired with sparkly hazel eyes, he's nothing to sneeze at. He was just born with charm, and it is simply a part of him, the same as his skill with the toolbox.

I had forgotten about this phenomenon, until Monday afternoon, when I returned from teaching a very satisfying master class and found Rafe in the parlor with Rosa and Sophia plying him with tea and a better assortment of baked goods than anyone short of Preston gets. Neither Tommy nor the ladies were in evidence; Tommy had left when I did for a badly needed men's afternoon with the sports writers, and the ladies were at a dutiful tea with some British acquaintance. If not for my master class, I might have been dragged along.

Thank heaven for a decently busy life of my own, I thought, not for the first time.

Rafe's appearance was a surprise and treat on many counts. He was happily enjoying the sweets and the company, and the girls were enjoying him. All innocent fun. It is Rafe's particular gift; he can charm a roomful of women and somehow manage to spread the attention around so that none of them is jealous of the others.

"Rafe?"

"Oh, miss!" Sophia exclaimed, blushing as she saw me.

"Mr. Coyne is here," Rosa added, with her own maidenly flush.

Rafe stood, meeting my gaze with a laugh, which I shared. "Good to see you, Ellen."

"Glad you came by. Haven't seen you in a while."

"Ah, it's been awfully busy." We hugged and he shook his head. "I'm taking some classes in accounting. Planning to spend my waning years fixing the books instead of the stairs."

Rosa and Sophia giggled.

"Quite a nice staff you have here. I'll need to visit more often."

"You're always welcome. How is your mother?"

"Oh, you know." He shrugged. "Busy making some kind of novena and helping the nuns. I swear she's more interested in the saints than her children."

"Well, they're better behaved," I teased. The Coyne cousins had spent most of their youth sneaking out to enjoy what Aunt MaryKat considered inappropriate amusements, which basically consisted of anything other than praying or helping her with her latest improving project.

"That much is true."

We exchanged bad-child grins.

More than once, Tommy and I had helped Rafe and his older brothers slip away for a little stickball after Mass, and even Aunt Ellen once assured Aunt MaryKat that the boys were with Uncle Fred on a bricklaying job, when they were actually at a baseball game. I don't remember how they got the tickets, but they were a true luxury for kids like us, and Aunt Ellen was not about to let the Coyne boys miss out.

Needless to say, the adult Coynes are fine upstanding citizens, and most even go to church, if rarely with their mother.

Rafe sipped a little tea. "Tom seemed well the other day and you're blooming as usual. Weren't you supposed to be in London?"

"Marie's family got scarlet fever."

Rafe's eyes widened. His youngest brother had died in an outbreak, and none of us would ever forget the funeral with that tiny coffin, sadly not uncommon when such terrible diseases strike.

"No, no," I said quickly. "All recovered, but she was worn-out from nursing them. We're going in the spring, and I'm staying busy here for now."

No more a fool than anyone else in our family, Rafe smiled. "Tom said something about a duke?"

"Yes, I have a beau." Fair enough, and offering no opening for further teasing.

The girls snickered.

Rafe grinned at them as he patted my hand. "Good on you."

"Thanks." I sat. "I see there's no need to ring for tea."

"Miss Rosa and Miss Sophia have been doing an admirable job of keeping me company."

"I imagine they have." I smiled at the young ladies in question, but then held their gaze for a moment.

"Um," Rosa started first, "I believe I have some mending to do, miss."

"And I have to dust the bookshelves," Sophia added.

"I'm sorry I kept you from your work," Rafe said, once again giving them that dangerous smile.

"Not at all, sir."

They spoke in near-perfect unison, and we all laughed.

"I'll hope to see you again soon, ladies."

They bowed quickly and scuttled off, and I shook my head at Rafe.

"What? I was just making conversation until you got back."

That, by the way, is why Rafe does not leave a trail of trouble and broken hearts in his wake. As far as he's concerned, he *is* just being polite and enjoying a nice talk, with no intentions whatever toward the ladies clustering around him. That obliviousness saves him, and the ladies, too.

I just smiled at him. "I know. And it was a nice break for the girls. They work very hard."

He gave me a sharp look. "Not as hard as they do elsewhere. You know for service."

"True." So did he; both of his sisters had been maids for a while before they married. No need to dwell on that. I topped off his tea and poured myself a cup. "You are looking happy and healthy."

"I'll be happier and healthier by fall, once I'm done with school. I've already got a line on a good post at an accounting firm."

"Marvelous."

"I think so. Happens to be a gent who I've done some work for. Irish, too, just a bit further along."

"Good on all counts."

"Much above the usual run of rich folk. Like that friend of Tom's, too."

"The Bridgewaters are so far up that they don't see most differences."

Rafe shook his head. "Not all of 'em."

"Oh?"

"The lady of the house treated me like dirt, shrank away from me as if I was going to assault her when she saw me checking a cracked stair."

Considering the matron's attitude toward me, I was not surprised to hear she was less than kind to a workman. But still. Even the coldest, stiffest people—women and men—warm to Rafe's smile.

Very strange, even allowing for all of the class preju- dice that would be in play. And stranger still, considering that we know the Widow Bridgewater appreciates a fine- looking man. Certainly we knew she appreciated *my* fine- looking man.

"Mama Bridgewater is a piece of work," I said finally.

"Indeed, she is."

"Her son is, too."

"Oh, he's a nothing." Rafe took a couple more cookies. "Just a nasty little rich boy."

"Nasty for sure."

"He hasn't been troubling you?"

"No, nothing like that. He turns up after shows on oc- casion is all." I spoke quickly, because like any sensible Irish woman, I recognized the set to his jaw, and what it meant. Truly the very last thing I needed in the world was one more man trying to protect me.

Rafe nodded but didn't relax as he picked up a cookie and toyed with it for a moment, thinking. "See, there was something a bit troubling at that house."

"There was?"

"I can't be sure, because the ladder is an antique—apparently from some college at Oxford, if you can believe—but it did not look like it had given way from age or wear."

"Really?"

"Really. I've repaired a few of those fancy library ladders before, and when they fall apart, it's usually in the center of the rung."

"Where most of the wear is."

"Exactly. This one gave way on the side. The join of the rung came loose, which really shouldn't happen in a fine old piece like that. People built them to last."

"You'd hope so."

Rafe laughed. "The rich folk are terribly precious about some of these things, but a lot of that antique cabinetry and such really is beautifully made. Hate seeing them abused and painted pink and all that sort of mess."

"Craftsman that you are."

"I can't do that level of work, Ellen. I'll be a much better accountant." He took a sip of tea. "The rung wasn't all."

"No?"

"There was also that cracked stair. It was on the flight from his floor to the main flight."

"Where he would be the most likely person to use it."

"If not the only one, other than a maid . . . who of course nobody would think of." Nobody but us.

"What do you—"

"I don't think anything. I am only passing on something that troubled me a bit because Mr. Bridgewater is a decent man and a friend of the family." Rafe's usually amiable face was absolutely grave. "I would never accuse anyone of doing something wrong, I'm just saying . . ."

I nodded. He had done his duty by passing on the troubling information, and now it was on us to figure out if there was anything to do about it.

"Anyhow," he said, reaching for the last jam tart, "I can't let these go to waste. I assume you're watching your girlish figure as usual?"

"Oh, yes. I'll have to button that doublet again soon."

"And perhaps a wedding dress one of these days?" He gave me a teasing glance.

"You sound like Aunt Ellen."

"Or my ma. She's been trying to marry me off for years, you know."

"You'll marry when you're ready . . . if you do at all."

"I will, but only when I meet my proper woman." Rafe's amiable face turned serious. "I'd like to have a proper life to offer her when I do."

"She might have her own ideas of a proper life, you know," I reminded him.

"Fine by me if she does." He nodded. "I'm not sure if I'm a New Man, but I don't have any problem with the New Woman, as long as she's the right New Woman for me."

Good on Rafe. I made a mental note to keep an eye open for appropriate young ladies once he finished that accounting course. "In the meantime, there are always sweets."

"And they'll do quite nicely for the moment."

We smiled together as he polished off the treat, and he checked his pocket watch.

"I need to get going. I have to hang a new door over by Horatio Street."

"Fair enough. Come by again soon, all right? I've missed you."

"I've missed you, too." The grin came back. "The cookies and the company are very good here."

I laughed. "Just try not to come on a performance day. Rosa will send me on stage without my shoes."

"We can't have that."

Chapter 12

The Course of True Love Ne'er Runs Smooth

"So," Tommy said, handing me the contract proposal from the Met, "they would be happy to have you for one New York production a year, spring or fall season. As long as the Ella Shane Opera Company does not compete directly with the Met, they have no problem with shows at other times, so you could easily do one more New York stand each year. Perhaps two, at least until you have a little one."

The three of us were in the parlor, at a coffee table full of calendars, lists, and other papers, working out the details of the marriage contract. So far, Gil had been as good as his word, agreeing to language acknowledging my right to work, and to retain the proceeds of that work, as well as control over my shares of the company and properties.

I'd brushed off any suggestion of allowances or settlements, since I did not need or want them. He brushed off any suggestion that I should contribute to the maintenance of the admittedly crumbling Leith Castle, since the entail was keeping it habitable, and he rarely used it, anyway.

We'd agreed easily enough on sharing financial responsibility for any children, and on splitting our time between the U.S. and Britain, with exact details to be decided by mutual agreement depending on my performance schedules and Gil's duties as a Peer and landowner.

Benefit performances on both sides of the ocean would be worked in whenever feasible, since Gil and I shared a commitment to charity, even supporting some of the same ones.

We had even agreed on a tour every other year, schedule to be determined by family and other responsibilities.

All that was left was hammering out the details of the New York stands, the bread and butter of my career. Starting with the Met, which had been courting me for years.

I had been resistant, because despite the prestige, it was unlikely that they would mount enough productions with trouser roles to keep me busy. Now that I would have other things to do, though. . . .

Quite a good solution, as it happened.

I nodded and looked to Gil. "So, a total of three New York stands a year?"

"Three?" He shook his head. "I have obligations at home, Shane. I cannot just wander away from the estate for half the year."

"It would not be half the year." It would also be less than half the work I was used to doing.

"It surely would. Two weeks travel, probably a month of production, how long for rehearsal?"

"So you expect me to live there more than half the year?"

"Well, you are going to be the Duchess—"

"But that's not *all* I'm going to be."

He sighed, his face tightening with irritation, an unmistakable patronizing note in his voice when he spoke. "You may find that two productions in the States is quite enough once we are blessed."

"Oh, the little woman will want to cuddle her baby?" I threw the Met proposal on the table.

"I did not say that—"

"It certainly sounded like—"

"Enough!" Tommy cut in. "Let's just leave this for now. We've agreed on everything else. Why don't we take a day or two to think about how to manage the question, and return to it?"

Gil and I were glaring at each other as we hadn't done since the very first day he walked into my studio.

"Look, you two," Tommy said calmly, putting the Met proposal back into his portfolio. "We are here, having this discussion and, apparently, this argument, because you love each other and want to be married. You would both do well to remember that."

Neither Gil nor I moved.

"Very wise, Thomas." Countess Flora appeared in the doorway, holding a book and a cup of tea. "Children, there is nothing you cannot work out if you love one another."

Gil and I shook our heads together. No matter what else we might disagree on, we were absolutely as one when it came to the countess's meddling.

"Right, then. Go have a nice fencing match upstairs and burn off all of the bad feelings so you can kiss and make up."

It was not the worst idea she had ever had.

Tommy was in the big overstuffed chair in the corner with his current book, a history of the discovery and settlement of California, when I walked into the studio perhaps ten minutes later, having traded my pretty lavender lattice-print dress for my favorite dark-blue cavalry twill breeches and a loose, fluffy, well-washed white shirt from some previous tour's Romeo.

"How do you do it, dear? You're pretty as a picture even in your boy's outfit."

Countess Flora was sitting on the piano bench. Tommy stifled a snicker.

"Thank you kindly." I bowed to her and moved to the cabinet to take out a couple of foils, as the countess idly plucked out a few notes on the piano, smiling as she heard its clean and perfect tone.

We have a very nice Lutz upright in the drawing room downstairs, but the truly good piano of the house is the studio instrument, which was both insanely expensive and incredibly difficult to build and place all the way at the top of the house. As far as I was concerned, it would stay there as long as we lived at Washington Square.

I would happily buy myself a good piano for London, and write *that* into the contract!

The countess soon had someone else to occupy her attention.

"Love the birdie!" Montezuma proclaimed from the rafters, flying down and lighting on the piano's music stand.

"Well, aren't you a sweet birdie? I have a friend much like you. He's called Robert Burns, naturally for the poet."

"Montezuma—and his name—came with the house," I told her, smiling as birdie and his new admirer beamed at each other. "We were quite glad for him."

"Montezuma makes friends rather easily, Mother." Gil walked in, carrying his jacket.

"*Alba gu brath!*" announced the bird.

The countess smiled up at her son. "You taught him that."

"Indeed, I did. He called me an English stick."

They laughed together.

I joined in with a small chuckle as I turned to Gil with foils in hand. "Ready?"

The tension between us was still simmering below the surface; I could see the tightness in his face as he stepped away from his mother, and put a hand up.

I tossed the foil, and he caught it, almost cleanly.

He smiled. "I appear to be improving my catching."

"You seem to catch quite well when it matters." I returned the smile. We knew, as no one else did, that the comments were a reference to our first kiss, when I'd swept him into an embrace after a duel with a murderer high above the stage. He had tossed me a dagger during the fight, and I told him that it was a good thing he threw better than he caught . . . and after the kiss, he observed that he'd caught quite well.

Which, of course, he does when it matters most.

Perhaps a way to remind ourselves that we don't wish to be at odds over the contract when there are so many other good things to do.

We stepped into position.

"En garde," I said as we crossed swords.

As usual, the first few parries were awkward, Gil inevitably having to accustom himself to dueling a woman, and one more skilled than he. This time, more awkward than usual. We were both holding back a little, cautious perhaps because of all the strong feelings that had been in play just minutes before.

"You were much better in our last match," I told him finally, referring to his last-minute appearance as Richard III in the climactic duel of our fall run.

He chuckled despite himself. "I was only going out there to let you kill me."

"And you did it beautifully."

He launched an attack, which I fended off easily. "Not so beautiful today."

"Rather higher stakes, perhaps." I started an attack of my own.

"The only stakes that matter." His eyes held mine for a moment, and I lost my advantage.

"Well played," I said as I backed up a little.

"We always seem to fight to a draw."

"We do." I saw no need to mention that I had in fact defeated him on at least one previous occasion . . . and often *gave* him the draw. I merely started another attack, hoping not to be distracted this time.

"Perhaps we can fight to a draw in other matters as well."

"It is one way to look at it," I agreed, as I backed him off.

He launched a new attack, pushing me back a bit. "Not the worst way."

"True." For several measures, there was only the sound of steel on steel as we parried back and forth.

"In the Lords, when we are dealing with a contentious matter, we sometimes table it—or put it off for a while to allow for further thought and cooling of tempers."

"We could table the contract for a bit," I agreed. "We are very close."

"We are."

"We are also fighting to another draw here."

His serious expression relaxed into a smile. "Yes?"

"Yes." Oh, that smile!

"Draw!" Tommy called.

"Well done, children!" The countess applauded.

Gil and I exchanged sheepish nods and a very appropriate handshake for the end of the match. But he held my hand for a half note or so after.

"A draw and an agreement to table the matter?" he asked.

"Yes." I smiled back, suddenly very aware that he looked like the very personification of every maiden's dream of a Wicked Duke, and very glad that I had every right to do something about it. If only our chaperones would give us a few moments . . .

"Excellent."

"*Bashert.*"

He leaned a little closer to me, and the countess cleared her throat.

Tommy chuckled. Wretch.

We broke apart, and I briskly moved to put away the foils.

The countess started idly playing an air on the piano, and Montezuma joined in on the melody line.

Gil started laughing. " 'Sweet Afton,' of course."

His mother joined in. "Naturally. I wanted to see if he was familiar with Robert Burns's repertoire."

"He usually sings opera," I reminded them as she stopped playing. "Mostly the soprano parts—he has a crush on Marie."

"Pretty music!" Montezuma snapped.

We all looked to Montezuma and laughed.

"I have my marching orders," said the countess, who commenced playing again.

While the music lesson went on, Gil slipped behind me. "I am meeting a friend from the Consulate for dinner. Walk me to the door?"

Which actually meant—shall we steal a private moment or two while the others are occupied?

"Certainly."

Tommy looked up from his book with a quirked brow, but left it at that.

In the landing between Tommy's floor and the foyer, we had a very nice little deep-green plush-covered bench that was never used. Until that day. Gil looked around for signs of aunts, and seeing that we were actually as alone as we might be, took my hands and pulled me over to sit beside him.

"I am told there are couples who argue just because the making up is so pleasant," he said, drawing me close.

"I've heard the same. Perhaps we should test the theory."

Whether it was the arguing or the fencing or the strong feelings in play, I didn't know, but certainly, it was a very pleasant, and passionate, makeup. Gil held me close, his kiss far less cautious and far more intense than our usual light and careful embraces.

Even for an engaged couple, we were likely reaching the bounds of propriety when we heard a whistle from above.

Tommy, giving us fair warning on his way down from the studio.

By the time my protector reached the foyer, Gil and I were standing near the door, a suitable distance apart, nothing to give us away but the twinkle in his eye and the blush on my cheeks. Not that Tommy had any illusions about how we had spent the last few minutes.

"Leaving so soon, Barrister?"

"Dinner engagement with a friend at the Consulate."

They shook hands.

"Have a good evening."

"Probably better than yours, since Mother is teaching the parrot new songs."

We all laughed together at that.

After the door closed, Tommy turned to me with a wicked little grin.

"No fighting just for the fun of making up."

"What?" I asked innocently.

He chuckled. "Never mind. Just be glad you managed to fight to a draw."

"Hopefully we can do that on the contract, too."

Toms's teasing expression turned serious. "You'd best. He's a good man and he loves you. Don't ruin it."

I stared at him.

"I'm not one of those fossils who thinks a woman needs a man to be happy, and you know that. But he's probably the only man you're likely to meet who's willing and able to find a way to fit himself into your life."

"I suppose."

"And you can always skip the argument and go straight to the making up." He gave me a teasing grin and smacked my arm lightly with his book. "Better go break up the countess and Montezuma's mutual-admiration society and clean up for dinner."

I sighed. "Another exciting night for us."

Tommy grinned. "You, Heller."

"What?"

"Rafe's got the night off, so we're going out for a pint and a gossip."

"Lucky you." I sighed. "I'll probably have to play whist and referee forty-year-old arguments again."

"Tribulation is good for your soul."

That gave me an idea. "Any chance you could send Father Michael over? All ladies love a clergyman."

"And he loves a good dinner."

"A happy ending for all."

Chapter 13

In Which We Dine With the Clergy

Dinner with Father Michael turned out to be quite fascinating, and not merely for the pleasure of watching the ladies' reaction to him. They quickly decided that though he was the very personification of Popery, he was actually quite like a handsome young village curate, to be treated with the same appreciative indulgence.

This led to inquiries as to whether he was eating properly and sleeping enough, and suggestions of improving books. If they had not been aware of priestly celibacy, they would likely have started offering attractive granddaughters.

Since Mrs. G took it as her religious obligation to provide a superlative dinner for the priest, even before she was joyfully working out her final days until marriage, the meal was both delicious and beautiful. Knowing that Father Michael has every healthy boy's fondness for beef, she'd presented a roast slowly cooked to perfection and escalloped potatoes, arranged with frizzled onions and herbs as an edible garnish.

Mrs. G likes things pretty, but not precious, as do the rest of us—and our august guests as well.

The thought occurred that it was going to be extremely difficult to find a new cook even remotely as good as Mrs. G. I resolved to ask Hetty to recommend an ethical agency that could help.

It had been ten years since we hired Mrs. G, when she was a newly widowed friend of a friend of Aunt Ellen's needing work, and I had been dreading the process of finding someone else.

Surprisingly, this time, Aunt Ellen's inquiries in her parish had turned up no one. I'd already asked Rosa if she had any friends or relatives who might be interested and available, and asked her to put the word out, too, but no success so far. This was new; we pay quite well and do our best to treat our staff as we'd like to be treated. But we'd never before had to hire anyone without a recommendation from a friend or relative; Mrs. G knew Rosa's family from her parish. Even in our large City, it's possible, and preferable, to stay within circles of connection.

As much as I hated turning to people I did not know, I supposed an agency was the best solution. Heaven did not just send one a wonderful new cook, after all.

None of that was suitable dinner chat, though. I am not one of those ladies who complains about the "Servant Problem." Usually that means servants who are insufficiently servile, and considering my background, I find the whole area of discussion insulting.

We had far more intriguing matters to consider in any case.

Conversation began in the usual neutral direction, focusing on the delectable meal and the chilly weather. The intrigue began when I asked after Cousin Andrew. Of course, the ladies took pleasure in discussing the happy news of an impending wedding for a time, but then Father Michael allowed as how his cousin had to solve the Waverly Place

Hotel murder before he could really enjoy planning his nuptials.

"Really?" asked the countess. "I would have thought they'd grabbed up the miscreant by now."

"How so?" I asked, her response leaving me genuinely surprised and curious.

"Well," Charlotte began, "it's quite clear that the poor young man surprised a burglar and the burglar killed him."

"Of course, a burglar would have no way to know that we do not travel with valuables," Caledonia added. "Which would not have prevented him from attempting a robbery."

Father Michael glanced to me. I shrugged. I had no idea where this was coming from, other than possibly the standard British perception of America as a wild and dangerous place.

Which seemed rather odd for three ladies from that most wild and dangerous of places, the Scottish Highlands.

"I suppose burglary is as good a theory as any," Father Michael temporized, a troubled expression clouding his handsome face.

"Though Eyckhouse, or someone else in the building, would have had to be in on it," I suggested, "since there was no sign of forced entry, was there?"

"Not at all," the countess nodded. "And that makes the case, doesn't it?"

"Perhaps," I said cautiously. Her barrister son would never have accepted that.

"Well, he was the son of the owners and would have had keys. If he was indeed working with some ruffian, the burglar might have turned on him when they realized they would leave empty-handed."

"That's probably exactly what happened," Charlotte agreed. "Some sort of foolish plot gone wrong."

"They assumed British ladies would have jewels," Caledonia added, "and quarreled when there was no jackpot."

"It's possible," I admitted, doing my best not to react to Caledonia's use of slang, or wonder where she'd picked it up. Perhaps they'd been reading sensational novels on the steamer.

From what I had heard of Darren Eyckhouse's character, the plot was not impossible. Though one did have to be quite careful in transferring faults in one area of a person's life to another. The fact that he apparently had no compunction in taking what he wanted from young maids did not mean he would also take what he wanted from the Highland ladies' jewel boxes.

It didn't mean he would not, either.

Father Michael shrugged, and when he spoke his voice was quiet and serious. I was not sure if the caution was priestly, or police family, but I recognized the warning note. "I am just glad all of you are safe, and I hope for Andrew's sake that the killer is found soon."

"An excellent thought, young man," the countess said approvingly.

"Would you like more potatoes, dear?" Caledonia passed the dish.

The priest smiled. "I never turn down Mrs. G's potatoes."

Dinner and a very pretty dessert of angel cake with violet icing, trimmed with sweet candied violets, moved to a relaxing conclusion after that, but I could not help marking the ladies' sharp determination that they'd figured out the crime . . . or Father Michael's discomfort with their theory.

Later, while the ladies drank a medicinal brandy and set up the table for cards, I walked Father Michael to the door.

"So?" I asked.

"I might ask you the same," he said. "I saw that expression when I asked after your beloved."

"We are sparring a bit over the marriage contract. It will keep. What is troubling you about the killing at the Waverly Place Hotel?"

"I cannot tell you all the details because some were told to me in the confessional . . ."

"Fair enough."

"But Darren Eyckhouse was not a good man."

"I suspected as much from what Andrew told us."

The priest nodded, his jaw tight and eyes sharp. "More than once, I have had to explain to young girls that something forced upon you is not a sin for which you have to atone."

"Oh, no."

"Yes, I have reason to believe he used his power as the son of the hotel owners quite mercilessly against the youngest and most vulnerable of his parents' employees."

"Bastard."

He blinked a little at my unusual, but not unprecedented, profanity.

"I'm sorry, Father, but I don't know many bad words. And I'd like to use them all for a man who did such things to children."

"And they *are* children. Girls in their teens, just trying to bring in a few dollars to help their parents, doing back-breaking work as it is, and to have that—*Eyckhouse*—come at them . . ."

He broke off with a shudder that I shared. His hands were tight, and I knew he was thinking of his sisters. I thought most of the five had been able to avoid domestic service, but perhaps not all.

"I told Andrew about it, of course. But the answer was always the same. If the girl would not bring charges, nothing would happen."

"And no girl would."

"Not at the cost of her reputation and any chance of respectable work."

I shook my head. "No justice."

"Not here on earth, anyhow. It is a good thing he was a Lutheran. I would have had a very hard time consigning his soul to God."

"God will take care of him," I reminded the priest.

"It's not God's hands I hope he's in." His face was hard and grim. "At times like this I console myself with the uglier sermons about what happens to the tormented souls in Hell."

"And hope that no one pays too dearly for sending him there."

"True. I do not share the ladies' confidence that this was a burglary gone wrong, and that some robber will be quickly apprehended."

"No."

"I worry it may have to do with one of those poor girls, and I fear for them."

I nodded. "Or their families."

"Yes, I can tell you without breaking any confidence that I know of at least one older brother who wanted to do harm to Eyckhouse. I told him to go to the police and find his sister another post."

"What did he do?"

"Once the drink wore off, he decided he did not want to go to jail. Or to put his sister through a complaint." The priest shrugged. "So he found the girl a husband who was willing to take what he persisted in calling damaged goods, and walked on."

"Is she—"

"I have no reason to believe the marriage is unhappy, and they will soon be blessed . . ."

I shook my head. Poor little girl. I prayed she would at

least find some solace in marriage and motherhood, but I doubted it. How can such important milestones be satisfying in desperation rather than in love and joy?

Father Michael patted my arm. "I know what you're thinking. People make the best of such things every day and I do my best to help. The man, against all odds, is a good and loving sort, and they were married most of a year before they had any expectations. They'll come out all right, even if they don't start as well as you and your man."

I blushed, not at the mention of my man, but at the Father's skilled reading of my mind.

"It's normal enough, Ella. When people are engaged, they compare everyone's life to their own felicity."

"What an unfair thing to say! Especially when it's true."

We turned to see Preston walking up from the kitchen stair.

"Well, if it isn't the bridegroom," Father Michael teased.

"Just had a few moments to see my fiancée, and I thought I'd step upstairs on my way out and see how our newly betrothed one is doing."

I sighed and shook my head.

"Apparently a bit of a donnybrook today over the contract," the Father told him.

"Greta said she had heard about a little unpleasantness. There was also—apparently—a happy making up."

My blush returned, and irritation with it. "Does everyone know every detail of my life?"

"Of course we do." Preston grinned. "It is a very small world, kid."

"No question on that," I agreed. "I would offer you coffee, but—"

"There have already been lemon tarts. Greta spoils me."

The joyful glow in his eyes was wonderful to see. I wondered if Gil lit up that way when he spoke of me.

"Yes, kid, he talks of you in exactly the same tone."

I didn't even bother wondering how he knew what I'd been thinking. "We are well matched, in general."

"Better than that, kid."

"Now what's this about the contract?" Father Michael asked. "Surely you are going to come to terms . . ."

"You'd best." Preston's warm smile turned stern. "If he's willing to let you keep singing, what else is there to argue over?"

"It's rather more complex than that," I said. "We have a few things to work out. I hope we can, but . . ."

Both of them glared at me.

"You *will* work it out," Preston assured me. "Because love always wins, unless you are too stupid to let it win."

Father Michael grinned. "I can't say it better than that."

Chapter 14

In Which Connor Coughlan Returns

The next afternoon, after escorting the Scots contingent to my favorite milliner just off the Ladies' Mile, I was reading in the parlor and they were resting upstairs when the doorbell rang. I looked up, only to hear Sophia answer it with a squeak. I put down my book, expecting to see Gil, after whom Sophia generally mooned with an entirely harmless crush.

But there was nothing harmless about this visitor.

"Ellen."

"A Mr. Coughlan, miss?" Sophia said, her eyes wide with something that looked like awe, but might have been fear, too. She probably didn't know his name, but any girl growing up where she did would recognize the look in his cool green eyes and the way he carried himself, even if Connor was doing his best to not seem menacing.

"Thank you, Sophia."

Sophia nodded and picked up her feather duster, turning to the bookshelves, clutching it like a weapon, with a ferocious set to her jaw.

"Calm down, sweetheart," Connor said, freezing her in her tracks. "I'm an old friend of the family, is all."

"Oh." Sophia relaxed a shade.

He smiled at her, the real, genuine one he saved for friends, turning him into any other handsome Black-Irish gentleman. "Go on about your business, little one. It's all right."

"Of course." She tried for proper demeanor as she turned back to the shelves, but her blush gave her away. I suspected Gil had just been superseded in her affections. Not that she had any better chance of catching this one, for which we could all give thanks.

"Good to see you, Connor," I said formally, holding out my hand. We both knew it did not mean good news for him to be here, but the forms must be obeyed.

He took my hand and placed a gentle, almost reverent kiss on the back of it. There had never been any attraction between us, but we shared a deep connection from growing up on the same Lower East Side street. I'd even once ripped out a handful of his hair helping Tommy in a scrap with him.

But while my life had led me to the most prestigious opera stages in the world, his had led to the underworld of Five Points. Connor was not exactly the kingpin of the City's most dangerous neighborhood, but he wasn't far from it.

He had maintained a loose acquaintance from afar with both me and Tommy, usually nothing more than the occasional bouquet and backstage appearance at a New York production. That might have been the end of it, except that during the run of the *Princes*, he and Gil had discovered a shared interest in a case that affected them both.

And on the final night of the run, I'd jumped in to help Connor in a fight, just as I used to do for Tommy back in the old neighborhood. Except that it's a much more serious thing when it happens among adults. Especially if you're fighting a homicidal maniac. Connor had clearly not forgotten my coming to his rescue. There was something new in his face when he looked at me, and I was not at all certain I liked it.

"You know I would not seek you out for social reasons, however much I might like to," he said as he sat down on the chair by my chaise, Gil's usual spot.

"I suspected as much."

The hand he had kissed was my left, and he looked at it for a long moment. "Is that a new ring?"

"It doesn't mean quite what you think it does."

A faint smile played about his lips. "Still fighting the poor bas—fool, are you?"

"Negotiating, rather."

"Ah. Well, you may want to tell him to look out for himself."

"Why?"

"I have heard that someone is trying to take out a contract on him."

"What?"

Connor patted my hand. "It's all right. Nobody will take the work now."

Which meant that he'd put out the word that anyone who did would pay with their life. "Thank you."

"I told you before. I owe you my life. I'll be taking an interest in your safety and happiness, Ellen."

"All right."

"Don't worry. I don't expect to dance at your wedding. I'm just making sure there is one."

"Any indication of who was looking to harm Gil—His Grace?"

Connor smiled a little at the slip. "None so far. I'm looking into it as I can."

"Again, thank you."

"And again, none necessary." He watched me for a moment, his face turning more serious. "One other thing, though, Ellen."

"What?"

"This one is something I can't do anything about."

"All right."

"I hear your reporter friend is poking about at the domestic service agencies."

"She is." I did not ask how he knew that.

"That's fine, as far as it goes, but a couple of them are run by some very bad people."

For Connor to describe someone as very bad people meant they were likely the incarnation of Satan on earth. Or at least someone who could be extremely dangerous to Hetty. "What kind of bad people?"

"The kind who find other uses for the prettiest and youngest girls who come looking for work while running a perfectly legitimate agency for the rest."

I didn't know the exact details of those other uses, but I knew they had to be both horrific and lucrative. And that anyone involved in such things would not scruple to make a lady reporter disappear if she looked too closely into their business. "Oh, dear."

"As far as I know, she hasn't stumbled into anything really dangerous yet. But as a friend, you should steer her away from that. She won't stop it, and she will die trying."

"It's wrong, and it should be stopped," I said slowly.

"No argument, Ellen." Connor shook his head. "I have three sisters. You know I would not traffic in that sort of thing. But there are a lot of wrongs in the world. Surely she's better off alive and pursuing ones she can fix?"

I sighed. I hated it, but he was right. "Thank you for the warning. I'll urge her to focus on the killing at the Waverly Place Hotel."

"The bounder who got himself stabbed in the eye?"

Connor nodded grimly. "Better for her. Maybe she can help make sure nobody pays for that."

"What do you mean?"

"I hear things, you know. Enough to say that Darren Eyckhouse had some nasty habits, and it's no loss to the world that he's dead."

The same sentiment as Father Michael expressed last night, just with less religious wrapping. And Hetty had said much the same.

"You are not the only person of that opinion," I said. "I hear things, too."

"I'm sure you do. There's quite enough with that to keep her busy."

"And away from worse."

"Far worse. But also far more than one woman with a pen can fix. Even that woman." He had crossed paths with Hetty before, and they shared a wary mutual respect. "If you steer her toward the big operations uptown, she should not run into any trouble."

"Will do. Thank you."

"Glad to." It was specific enough to keep her safe but left room for Hetty to work. While Connor was hardly in the habit of courting the press, he knew he might someday want to have a friendly reporter nearby.

"I won't tell her what I know, or how."

He smiled. "I had no doubt."

For a full measure, we sat there looking at each other, Connor's expression unexpectedly gentle.

"I didn't offer you tea. Would you like—"

"No, Ellen. I should be going. I only came to inform you of what I'd learned. And apparently to offer you at least a little congratulations."

He nodded to my hand.

"Not officially yet."

"Fair enough." He watched me again for a couple of measures, something I could not figure out flickering in his eyes. "You've read all of those medieval romance things, haven't you?"

"Many of them."

"Then you know that sometimes, when a man cannot be with the woman he admires, he might make certain that she is happy and safe with an appropriate husband. That perhaps it is his way of caring for her."

"Yes."

We both understood what had just been said, and what never would be. And that I would never take advantage of that.

"Be careful, Ellen."

Connor met my gaze again as he stood. If we had taken different turns off of Orchard Street . . .

He bowed, as elegantly as any society gent, turned and walked out of the room, as the door opened and familiar voices filled the foyer.

"Tom. Saint Audrey." Connor had always deliberately gotten Gil's name wrong, and it was somehow soothing that he hadn't stopped that.

"Connor."

"Just sharing a little important information with our Ellen." His description of me was a common enough usage, but carried a troubling new meaning after our latest conversation.

"Good to see you, Coughlan," Gil offered neutrally.

"Same, Saint Audrey."

They all exchanged bows and nods, and Connor walked out the door without a backward glance.

"Do we want to know?" Tommy asked me as he turned for the parlor.

"Probably not." I shook my head to clear it. At least

part of that conversation was clearly covered by Gil's and my agreement that we could hold back things the other had no need to hear. Not all, though.

"But?" Toms asked.

"But you'd best know, anyway. Someone tried to put a contract on our Barrister and he stopped it."

Tommy whistled.

Gil shook his head. "Who would want to kill me?"

"He could not—or would not—answer that." I was happy enough to keep the conversation on that ground. It was what mattered, after all.

Tommy's eyes narrowed as he looked toward the door. "Something related to the unpleasantness last fall?"

Our Barrister's unexpected autumn in New York had owed little to a desire to see me and a great deal to a need to find the killer of a friend. He had indeed made certain that the right person was sent to the Queen's Justice . . . but now, I had to wonder at what cost. And who might be left to seek a less lawyerly vengeance of their own.

"I hardly think so." Gil shook his head. "No one else had anything to do with it."

"As far as we know," I said. "Hetty said that whole case was a snake pit."

Tommy let out a long breath. "If there was anyone else, they'd have to be sitting around waiting for the Barrister to return—and have plenty of cash lying around for the contract."

"True," I admitted.

"What about last spring?" Tommy asked.

Gil and I both tensed a bit at the memory of our first misadventure, which had come far too close to ending in death for us both. Probably more for me, since I was the one who ended up dueling the killer on a catwalk. Although, Gil *was* almost shoved in front of a grocery wagon.

"That ended in a life sentence," I reminded Tommy. We'd read the *Beacon*'s article together.

"As it should have." Gil nodded. He, like Tommy and I, is resolutely opposed to capital punishment, and would have been willing to ask for clemency, even in the tragic death of his cousin.

"That judge almost never imposes the ultimate penalty." Tommy shrugged. "But there might be a brother, or sister, or friend of the killer . . ."

"There might be for any number of people I've annoyed over the years," the Barrister mused.

"Really?" I turned to him with a concerned glance.

"I have assisted my friend Joshua several times in the past. It's not impossible that someone who believed I helped cause an injustice might wish to take action."

From the very formal way he put it, I knew he had no intention of saying more about his efforts with his good friend, one of the top defenders in London.

Tommy was watching me, and not him. "I'm sorry, Heller, but it also might be you."

"Me?"

"As a motive. Some of your stage-door admirers might be unhappy about the idea that you may have found a suitable husband."

"Really?" I stared at him. "If they even know, it's the silliest—"

"Mr. Duquesne did not seem silly at all," Gil observed.

"I was not thinking of him, however unpleasant he was the other night." Tommy shrugged. "I suspect if it is one of Heller's admirers, it's someone we don't see. It's rarely the person you see that you have to worry about, after all."

Gil and I nodded.

"Wise advice, that." Gil's mouth twisted a little. "It's why I keep my mother and aunts where I can see them."

"Gilbert! What a thing to say!"

We turned to see the three graces in question, rested and revived, proceeding down the stairs, signaling the advent of teatime and, more importantly, time for the children to amuse their betters.

Later, after Gil had made his escape for a quiet evening at his hotel, and the ladies had adjourned to their whist and arguing, Tommy and I returned to our troubling conversation over a much-needed medicinal sherry.

"Connor would not warn you if it were not a serious threat," Tommy said. "We'll have to watch out for your man."

"Absolutely."

"He'll watch out for himself, too." A faint smile as he took a sip of his drink. "I think our Barrister is a bit tougher than he plays."

"I tend to agree." I took a sip of my own. "It's all a bit odd, though."

"What?"

"That he's the one Connor says is in danger, when it's our friend Cabot who seems to be having a run of nasty mishaps."

Tommy's face tightened. "You think?"

"I don't *think* anything, but remember, Rafe said the rung and the stair troubled him."

"He did, at that."

"It's probably nothing, but you should keep a bit of an eye on Cabot, the same as I'm going to do on Gil."

His grim expression relaxed slightly, and the gleam returned to his eyes at the thought of his friend, and perhaps further amiable wrangles over historical controversies and baseball rules. "Such difficult tasks we set ourselves."

"Indeed."

Chapter 15

In Which Miss Hetty Shocks the World

While the phone rarely rings in our home, still I did not think much of it when I saw Sophia answering with her best sweet voice the day after Connor's disturbing visit: "Hurley residence."

Teaching Rosa, and later Sophia, telephone manners had been a bit of a challenge at first, since—like us—they had not grown up with such new-fangled things. Unlike us, though, they suspected that telephones might just be the work of the Devil.

Once Father Michael assured them that he had one of his own in the rectory, and that the devices were actually a gift from God for reaching people speedily in emergencies, we were left with the practical matters. Both naturally soft-spoken, they thankfully did not fall into the habit of yelling into the receiver as so many did, but did require a bit of encouragement to speak loudly enough to be heard.

When Tommy and I got our telephone line, we decided to put it in his name and answer it likewise, since the Champ was far less likely to draw unwanted attention than I was. Rosa and Sophia were trained to ask if the matter was urgent, and if not, to take a message, because really, as good as the phone is in emergencies, it can be terribly intrusive at other times.

Tommy and I both have more than one casual acquaintance who enjoys calling simply to chat. As fond as I am of a good conversation, I firmly believe that it should take place in person. I do not see new inventions changing my opinion on that.

All of this to say that we had no idea what was coming when we heard the ring that afternoon. Sophia came running into the parlor, much upset.

"Detective Riley, Mr. Tom. He says it's urgent—involving Miss Hetty!"

"Miss Hetty?" Tommy and I spoke in unintentional unison, as he rose from the checkerboard, where he had been getting the better of Yardley, and I put down my book.

Gil and the ladies were on yet another museum visit. Poor man, he was going to be terribly sick of Ancient Egypt and the decorative arts before this visit was done.

This was all most peculiar. We had not heard from Cousin Andrew for a few days; he, Katie and Mack were due to join us for dinner some night soon, but of course he had less pleasant matters to consider as well. If I had thought about it, and I hadn't really, I would have assumed that he was busy with some sort of lead that had nothing to do with us.

More fool I.

"What about Hetty?" Yardley asked, standing with a concerned face.

"Well, let's find out." Tommy strode into the foyer and took the receiver. We followed, watching the short conversation, during which my cousin's eyes narrowed and his voice became softer and calmer with every brief sentence, mostly a series of "I see's" ending with "Thank you for telling me. We'll be right down."

Tommy shook his head as he put down the receiver.

"What happened?"

"She's been arrested in the death at the Waverly Place Hotel."

"Arrested?"

"Hetty, kill someone?" Yardley gasped.

"It's a manslaughter charge. Apparently she confessed to stabbing Eyckhouse because he tried to assault her."

"Assault as in . . ." Yardley began, his eyes widening.

"Yes," Tommy said quietly. "Exactly what you think."

Yardley looked as if he'd been slapped. I wasn't sure what offended him more, the idea that Hetty had harmed someone or that the someone in question had been attempting an outrage. I did *not* sense much concern for Hetty's well-being. It was not the time to sort it out, but it did nothing to improve my opinion of him.

"Good Lord," I said. "Poor Hetty."

"Poor Hetty, indeed," agreed Tommy. "She's to be arraigned late today, and if she can't post bail she'll end up in the women's jail."

"No, she won't." I picked up my purse and walked over to the coat rack. "Her family may or may not be able to afford bail, but we can surely help."

Tommy nodded. "Absolutely."

"What can I do?" Yardley asked, recovering his balance a bit.

"Well, she's going to need a good lawyer." Tommy thought for a moment. "Rowan Alteiss is the best defender in the City."

"Specializes in women in trouble," I added, remembering that he'd been involved in several sensational cases. "And his office is right up the street."

"That's right." Yardley gave me a sheepish shrug. "I've seen him at the pub downstairs of it."

"Well, pub or no pub, Mr. Alteiss is the just the right

lawyer for Hetty." I nodded to Yardley. "You go see if he's available. We'll meet you at arraignment court."

"Should we leave a note for the Barrister and the ladies?"

"Good idea."

I left the note, and word with Mrs. G that we would be quite late for dinner, if we appeared at all, and she should see to the ladies and just leave us something we might warm up for ourselves, and so we blasted out on our missions.

It turned out to be a long, dirty and ugly afternoon and evening, and a grim education for us all. Innocent Hetty was until proven guilty, but no one feels the obligation to treat a defendant like a lady.

Worse, the nature of the incident required reference to exceedingly indelicate matters, and her profession already raised questions about her status as a good woman. It's fair to say that despite Cousin Andrew's best efforts, her treatment was less than dainty.

Arraignments were held in a dingy, packed room, far from the grand venue used for important murder cases. Most of the defendants were men, and the few women were the sort I wasn't supposed to know existed. None of the offenses was especially serious—mostly public drunkenness, minor assault and the like.

Rowan Alteiss, a tall, rawboned man with a salt-and-pepper mane who always seemed to look just a little disheveled despite well-cut clothes, blew in a few minutes before the matron escorted Hetty to the defense table. He shook hands with Tommy and me, and expressed amazement at Hetty's arrest. As it happened, he was a regular reader of the *Beacon* and enjoyed her work.

Yardley was not in evidence, apparently having had to get back to the news office to finish an article. Well, a man does have to keep his job.

"I've read her work for years. They should give her

more exposé's and fewer hats." Alteiss shook his head, his gray eyes genuinely concerned. "She seems so smart and cultured. How did she get mixed up in manslaughter?"

"She was posing as a maid while working on an exposé story," I explained. "The victim apparently tried to assault her as he'd assaulted other maids."

"We can't prove all of that yet," Tommy put in, "though we strongly suspect it."

Alteiss's face tightened. "Poor Miss MacNaughten. Well, we'll get her bailed out tonight and then see where we are. I don't know many juries who would convict a woman for defending her virtue."

Tommy and I nodded.

"But I will tell you, folks," continued the defender, his eyes narrowing a little, "that some people still don't think of a reporter as a good woman, and we may have a bit of ground to make up on that."

I bit my lip.

"I did not say *I* believe that, Miss Shane. Some jurors might, though, and we need to be aware of it."

"True enough." Tommy didn't like it any more than I did, but we could not deny the ugly facts.

A murmur as the matron brought Hetty in, and the bailiff yelled: "Henrietta MacNaughten, Manslaughter!"

Alteiss looked at her and shook his head. "Let's just get the lady home tonight."

The lady would have voted strongly for that herself, I suspected. Hetty's red hair was trying to straggle loose from its knot, and her gray plaid dress, thankfully not one of her best, looked dusty and much the worse for wear. It was probably wise not to inquire too deeply as to the nature of the stains at the hem.

Despite all that, her face was calm, and her posture straight, though there was undeniable fear in her eyes. When Alteiss walked over to her, shook hands and nodded to us, she let out a sigh of relief and managed a tiny smile in our direction.

"Rowan Alteiss, of counsel for Miss MacNaughten."

The judge, an immensely fat gentleman of middle years, grinned at the defender. "Well, well. We don't generally see your caliber at arraignments these days."

"A favor for a friend."

I was not sure which of us Alteiss was counting as a friend, and it did not matter. He was Hetty's defender, and he was more than welcome in our circle.

"Well, then, do your magic, Alteiss."

"Merely pleading not guilty and requesting freedom on recognizance, Your Honor."

"Oh?"

"Miss MacNaughten is a noted newspaper reporter and no danger whatsoever to the community."

"Darren Eyckhouse might disagree," cut in the prosecutor, a stiff-necked man in a pair of painful-looking pince-nez.

"Really, Johnrow?" The judge shook his head. "She's accused of stabbing a man who was attempting an outrage."

"That's her story, anyhow."

"And if a jury agrees, they'll give her a medal." The judge chuckled. "I'm not inclined to set high bail in a case like this. Stay in town and out of trouble, Miss Mac-Naughten, and don't miss any hearings, no matter who your lawyer is."

"Yes, sir." Hetty's voice came out as a tiny thread.

"And of course, leave the stabbing to your male protectors for a while."

No one was sure what to do with that, and the judge just gave Alteiss a grim nod. The matron took Hetty's arm and guided her over to the lawyer, Tommy and me, and I embraced her. She was shaking like a leaf.

"Are you quite all right?"

"I'm a professional. I'm fine." She pulled away from me quickly and smoothed her dress.

"Of course you are."

"Miss MacNaughten," began her defender, "why don't you come around to my office in the morning and we'll talk about what's next."

"All right."

He shook her hand again. "It will be fine, Miss Mac-Naughten. Just do as the judge tells you and stay calm."

"Thank you, Mr. Alteiss."

"It's a pleasure." The lawyer gave us all what certainly seemed like a genuine smile. Well, we love our work, why shouldn't he love his? He bowed. "Try to get some rest. Things will be better, or at least different, in the morning."

He took up his brief bag and headed out of the courtroom.

"I can't afford . . ." she started, nodding to Alteiss's retreating back.

"All taken care of," I assured her.

Tommy patted her hand as she tensed. "No point having money if you can't use it to help a friend."

"All right. For now."

"Would you like to come to the town house for some tea?" I asked, shepherding her out of the courthouse.

"No, I want to go home for a good wash, and I have to tell my parents."

We both stared for a moment and just kept walking.

"They thought I was working on a story about planning society parties. I didn't want them to worry about me."

"Oh, dear," I sighed. "You're going to have quite a conversation."

"They won't be happy. Father may even yell a bit." She shook her head. "But it will all blow over."

"Make sure to tell them that Rowan Alteiss is your defender," Tommy suggested. "Everyone knows what that means."

"That's something. They'll be upset about what happened."

"Any parent would," I assured her. "Someone trying to harm your little girl . . ."

"It's not that bad."

The calm tone of her voice made me just stare at her. The one time I'd come close to such a thing—that artistic director who cornered me before Madame Lentini walked in—I'd been wobbly inside for weeks. It wasn't what had actually happened, which was nothing at all, but the fear of what might have, and the feeling of utter powerlessness in the face of determined male lust. Even now, nearly two decades later, I could not discuss the incident without a twist in my stomach.

It is of course never fair to judge someone for reacting to difficulties differently than you do, but her calm made me suspicious. I doubted this was simply journalistic objectivity.

"Hetty, is there something you want to tell us?" I asked.

"What do you mean?"

Tommy looked slowly from me to her as we all stopped near the door. "You *did* stab him when he was trying to assault you?"

"Of course I did. The creep had his hands on me, and I wasn't going to stand for that."

Tommy flicked his eyes to me so quickly that Hetty didn't see it. I couldn't tell what was missing from her tone, only that it was, and there was no longer any doubt in my mind.

The poor little maids who went pale at the mention of Eyckhouse. I would not put it past Hetty to cover for someone she thought was unable to protect herself. She might even be right. If it would be hard to convince a jury

that an educated woman working as a maid for an investigative report had a right to defend herself against a man's
lust, how much harder would it be to convince them that
some poor little skivvy did?

Not to mention the fact that the girl's life would be ruined even if she weren't jailed. Simply being caught in the
situation would be enough to get her dismissed without a
character and unable to find any respectable work. Yes,
service was an awful life, but it was still a decided improvement over the street.

Hetty would see all of that, but many others might not.

To plenty of people, including the men who would sit
on the jury, those girls are expendable, and expected to act
like it, after all. They would not give much thought to the
few terrible choices the girl had, cornered by a predator in
that bright white bathroom.

But Hetty would.

What a noble—and foolish, and incredibly dangerous—
thing to do, to take responsibility for it. And how completely in character for Hetty. I looked to Tommy.

"Why don't we see you home, and you can have a nice,
quiet night with your family," I suggested. "Maybe you'd
like to come over for tea tomorrow after you see Mr. Alteiss?"

She nodded, apparently unaware that I'd figured it out.
"A good idea. I will want to stay away from home for a
while, and I doubt the *Beacon* will want me on assignment
until this is settled."

"You never know. Maybe they'll want you to write up
an account," Tommy said.

We shared a hansom to Hetty's home, where she slipped
in alone to face the parental wrath. Tommy and I walked
the last block and a half to clear our heads before returning to the maelstrom that our home had become.

"She's lying," he said as soon as her door closed.

"Up, down and sideways," I agreed, taking his arm. "I think she's covering for one of those poor little maids."

"Can you get her to admit it?"

"I'm going to leave that to Mr. Alteiss for now."

"What makes you think he can do what you can't?"

I shrugged. "Barristers have magical powers?"

Tommy laughed. "Well, some of them do."

Chapter 16

Companionship and Concern
in Brooklyn

The next morning, Hetty stopped off for a cup of coffee after meeting with Rowan Alteiss and proceeded to both stick to her story and deflect any attempts at discussion of it. The only consolation was, since she'd managed to get herself arrested—as Morrison, her very enlightened editor, put it—she was back to hats.

Normally, of course, I would not rejoice in Hetty's forced return to millinery, but it neatly removed her from the investigative report about domestic service agencies—and thus from any danger from their owners. Not to mention sparing me having to warn her off and give some oblique yet believable explanation of why it was a bad idea to pursue some of the agencies.

Probably the only positive outcome from the previous day's events.

The *Beacon* ran a short article about the arrest, below the fold on the front, describing the suspect only as a lady employee who claimed Mr. Eyckhouse had been attempting an outrage. I doubted the other papers would be so reserved, though none, of course, would use Hetty's name, given the nature of her defense.

Still, I had to agree with Morrison that she was much better off with hats and handbags for the moment.

Once Hetty was on her way to her latest article on accoutrements, I took myself off to Brooklyn for a visit to chez Winslow, otherwise known as the home of Madame de l'Artois and her family. We were trying to stay in trim, and not incidentally to enjoy a little relaxing time together now that everyone was healthy and happy again.

Some, admittedly, far happier than they'd been.

Marie and I had a lovely little practice of our major duets, and a lovelier tea, complete with appearances by the wee Winslows, who were back to their cheery and lovable form. I brought books, as I often do: a volume on tigers for Jimmy, who was currently mad for exotic animals; a biography of Queen Victoria for Polly, who was determined to grow up to be a queen—*not* a princess; and a delightful little picture book of letters for small Joseph, nearly a year-and-a-half old and thrilled to be allowed to play with his older siblings again.

My cup of tea was mostly gone, and the one small fairy cake I'd permitted myself a sweet memory by the time Joseph pulled on my skirt and climbed into my lap. He is a tiny dear creature, white-blond with his father's brown eyes, wide with interest at the world. For whatever reason, likely the mere fact that he can play with my charm bracelet, he's taken a liking to me.

He snuggled right into my arms and commenced looking at the charms, as Marie grinned. "You are going to be a wonderful mother."

For probably a full measure, I just sat there, frozen. Until she said it, I had not actually allowed myself to consider the idea. But of course, I had indeed moved a very long way from the theoretical hope that I would someday have a child toward the real possibility of one. "I suppose I might just be."

"You hadn't thought about it. Even now."

"I guess not."

She chuckled. "Ah, well. Just make sure to keep a good full schedule as long as you can."

My blush and confusion made her shake her head.

"Once you're in a delicate condition, especially the first time, it can be very nerve-wracking. Most doctors won't agree, but I have always found that staying as busy as they will let me is exceedingly soothing."

"That makes sense." I had given no thought at all to this, but of course, the process of growing a small life for months on end would be quite fraught. It's likely why people tend to wrap women in cotton-wool even more than usual at such moments and force them to stay indoors on a chaise somewhere until the little stranger comes. Even my aunt Ellen, who had to work as much as possible to keep the family fed, would stay inside, only taking in laundry, picked up by one of the older children, as she approached the arrival of a new cousin.

"A delicate condition is also good for the voice in the early stages." She smiled. "I made sure to make a few recordings when I was expecting Joseph."

"Good to know." Phonograph recordings are a very nice little sidelight for singers, and the money associated with those recordings no doubt formed the beginning of Joseph's college fund.

"But first, you'll have the fun of the wedding and honeymoon. Any plans yet?"

"No, much too early for that." I shrugged. "First we settle the contract, then we get to the enjoyable things."

"You're still negotiating?"

"He is irrational about New York dates. I've agreed to one production a year with the Met, and I want two more stands here."

"He doesn't want anything but the Met?"

"No, he'll agree to one more local run and a tour every other year, but—"

"That's more than I did during the first few years Paul and I were married." Marie shook her head as she picked up her teacup. "Don't ask too much. He'll also accept benefits and other one-night events, right?"

"Of course, whenever we can work them in, here or London."

"Take it."

"I have to have the freedom to maintain a career."

"Once you're married—and especially after you have little ones—you naturally have and *want* a lot less freedom." She took a sip of tea. "Your life is going to change. Singing will still matter, but it will no longer be the only thing that matters."

"I know—"

"You think you do, but you don't. I didn't, either. You're right to want to keep your career and have something of your own, but don't push him too far."

"I'll think about it." I gave Joseph a cuddle, and he nestled into me.

"It's not just thinking, Ells." Her smile was different, softer. "It's feeling, too. You think you have terrifying feelings now, wait until you hold a baby of your own."

"Always watch out for the mama," I teased.

"You watch out for Mama!" Joseph piped up.

Marie laughed, and I joined in. It was, it turned out, young Master Winslow's first complete sentence, an occasion to be applauded. The rest of tea consisted of Joseph basking in the approval and applause that went with mastering subject, verb, object. Tommy and Cabot came to collect me just as everyone was beginning to tire, and Marie, the baby on her hip, walked me to the door.

"Well, who have we here?" Cabot asked, bending down to greet Joseph.

"Master Joseph Winslow, meet Mr. Bridgewater," started Marie.

"Watch out for Mama!"

We all laughed.

"An excellent warning," said Cabot. "I'm quite impressed with your speaking skills, Master Winslow."

Cabot might as well have been speaking Latin. Joseph had just noticed Noble hanging back in the foyer and started squirming in Marie's arms.

"Big doggie!" Joseph said, reaching out. "Pet doggie!"

"Is it quite safe?" Marie asked. She had met Noble before, but he had never been around her children.

"Mastiffs are extremely gentle and protective of children," Cabot assured her. "Let me bring him over for a quick pet."

Noble loomed over wee Joseph and accepted a small, awed pat, which he repaid with a generous lick on the cheek. That made the little angel giggle, and the big ones, too.

Soon, since children and animals do best in small doses, we made happy good-byes and took our leave.

It was a cold but not impossibly frigid night in that rather nice precinct of Brooklyn, so the three of us took the short walk to the Bridgewater lending library, where Cabot and Tommy had started an evening reading group for newsboys. Most of the poor fellows could no longer go to school because they had to work to support their families, but they still hoped to better themselves. With that goal, Cabot was paying a schoolteacher to spend three evenings a week with the strivers, helping them find good books, encouraging them to study whenever they could and urging them toward better opportunities.

That night, Cabot had invited Tommy and me to see the

group's meeting, because he was hoping to set up similar reading groups at other libraries in the City, some for newsboys, some for factory girls or maids.

After, we picked up Noble in the library entrance hall and walked out into the cold night warmed by inspiration. The boys were doing well, and one had even lined up an apprenticeship at a print shop.

"Wonderful boys, Cabot," I said as we stepped down to the sidewalk.

"And so eager to better themselves." Tommy smiled.

Cabot didn't. "I see boys like these, and then I go home and see my nephew, who is happy to waste money any way he can and appears to have no desire to make anything useful of himself, and it troubles me, truly."

"Teddy's not even twenty yet," I reminded him. "He could yet turn out well."

Cabot shook his head. "I dare say you and Tom were well on your way in your lives by the time you were his age."

"We came from a rather different world." Tommy's tone was gentle, no slap intended. He looked up the street for a hansom. There were none, so we started walking.

"I probably should have brought the carriage," Cabot said apologetically, as Noble fell into the same easy pace as the humans, "but I didn't want the coachman to stay too late."

Tommy and I smiled. Cabot, raised at the top of the social scale, had no need to even be aware of his coachman's time, and it spoke very well of him that he was.

"Lantana is busy in her potting shed, and Teddy took off in his horrid motor, so there was no need for the driver to attend to us."

"Lantana?" I had not realized Mama Bridgewater even had a first name, never mind such an outlandish one.

"Teddy's mother is originally from some awful little city

in Georgia. Fancies herself a Southern belle. She grows orchids. Nasty things."

"Orchids are quite a lot of work." I had heard of a few society ladies who grew them.

"Yes, and she doesn't grow the pretty, bright-colored ones you'd think of. Hers look like spiders and have these awful cloying scents." Cabot shuddered as we started to cross the street.

"LOOK OUT!" Tommy grabbed my arm and gave Cabot a shove toward the other side of the street. It was unnecessary, since Noble had heard the warning and started pulling his master to safety.

We didn't see anything but the back of the motor speeding past us, as Noble barked furiously at the thing. It was the first time I'd ever heard him bark, and he did indeed recall the Hound of the Baskervilles as he called down canine vengeance on the machine that had endangered us all.

Really, the city was far safer before people started running about in motorcars. None of us fell, and none was hurt, but what an annoyance!

"If you are going to have one of those damnable things, sorry, Miss Ella, you should have to be able to handle it properly." Cabot shook his head as he patted and soothed down the dog.

"Or else." Tommy patted the dog, too, and I was not surprised to see Noble become almost instantly calmer with the reassurance. Tommy has the very real gift of making just about all creatures feel safe with him. Because they are. After perhaps a stanza or two, everyone seemed almost back to their normal calm.

I took another glance up the street. "I think I see a hansom. Let's get back to our own borough."

"Had enough of the wilds of Brooklyn?" Cabot teased.

"It is part of our City now," I admitted reluctantly, "but that does not mean it is as civilized."

We all laughed, then, at our Manhattan pretensions.

"Come back to the house, Cabot," Tommy offered, "and we'll scare up some cocoa in the kitchen."

"There is even shortbread in the cookie jar," I added. "And a nice bone for Noble."

"I can think of no better way to end the night."

Chapter 17

Walking Out on a Cold Day

As often happens after such dramatic events, the next day started uneventfully, aside from a moderately lurid feature on the killing at the Waverly Place Hotel in one of the *Beacon*'s competitors, promoting the burglar theory, undoubtedly from the sheer need to upstage Hetty and her employer. Even though there was still no mention of Hetty's name, the poorly written and yet more poorly sourced article clearly intimated that the confessed killer was really nothing but a sensation seeker, and the *Beacon* had swallowed her story simply to sell papers.

Not that the *Republican Star* wasn't hoping to get its own piece of the pie; it trailed the *Beacon* in readers by a wide margin, and the publisher was clearly hoping to make a move. This did not bode well for Hetty. A good rule of thumb: never get into interesting trouble in the midst of a newspaper war.

Despite the heat and light from the presses, most of us were merely working to stay warm and out of trouble. It was that one week that New York suffers every February, with viciously cold temperatures accompanied by cutting winds. So I was surprised, and quite curious, when Gil suggested a walk in the park before tea that Thursday.

Anyone but Gil could have waited until the mercury rose to a decent level, thank you, but my (unofficial) fiancé deserved some consideration.

It was so cold when we left the house that Mrs. Early was not in the park. Father Michael kept the church open and warm on such days, and many of the neighborhood unfortunates sought shelter there.

As soon as I saw Gil, I understood the game. Walking in the park was really the only place the two of us could have an even remotely private conversation, thanks to the Highland ladies, not to mention Tommy, Preston and Cabot, running about the house at odd times. It was worth braving the cold for a few uninterrupted words.

For a short while, at least. I bundled up in my heaviest coat, with my fur stole and muff, but it was still brutal enough that I had no desire to stay out for long. Gil, in his own thick coat, with a muffler and gloves added to his usual dapper hat, did not seem any more inclined to dawdle.

"Is there, by any chance, a respectable tearoom nearby?" he asked.

"No closer than our parlor, and none nearly as good." I smiled up at him. "We shall have to keep moving to stay warm."

"And perhaps huddle together." He pulled me a bit closer, which I did not mind in the least, even if it was not entirely appropriate for a couple not yet publicly engaged.

"Perhaps."

"It is worth the cold to have a few moments to converse outside my mother's watchful eye."

I chuckled at that.

"It's not that I wish to whisper sweet nothings, though that's always a good thing."

"Always."

"But something is still troubling me about the incident at the hotel."

"What?"

"Ah, if I knew, I would have the answer to all. We are reasonably certain that your friend Hetty did not do what she confessed to."

"We are."

"Her story is weak. A man known to prey on young girls suddenly attacks an adult woman?"

"Known, I thought, to prey on any nearby woman with no recourse."

Gil shook his head. "I've asked a few questions here and there. Eyckhouse liked young girls."

"Surely predators devour whatever is in their path," I said, somewhat puzzled as to why he'd seized on this detail.

"Not quite, Shane. Predators generally have a preferred prey. Men like this are in the habit of selecting a particular sort of victim."

"So . . ."

"So if Mr. Eyckhouse was in the habit of assaulting very young women, it's highly unlikely that he would have suddenly pounced on Miss Hetty, however appealing—"

I patted his arm as he colored a little. "It's all right. Neither Hetty nor I would take it as an insult that such a vile creature did not find us an attractive target."

"Quite so." He took a breath and continued. "I assume, as I'd imagine you do, that she is taking the blame for one of those unfortunate little girls."

"A very reasonable assumption."

He nodded as we circled the fountain, empty and silent in the cold. "Does she think she will be acquitted on grounds of self-defense?"

"I think so. It's a terrible gamble, of course, but with Alteiss on her side, her odds are better. I am still hopeful that they can clear this up soon and spare her from jail."

"I am not as versed in the American criminal justice system as you, sweetheart, but I would not count on it."

"I know."

"Miss Hetty is not my only concern."

"Oh?"

"My mother and her sisters."

"This again?" I still could not understand what he was expecting of them. "All they did was find the body."

"As far as we know."

I looked sharply up at him. "What do you—"

He sighed. "I have no idea. But I have spent my life dealing with those excellent ladies, and I am quite certain they are not being entirely truthful."

"You think so?"

"No, I know so. When they saw your note about Hetty's arrest and the hearing, they all became very quiet. You'll remember they did not come down to dinner that night even though you had made arrangements for them."

Mrs. G had told me about it the next day, and it had struck me as more than a little odd, as well. I had assumed they were just tired from a long day out. But now? "Oh, dear."

"So I have no idea what they may have done, or may be doing, but I know something is wrong." Gil's face was tight with concern.

I patted his arm again, unsure of what to say. I did agree that they gave far too much credence to the silly burglar theory, but that surely implied nothing more than minor misconceptions. And really, choosing rest over dinner, even one of Mrs. G's admirable repasts, was no evidence of anything other than questionable judgment.

"Please keep a good eye on them, Shane. They may give something away around you."

"I will. Please be careful in your inquiries, whatever they may be."

He nodded. "Has Mr. Coughlan given you any further insight on his concerns?"

"No, he would not. We will just have to trust that all is well."

"I do not like having that man come near you. There is something in his aspect . . ."

"We grew up together," I reminded him. "More, he believes he owes me his life. He looks after me a bit."

Any more than that, Gil would never need to know, and I would surely never tell him.

Gil scowled. "I do not mind him looking after you. I mind him looking *at* you."

"Well, he warned us of a threat to you."

"And I appreciate it, as far as it goes."

We had walked quite far afield, and I realized I was getting very cold. Too cold.

"Why don't we go back to the house?" I suggested, carefully keeping my voice light. "I'm sure Mrs. G has the teakettle going."

"An excellent idea."

Though we walked quickly, we did not move quickly enough. About a block from the house, I started shivering. I am always careful to avoid getting too cold because it reminds me of the final days with my mother.

We were barely surviving in the last months, living in a tiny, frigid room in a corner of a tenement. Every day, she was thinner, paler and more tired . . . she slept longer. Every day, though I was just a little girl, I tried to take up more of the piecework that was our only income. More than once, I remember her saying she wasn't hungry when she put out bread for me. There wasn't money for anything else.

And there was almost never money for heat.

Every night, we'd huddle together in the pile of blankets on the floor that passed for a bed, sharing what warmth there was. I would burrow into her embrace, willing myself to ignore how small and bony and fragile she felt, and she would tell me stories, either of her meeting and marriage with my father or of the glorious future she imagined for me.

"You're an American girl, Ellen, you can become anything."

Dreams and stories were all she could give me, and in the end, it was more than enough.

She would always kiss me on the top of the head and tell me she loved me before we fell asleep. I always said it back. I hope.

They found me curled up beside her body one frigid morning, believing, probably pretending, that she would wake up and everything would be all right. I would have ended up in the orphanage, and probably my own small corner of potter's field soon after, if Aunt Ellen had not swept in, saying she wasn't going to let Frank's girl go to strangers.

But as much as I love Aunt Ellen, and as safe and protected as I feel with Tommy—and now Gil—a small corner of my soul will always be that little girl who awakened cold, hungry and alone one winter morning.

"Shane, are you all right?"

Gil's voice brought me back, and I looked up at him, unable to hide the shivering. "Just . . . just cold."

His eyes sharpened on me, and I realized that he understood. I'd had a similar upset before when I foolishly offered to sew on a button for him, and I'd told him some—but not all—of the story, holding back the worst partly because I had such a hard time speaking of it, but also because I was unsure how he would react.

"We're almost there, *mo chridhe*. I'll see you safe home."

"Thank you."

He took my other hand and practically towed me the last few yards to the house.

Inside, all was warm and bright and safe. Tommy and the ladies in the parlor were laughing about something. Mrs. G was baking gingerbread, or possibly sweet rolls, filling the entire building with the delicious, homey scent.

Gil guided me to the foyer chair, holding my hands as I sat, then leaning over me, rubbing my fingers between his. "See? Safe and warm, sweetheart."

I nodded. Logically, of course, I knew I was safe and warm and far from the tenements. But reason had little to do with this.

"The cold?"

"Yes," I managed.

"When you were with your mother?"

"We had almost no heat that last winter." I took a breath, relieved to feel the shivering starting to subside.

His eyes lingered on my face. He knew there was more than I'd told him, and he was waiting for the full story.

If I could trust him with my heart, I had to trust him with the truth.

"She . . ." I started, pulling back a little, my voice raspy and hard to control. "She died in the night, and they found me clinging to . . . to her in the morning. I hoped she'd wake up when it was light—"

I put my head in my hands then, unable to stop the tears.

"Dear God, *mo chridhe*." Gil knelt in front of me, drawing me into his arms, patting my back as if I were still that frightened child. There was nothing he could say, and to his credit, he did not try, just holding me until the storm passed.

"I'm . . . I'm sorry," I stammered when I could speak again.

"No, sweetheart." He moved back a bit and took my hands again, and I could see that his eyes were full. "You have nothing to apologize for. I'm glad I can comfort you."

"All right."

He held my hands tightly then, gazing up at me. "You will always be safe with me, Shane. Always."

It felt like a vow, with his hands around mine, the way they would be at the altar.

I nodded and took a breath. "Thank you."

"No thanks desired or required." His eyes burned into mine. "A man protects his woman."

"I am usually better at protecting myself," I admitted. "I do my best to avoid becoming too cold."

"Very wise. I will do my best to help you." He smiled faintly. "Even at the cost of keeping larger fires in the country house."

I returned the smile. British homes are notoriously cold, of course. "As long as I have you to keep me warm."

He stood then, and I let him pull me up, and burrowed into his arms, not just for the warmth but for the affection and reassurance. For what seemed like, and might well have been, quite a while, it was nothing more than care and comfort, entirely innocent.

Then, though, he looked down at me. "Are you—"

I did not give him a chance to finish the thought, getting on tiptoe and pulling him into a kiss. Whether it was the honest adoration in his eyes, or the care he'd shown at such a terrible moment, or just the usual attraction between us, I'll never know. No matter, it was an absolutely welcome advance.

He drew me closer, meeting my kiss with the same passion, his arms tightening around me.

"Gilbert, really!"

We broke apart instantly, guiltily, as the countess let out a musical chuckle.

"It's all right," I said quickly. "I got chilled outside, and he was helping me warm up."

She shook her head and patted my arm, a gleam in her eyes. "Don't try that excuse with your cousin or Mr. Dare."

"Mother." Gil managed a growl.

"If you are cold, dear, Mrs. Grazich has laid on a very nice tea." She grinned. "A cup and some polite conversation would do you both good."

"No doubt," I agreed quickly, doffing my coat before Gil could help with it.

As we followed the countess into the room like the bad children we so clearly were, Gil brushed my hand with his and gave me a very serious, assessing glance.

I nodded, warmed once again by his need to make sure I was indeed all right. While we might have many matters to settle between us, and I would not, could not, surrender too much on my career, I also knew I did not want to give up his love, not only the unavoidable passion but the caring and protectiveness that was like nothing I'd ever imagined.

Chapter 18

Mr. Lincoln and Mrs. G

The weekend found the Highland ladies spending Sunday afternoon at Aunt Ellen's for the promised shortbread lesson and decades of family gossip. We escaped the worst of the consequences thanks to the Met's continuing courtship: an invitation to the Grand Sunday Concert. It was a most spectacular event, but like many performers, I am far happier on a stage than in the audience. Nonetheless, it was quite a treat to put on a lovely violet satin evening gown and go out on Gil's arm for an evening of amazing music.

It was not, however, intended as a public announcement of anything, since Cabot invited Tommy and the ladies to his family box, and it was easy enough to play it as entertaining visiting friends. Which is precisely how I described it to the *Illustrated News* gossipmonger when she asked . . . knowing full well it would still be an item in the yellow paper's column, the "Lorgnette."

And indeed I was not disappointed Monday morning, when Lincoln's Birthday began with a new crop of intrigue, starting with the papers. Rosa, being the aspiring writer of the house, read the newspapers before the rest of us got to them, which in some establishments might be cause for complaint, but in ours was simply her prerogative.

Tommy and I are not the usual employers, and we like it that way.

"Well, miss, you knew you'd end up in the papers if you went out last night," Rosa said, handing me the *Illustrated News* with a sigh.

She had folded it to the "Lorgnette." Most of its alleged reporting consisted of wild speculation about the lives of various prominent New Yorkers, though occasionally the paper did print relatively accurate, if highly sensationalized, accounts of backstage dramas in the arts world. Over the years, I'd come to the "Lorgnette's" notice every so often, usually for untoward or interesting incidents during my various productions.

Months ago, though, the column had taken note of my walking with Gil in the park, and soon after followed that item with wild speculation, no doubt fed by a society mama, that he was actually in town to court a young heiress. The miss in question had since eloped with a more congenial husband, a livery driver as it happened, but I suppose I should not have been surprised to see us drawing attention again after the Met concert.

> *Is our tomboy diva ready to trade her sword for a coronet? Miss Ella Shane appeared on the arm of a tall, dark British gentleman at the Met's Grand Concert last night. Adding fuel to the fire, sharp eyes had spotted her walking out with the same gentleman a few days before. He certainly looks like the fellow who attended many performances of The Princes in the Tower this past fall. Rumor has it he's a*

*genuine duke, and genuinely taken with
Miss Shane. Certainly, our beloved diva
seemed to be enjoying his attentions at the
opera last night. Could a true Cinderella
love match be on the horizon?*

"I'm not sure if a Cinderella love match is on the horizon, Rosa," I said grimly, "but some very bad sensational writing surely is."

She giggled. "I know now why it's an anonymous column—who'd want their name on that mess?"

"Definitely not you."

We nodded together.

"Look at it this way, Rosa, you've got another example of awful writing to add to your collection."

She sighed. "I'd like a few more examples of good writing."

"Maybe Miss Hetty should bring you to the morgue one of these days."

"Newspaper morgue, of course, miss?"

"Naturally."

"Lovely." She grinned. "When Miss Hetty is a bit less busy, perhaps."

"Probably best to wait."

Another shared smile.

"Would you like to take off early this afternoon? The gents are going out tonight, so it will be very quiet."

"Thank you, miss." Rosa returned to her mending with a happy smile.

I knew she was fantasizing about a quiet night with a book. So was I. It was the best I could hope for that evening.

Long before Gil appeared and upset all applecarts, Cabot had invited Tommy to the Republican Club's annual Lincoln's Birthday dinner. At tea, a few days before the concert, he expanded the invitation to Gil, with a significant smile, noting that our British visitor should see how Americans honor their martyred hero.

The dinner, I hardly need tell you, being a political event, was also a strictly male one. I, of course, found this annoying and offensive, but there was not one blasted thing I could do about it, so I determined to enjoy a relaxing night at home. Or at least as relaxing a night at home as one could enjoy with the Highland ladies playing whist in the parlor and arguing over which long-dead swain had fancied which of them most.

Ciphering has never been my strong suit, but I was reasonably certain that there was no way any of them could really have been courted by Lord Byron. At least not the Lord Byron we generally mean when we use that title.

In any case, soon after the card table coffee was poured, I left the ladies to their pleasure and slipped downstairs to see what Mrs. G might be doing.

"Well, Miss Ella. Was dinner—"

"Absolutely magnificent. And you need to stop calling me Miss Ella, since you will be Preston's wife in less than a week."

She blushed. "I can't very well call you kid."

I laughed. "Ella is fine. It will take me a while to stop thinking of you as Mrs. G."

"Greta is fine, too. Would you like to sit and talk over tea—Ella?"

"I would like that, but only if you let me start the pot."

"Fair enough."

I noticed as I brought the tea and cups over that she was sitting at the table with a piece of paper and a pencil, working on some kind of list. "Wedding planning?"

"Just so. We're having the breakfast at Holy Innocents hall, of course, and I want to bake as much as I can in advance."

"Tommy and I would be happy to get someone else to handle confections. Surely the bride shouldn't make her own cake."

Greta Grazich, soon to be Dare, grinned. "I want to make my own. It's the only way I know it will be perfect."

I returned the smile. It takes a perfectionist to know one. "Quite understandable. How are the dress fittings with Anna going?"

"It's almost done." She gave a dreamy smile. I'd asked my costumer Anna Abramovitz to make her dress as a wedding gift, knowing that no one could make anything prettier. "I haven't worn anything but black since . . ."

"Really?"

"Really. It's what's expected, and it's serviceable."

"Ah." I nodded. "So what have you chosen for your return to color?"

"Moire silk in the most beautiful sea-green shade." She sighed. "Anna is trimming it up with lace and ribbons, and making a hat to match."

"Perfect with your coloring." I nodded. With her silver-blond hair, clear green eyes and peaches-and-cream skin, it would be spectacular.

"I think so. Preston has already told me that he expects me to get several dresses in color as soon as we're wed."

Meaning he would buy them for her, of course, which he could not in propriety do before the marriage. "Well, as soon as you get a chance, we'll go up to the Ladies' Mile and pick out some fabrics."

She blushed a bit. "We're going to a hotel on Long Island for a little wedding trip, so it will be a few days."

"No hurry. I'm sure you won't need many new outfits to walk by the water."

A rather wicked sparkle came into her eyes. "We're not planning many social engagements."

Of course I was aware that newlyweds liked time to be

alone together, but I had not made the specific connection that these two newlyweds would enjoy their private moments. Naturally they would, and good for them. I covered my embarrassment with a smile. "Honeymoons are not a time for the social whirl."

"As you'll learn soon enough."

That did make me blush. "I suppose."

"All *is* proceeding well with the duke, isn't it?"

I sighed. "There are some difficulties to settle in the marriage contract."

She sighed, too, and took a sip of her tea. "It's likely harder for you, since your work is so important."

"True."

"But he loves you as much as you love him. Surely you'll find a way."

"I hope so."

She smiled. "Maybe you let him think he's in charge."

"What do you mean?"

"Oh, we all know you can't force a man to do anything."

"Right . . ."

"But if he surrenders on his own, he believes he won."

"Isn't that rather underhanded and manipulative?"

Greta Grazich, soon to be Dare, sweet and lovely future wife of my beloved Preston, gave me a very wise glance. "Ella, dear, a certain level of manipulation is required in any happy marriage. I promise you, the men are doing it to us."

"Self-defense, perhaps?"

"Just so." She clinked her teacup against mine. "Every woman for herself."

The ladies were still at it when I peeped back into the parlor, and I decided my best play was to slip upstairs, even at the cost of the medicinal sherry I wanted. I would do fine with my book without it.

I had just changed into my wrapper and taken my hair down into a braid when I realized the new library book I wanted was still in my bag in the foyer. I decided to risk the ladies seeing me in my purple wrapper and slippers because I really did want to find out exactly how Anne of Cleves had managed to escape Henry VIII with her head.

Naturally, as I picked up the book, the door slammed open, to the sound of laughter and footsteps.

"Come along, Barrister, we'll at least end the night with some decent whisky."

"Yes, please."

"And for me as well."

The three froze at the sight of me, all blushing and squirming like bad little boys.

I couldn't hold back a laugh. "It's quite all right, fellows. I'm glad you enjoyed your evening."

"Well, we surely enjoyed the presentations," Gil said carefully, with something odd in his aspect. "The speeches were very fine, and Mr. Bridgewater was quite the centerpiece."

Cabot gave a small, self-deprecating shrug.

"Don't be so modest, Cabot," Tommy cut in. "You did a magnificent rendition of the Gettysburg Address."

"Thanks, Tom." His grin made it clear that Tommy's opinion mattered a great deal to him. But then he coughed, as if he were stifling some sort of gastric unpleasantness.

I noted that all three gentlemen looked a bit pale.

"The refreshments did not quite measure up to the occasion, I'm afraid." Cabot shook his head and swallowed hard.

"No?"

"New caterer. Not nearly the standard of our previous one."

Neither Tommy nor Gil would ever be so rude as to complain of the quality of a dinner he had attended as a guest, but both looked as if they were preparing to join Cabot in a bout of dyspepsia.

Whisky was not known for settling the stomach, and I suspected the true issue was as much the amount of libation enjoyed with the unfortunate refreshments. But men must have their nights out, and I decided there was no point in that discussion at the moment.

If ever, really. It was harmless enough, and I knew from Tommy's occasional misbehavior with the sports writers that such things carried their own punishment. The gents would be sipping lukewarm tea and begging for quiet in the morning.

I stifled a snicker and very gracefully bowed to the ensemble.

"I am going to bed with my book. I'll see you later, gentlemen."

"Good night, Heller."

"Sleep well, Shane." Gil moved toward me and took my hand, but then something in his face changed. "Er—I had best be going."

He walked to the door with a speed I had not realized he was capable of. Cabot and Tommy exchanged glances, then turned to me, clearly defending their own.

"A man doesn't wish to be seen at less than his best by his beloved, Miss Ella."

"A bit late for that." I sighed. "Good night, gentlemen."

Cabot and Tommy headed, sneakily—they thought— for the parlor and the liquor cabinet. From the drawing room, though, the countess and her sisters, who had naturally not missed an instant of the drama, gave me knowing smiles as I swept upstairs.

I did not give in to the laugh until I had closed my door, certain that the fellows' indisposition was a matter of amusement and not concern. It was clearly just the nasty consequences of a night out.

Nothing like men being boys. And, as I had learned long ago with Tommy and the sports writers, no smarter play for a woman than to leave them to it.

Chapter 19

In Which His Grace Is in Need of Care

The next day dawned chilly but dry, with the early-winter sunshine that seems especially cruel with cold temperatures. It probably seemed crueler still to any gentlemen who had forgotten to close their blinds before retiring to their couches to sleep off their libations.

I did not expect to see Tommy early in the day, and I was not disappointed. He would likely appear at luncheon, perfectly turned out and back to his usual charming self, with only a few shadows under his eyes to betray his activities of the previous evening.

While I did not know Gil or Cabot well enough to know how they might behave after a gentlemen's night, I suspected neither of them would be in evidence that day. That was quite all right; I had any number of things to do, including a chat with Anna Abramovitz and a very quiet and personal mission to the stationer's, about which more later.

Since *I* had not been out until all hours misbehaving, I was up quite early, and Rosa handed me the *Beacon* the minute I arrived downstairs.

"Miss Hetty's gone and done it now."

"What?"

She pointed to the front, right side, below the fold. It probably would have been the banner, except that one Congressman Charles Chickering had fallen to his death—in his nightclothes, yet—from a hotel window on Park Avenue. While I offered a quick prayer for the repose of the unfortunate lawmaker's soul, I also could not restrain myself from adding one of thanks that he'd shuffled off the mortal coil, and taken the top headline, at this exact moment.

Hetty had given an interview. To the only other woman reporter on staff, who had clearly learned her writing skills from reading Gothic novels. It would have helped if my friend could have managed to play along as the poor threatened heroine. Instead, it read about as cold and clinical as an account of road construction:

"He put his hands on me, and I could not stand for that. So of course I stabbed him."

At least according to Amelia Brayhall, Hetty wiped a ladylike tear from her eye at that moment. I rather doubted it.

"God forgive me for saying it, miss," Rosa began, "but I don't think he attacked her."

"No?"

"In my first job, the grandfather chased me around. I was faster—except for the time he got me behind the scullery door. If the cook hadn't walked in . . ."

Her little face was tight, but her voice absolutely cool, as if it had happened to someone else. Everyone isn't left shaky by terrible experiences . . . but we all have marks.

"I was cornered by an artistic director," I said.

"Do you still feel sick and nasty inside thinking of it?"

"I do. Even though it wasn't my fault—as you know it was not yours."

"I do. Father Michael says the occasion of sin is the evil in a man's mind," Rosa nodded. "But there's just something in the way Miss Hetty describes it that tells me it didn't happen that way."

"I agree."

"What's going to happen to her?"

"She has a very, very good lawyer. Hopefully he will convince her that she needs to tell the truth."

"I'm not saying she wasn't right to stop that man, you know. If she did."

"Whoever stopped Darren Eyckhouse was absolutely right." I joined Rosa in a definite nod. "But Hetty's playing a very dangerous game, and I hope she finds a safe way out."

"Me too, miss."

After that troubling beginning, the day moved in a more pleasant direction, with a lovely ladies' breakfast, in which my guests and I enjoyed a most enlightening discussion of their latest excursion to the Metropolitan Museum—and pointedly ignored the story in the *Beacon*. Properly fortified, I was preparing to run upstairs to vocalize, when I heard the telephone.

The ladies were reading and generally considered such new-fangled things beneath their notice. Far be it from me to argue.

"HurleyResidenceMayIAskWho'sCalling!"

Someone perhaps needs a review on phone manners. Or elocution. Or both.

Sophia looked up to me on the stairs, her aspect a tick more frantic than usual when dealing with Mr. Alexander Graham Bell's invention. "Miss? It's for you."

"Who is it?"

"Someone named Lacey? A Scotsman?"

I stepped down and took the machine, wondering if a friend of the ladies was looking for them. "It's Ella Shane, may I help you?"

"Shane? Is my mother about?"

Of course. It was not a Scotsman named Lacey but a Northerner named Leith. Dukes generally use their title as their name in their own circles, and poor Sophia would never have figured that out. Unlike Rosa, she was not a regular reader of the papers, and for all I knew, she thought Gil was the Prince of Wales.

We are all quite thankful that he is not.

"The dowager countess is upstairs. Should I—"

"Absolutely not. And I will teach Montezuma things that will make the sports writers blush if you breathe a word to her."

I would have laughed except for the odd gravelly note in his voice. "What?"

"My indisposition of last night is turning out to be rather significant. I must have had a bad oyster, though I have no idea how."

"I'm sorry."

"Not nearly as sorry as I am." He cleared his throat. "Normally, I only eat oysters when I am at home in the North, where the waters are very clean. I must have taken one without thinking, because it's the only thing that would make me this ill."

"How can I help? Shall I come—"

"Please no."

"Then . . ."

"Can you send to your doctor? I do not know the American name of the remedy one uses to settle the stomach at such times, and I would rather not rely on the intuition of a chemist."

"All right," I said in a notably dubious tone.

"It really is not that serious, Shane. I do not need nursing or, God forbid, my mother and aunts. I simply need a competent doctor to recommend the correct medicine."

"My doctor is exceedingly competent. She is also a woman."

"Excellent on both counts."

"Really?"

"Quite. Please send to her, and not a word to my mother."

"Not a one."

He was silent for a moment, and then: "I do love you, Shane."

"I love you. Now let me get to work."

It was a simple enough matter, all settled before the ladies even looked up from their books. Dr. Silver was able to arrange a quick visit to the Waverly Place Hotel at midday, since she was already coming out to check on a new mother a few blocks away. Gil sent word to his mother that he had an unexpected matter of business to tend today, and his relatives decided to take that as their cue to go back up to the Ladies' Mile and explore the department stores in more detail, an expedition that he would never have joined.

I might have, but I was frankly glad to have a quiet house for a while. By the time I finished vocalizing, with much happy help from Montezuma, and slipped out to do my own little errands, a pale and greenish Tommy had indeed surfaced, just before lunchtime. He brushed off any suggestions of food and promptly headed uptown to see how Cabot was faring with his sickness, making the place mine, all mine.

And what sort of decadence did I indulge in? I suspect you know me well enough by now to know exactly what sort of luxurious misbehavior I had in mind. I wrapped myself in my favorite afghan, curled up before the fire with that neglected book on Anne of Cleves, and settled in for another reading session.

It started off feeling rather marvelous, but I had spent a great deal of time in recent weeks in such occupations, and I was beginning—horrible thought!—to actually be bored by my free time. At that, I had to laugh at myself; once we were in London for the run, I would surely be quite desperate for even a few minutes of quiet to read.

And who knew how I would arrange my days once Gil and I married? If we could agree on marrying.

Best to enjoy this time while I could.

Even so, the quiet was just starting to feel like a bit much when Dr. Silver walked in, Sophia trailing behind her.

"Dr. Silver, miss."

The doctor and I smiled at each other, and she gave Sophia a gentle nod, clearly seeing something of her own young daughter in the girl. "I was in the neighborhood, of course, and thought we'd talk a moment about the children's hospital benefit."

"Wonderful. Perhaps over coffee?" I offered. "Mrs. G always keeps a fresh pot."

"Oh, yes, please." She unwound her scarf and sighed a bit. "It is going to be a long afternoon at the office. There is a particularly nasty little cough going around, and I will likely spend the next several hours reassuring parents and telling them to give the children tea with honey."

With the encouragement of coffee, happily delivered by Sophia, and a small plate of meringues sandwiched with fig jam, we quickly disposed of the business of the hospital benefit. Dr. Silver is on the hospital board but had no intention of attending, preferring the actual good works to the society events that support them. I gave her my customary thumbnail sketch of the plans, so she could nod astutely at later board meetings.

"You're giving Joan of Arc? I don't know that I've ever seen you do it."

"It's not one of my usual pieces." I scowled a little. "I hate burning at the stake, but one does need to show a bit of range."

Dr. Silver chuckled. "Maybe you should try playing the pretty princess sometime."

"I'm rather long in the tooth for that."

"Aren't we all?" She took another meringue and gave me a wicked smile. "You do seem to have snared the romantic lead, though."

"That's right. You did not meet His Grace before today."

The wicked smile became a faint snicker. "I'm sorry. I know British titles and all, but I find it incredibly silly."

"So does he."

"I gathered that." She nodded. "He seems like a very good sort, and very smitten with you."

I busied myself with topping up the coffee cups. "He is."

"I do not think it a violation of his confidentiality rights to observe that there is something in the way he says your name."

"There is." My blush, I'm sure, was unmistakable, especially to a trained medical eye.

"Well," she said, giving me a significant look, "he seems to be recovering nicely from whatever this is. Bad oysters, perhaps?"

"Perhaps. Cabot Bridgewater was at the same event and also took sick. Tommy was ill last night, too."

"Florid gastrointestinal distress?"

"From what Tommy told me, quite florid."

She put down her coffee and contemplated. "It's probably just some sort of problem with the food. You know how men are at these events. They drink more than they should and eat things they should not and make themselves a bit sick."

"And if there did happen to be an oyster that was a bit off in the middle of all that . . ."

The doctor nodded. "Florid gastrointestinal distress."

"So nothing serious." Despite my best effort, I could hear a note of doubt in my voice. A long afternoon to think and contemplate between reading my improving book had left me turning over just a faint hint of doubt.

"No. Why?"

Nothing gets past Dr. Silver.

"Well," I began, "I've been warned that someone means His Grace harm, so . . ."

"Oh?"

"I don't know much, and can say less. But we are looking to his safety."

The doctor nodded. She also has a few connections on the rough side of town, as one might expect of a lady who patches up the neighborhood miscreants at all hours. "Well, if it's the kind of harm one might seek in Five Points, I don't think they'd trouble with something as scattershot as bad oysters."

"True."

"And if someone cared enough to warn you and look to his safety, he will be well protected."

"All true," I nodded. "But I worry."

She was probably the only person in the world to whom I could admit that.

"Find something else to worry about, Ella." Her eyes were reassuring as she picked up her coffee cup, and then she gave me a small, teasing smile. "Like burning at the stake, maybe."

Dinner that night was quite uneventful, other than one odd moment when the countess mentioned that she'd read a delightful article on the new spring hats, and I informed her that it had been written by Hetty. The mention of Hetty brought an uncomfortable silence to the table. Tommy and I had no intention of sharing our suspicions about Hetty's actions, which kept us quiet, and the ladies also seemed suddenly to have little to say.

After perhaps a measure of that, I quickly reminded everyone that Mrs. G had quite outdone herself, and sent the tureen of chicken and dumplings down the table once again. I could not help thinking that Gil was definitely right about the ladies' odd behavior.

I could also not help thinking that if Gil had not overindulged at the Lincoln Dinner, he might have been with us to mark it . . . and enjoy Mrs. G's much more wholesome feast.

Chapter 20

A Victorian Valentine's Day

Two days after Mr. Lincoln's day falls another important date on the calendar, at least if one is half of a courting couple: St. Valentine's Day. Until this year, it was an occasion to dread, with extravagant floral offerings from stage-door Lotharios by day and an unavoidable moment of loneliness by night. Many maiden ladies despise the holiday, but they do not have to spend it making appropriate thanks to inappropriate men while perhaps hoping for a better contender.

This year, however, the better contender had arrived.

The countess and her sisters made what I'm sure they believed was a subtle interrogation of me at breakfast.

"Are you planning a trip to the lending library today, dear?" the countess started in a carefully casual tone as she plucked the most heavily iced cinnamon roll from the platter. Her sisters were watching me rather too closely.

"I hadn't intended one. I have a fencing lesson this afternoon, and of course my daily vocal work, but I had intended to stay close to home today."

"Delightful. Gilbert has apparently concluded whatever

unexpected business he was tending to yesterday. He may come to tea."

"Lovely." I kept a neutral expression, even though I saw the sparkle in her eyes.

The previous day, I had slipped away to the stationer's to buy my first-ever romantic Valentine card. I'd already been to the bookseller for an appropriate gift to go with it, a volume of Shakespeare's sonnets. With Gil's indisposition, I had not been sure when I would have a chance to give it to him.

From all that I'd read, I understood that Britons, if anything, make more of Valentine's Day than Americans do, and I admit to being rather curious to see what Gil might produce. The behavior of the countess and her sisters gave me reason to hope for at least some consideration. The fact that those three sensible and excellent ladies were beaming like happy cupids strongly suggested my first real romantic Valentine's Day might be a success.

Other less pleasant duties took precedence, however.

The inaugural florist's boy arrived before we finished breakfast, and by midmorning, I had offered tips and signatures for close to a dozen overdone arrangements, including the usual red roses from Grover Duquesne and lilies of the valley from Teddy Bridgewater. They, along with most of the others, went straight to the women's hospital—where the poor mothers in the lying-in ward might get some well-deserved joy from them.

Only a lovely fresh nosegay of spring flowers from Cabot and a small formal arrangement of gladioli from the Met stayed in the drawing room for all to enjoy. Friendship and professional tributes are always welcome in my home; the florid importunings of men with ill intent never are. Despite that, I, of course, saved the cards to write proper thank-yous, because a lady *always* sends an appropriate note.

Teddy had apparently scrawled his own card, with thick black ink: *Do not forget the one who adores you.* The Captain of Industry's card was the same as every other, neat and unremarkable copperplate, likely from his social secretary: *With fondest wishes.* Somehow, it always managed to remind me that his actual wishes were unprintable.

There was one bouquet for which I could not send a thank-you. A dainty little arrangement of white roses, with a small newspaper clipping attached to the unsigned card: *Consider it my gift, and my way of making the world a bit better.*

The clipping, just a couple of lines, was an anodyne account of a fire at a domestic service agency off Fourteenth Street, leaving its owners badly hurt and putting it completely out of business. Connor's "gift," of course, was not nearly as much for me as for the unfortunate young girls the agency had preyed upon, likely the same sort of little Irish starvelings that I, his sisters and so many others had once been.

I probably should have been horrified, but no. Justice takes many forms, and they do not all come in a court of law, whatever my barrister beloved may believe.

I took the little nosegay up to my room between deliveries. No need for anyone to see and remark on it.

Once the rest of the flowers were sent on, I put the cards with the others, in my lap desk, with plans to write notes later in the day, and left the Highland ladies to their pleasure in another whist grudge match. I truly did have a good bit of vocal work to do before the fencing lesson, but I also did not wish to appear to be mooning about the house waiting for my swain to produce a Valentine.

In any case, I had a pleasant duty first. Mrs. G—Greta!—
was bustling about the kitchen, preparing a very pretty tea
when I stepped belowstairs.

"Miss—Ella! What do you think?"

"Absolutely lovely. You *are* leaving early today . . ."

She turned a bit pink. "Mr. Dare mentioned something
about dinner."

"Perfect. Give him our best."

We smiled together.

"And you?" she asked, her smile widening a little.

"I'm told Britons are quite fond of Valentine's Day. I
shall have to wait and see."

Whilst waiting, Montezuma and I went through a very
good vocalization session. I did a full sing-through of the
Joan of Arc aria I was planning for the big benefit for the
children's hospital, because I didn't do it nearly as often as
other pieces. It did not sound quite right to me, and I decided I might well want to book Louis for a session at
some point before the show.

Joan is not my favorite, but it's important to offer a variety of pieces, lest one get stale. Louis's finely honed ear
would help me bring the aria into shape; he could see and
hear things I could not.

"I'm not ready to be a good martyr, Montezuma."

"No martyr!" he agreed. "Love the birdie!"

"Mademoiselle Ella?"

The Comte du Bois (Mr. Mark Woods of the Bronx)
stood in the doorway.

I bowed. "*Tres bien, Monsieur le Comte.*"

We were well into our session, the *comte* clearly working hard to avenge his loss, as he'd been since my victory a
few weeks ago, and having some success, when Gil walked
in, Sophia a step behind as always.

"The duke, Miss Ella."

"Thank you, Sophia."

The *comte* and I broke. Gil and I exchanged smiles. The *comte* glared suspiciously at him.

"Is that your weapon of choice, *Monsieur le Duc*?" he asked with a wry little scowl.

Gil looked at the bouquet of lilacs in his hand and chuckled. "No, *Monsieur le Comte*. I'm sure you are aware that this is St. Valentine's Day."

"Yes." The *comte* smiled devilishly. "I plan to celebrate later."

"That's as may be, monsieur," Gil said, giving the alleged Frenchman a lightly dirty look for what he was hinting at, and bowed to me. "I am paying appropriate tribute to the lady of my heart."

I accepted the flowers and took a deep breath of the lovely scent, so fresh and perfect—and impossible to preserve or duplicate. Only Gil knows how much I love lilacs. "Thank you kindly. I have a gift for you as well."

"More to come, but I hoped we might work in a match before tea."

"Lovely." I turned to the *comte*. "You don't mind?"

"We are almost done with our lesson. I will happily observe."

I put the flowers on the piano for the moment, Gil doffed his jacket and we stepped into place, still smiling at each other.

"I am glad to see you looking better," I said as we crossed swords.

"You never look anything but glorious." He had a right to the diversion, considering the unpleasantness of his indisposition.

"Ah, pretty words to match the pretty flowers." I attacked.

He blocked it easily. "I should perhaps have brought you rhododendron—dangerous but beautiful."

"Not on Valentine's Day."

"Does my woman warrior have a soft heart?"

"You already know the answer to that." I backed him up a bit.

"I do." He started his own attack. "So what do you Americans do for your loves on this day?"

"Almost everyone exchanges cards." I smiled a little as I fended him off. As I did every year, I'd left a hilarious vinegar valentine on Tommy's desk this morning, and he'd left an equally comic one on my piano. "Mostly very silly ones among friends and family."

"Ah." Parry. "And what do courting couples do?"

"Usually cards, perhaps flowers. It was not an issue for me until this year." I started another attack to hide my blush, and as he blocked the thrust, I noticed him watching me very closely. "What?"

"I sometimes forget how innocent you really are, Shane."

I almost missed the next parry and came back a little harder than necessary.

He only barely made his own. "I mean no insult, sweetheart. But in so many respects, you are a woman of the world, and yet in others . . ."

There seemed little to say to that, especially since I'd cornered him.

"Draw, in the spirit of St. Valentine's Day?" I offered.

Gil nodded with a small smile. "Thank you, yes."

We bowed, and I realized he was still watching me with that sharp intensity, somehow much like his barrister's assessing gaze, but more so. He took my hand and kissed it, holding it for a long moment.

"*Monsieur le Duc,*" the *comte* growled.

"*Monsieur le Comte*, Mademoiselle Ella and I have an understanding, with Mr. Hurley's approval, and if my beloved permits a kiss on the hand, you may keep your own counsel."

For a second, the two glared furiously at each other. Then the *comte* gave him a wicked grin. *"Naturellement."*

Gil let go my hand and we all bowed.

"Would you care to stay to tea, monsieur?"

"Ah, *non*. I have an engagement of my own."

Perhaps ten minutes later, I came down to the drawing room, having changed into a new silk and wool floral jacquard day dress in a luscious shade of heliotrope, with a wide lace collar. Rosa had helped me twirl my hair into a puffy knot, adding a little rose-and-cinnamon-scented oil to smooth it, and of course I'd put on a bit more rose petal lip salve.

When I walked into the room, I heard a little musical ruffle from the ladies, and Tommy grinned. Gil, though, just stood and stared at me for what seemed like a measure or more, then gave me a sheepish smile.

"You do look amazing in clothes."

"Gilbert!" his mother chided. "What a thing to say to a lady!"

Gil, Tommy and I laughed, knowing why he'd said it.

"It's quite all right, Mother. Miss Shane was in fencing garb when I met her, and I did not recognize her the first time I saw her in women's clothes. Of course, I foolishly said so."

The countess and her sisters joined the laugh. "Well, romance makes fools of us all. Let's enjoy this lovely tea."

Tea was as lovely as promised, with heart-shaped cookies iced in pink and little raspberry tarts, as well as pink-tinted meringues, all accompanied, of course, by perfectly brewed Rose Pouchong. But I admit I was far more interested in giving my swain his Valentine . . . and seeing what he might have for me.

Finally, the ladies and Tommy exchanged glances.

Caledonia spoke first. "Did you tell me, young man, that you have a good book on Mr. Lincoln?"

"We have several. Perhaps you'd like to see the shelves in the drawing room?"

It was, of course, a deliberate effort to leave Gil and me alone in the parlor.

"I could do with some new reading matter as well," Charlotte added.

"As could I." The countess could not resist a sunny smile at us as they swept out. "We'll be looking at books across the hall, children."

Gil shook his head with a wry laugh. "Well, this is apparently our private moment for St. Valentine's Day."

"Apparently so." I rose and took the package from my chaise. "A card and a very appropriate gift."

He went to his coat and extracted a card and a tiny, flat box. "Much the same, my love."

We started laughing almost immediately. The envelopes were the same size and shape, and despite the wide selection available at the stationer up the street, we had settled on the same card inside: a rather flowery thing with a wreath of paper lace encircling the words: *For Our First Valentine's Day.*

"I think we can at least hope we did not buy the same gift," Gil said, handing me the tiny box as I turned over the parcel.

I waited for him to open first.

"Shakespeare's sonnets. Very nice."

"Of course I expect you to read them to me."

"It will be a great pleasure." His eyes told me that he would likely take as much joy in reading to me as I would in being read to, and that was quite a lot. "Now you."

"A charm!" I took out the wee silver piece, a design I'd never seen before. "A crowned heart . . ."

"Not just any crowned heart, *mo chridhe*. That's a luckenbooth, the traditional Scottish symbol of love."

"How perfect."

"I planned to send it to you before Mother took off on her flier, and had the sense to bring it along when I came after her."

"It's beautiful." I took off the bracelet and threaded the new charm into place, next to his gift from our first misadventure, an oval adorned with crossed swords and the legend *Until We Duel Again*. "Put the bracelet back on for me?"

Of course, I needed no help in clasping it, but I wanted him to do the honors. He did more, bending down and kissing the palm of my hand after the bracelet was fastened.

I caught my breath at the warmth of his lips and the surprising intimacy of the gesture, and he looked up, a hot glow in his eyes that seemed more intense than anything I'd seen before. Without a word, he pulled me to him and kissed me, slowly and gently, but with considerable passion. Happy Valentine's Day, indeed.

Eventually, the thought of the ladies and Tommy across the hall occurred to me, and I very reluctantly pulled away, whispering with the thread of voice I could manage. "We are not truly alone."

"Someday we will be." His voice was low and thick, and as he took a breath and backed away, I saw something exciting and a tiny bit unnerving in his eyes. What would happen if we *were* truly alone? He straightened his tie and cleared his throat, his gaze sharp on my face again. "I hope I've done well for your first romantic Valentine's Day, Shane."

"Very well, indeed." I blushed a bit. "I hope I've met expectations."

"*Mo chridhe*, you never disappoint." He took my hand and ran his thumb gently over the ring. "Nor could you."

"Nor you."

For several measures, we just gazed at each other, enjoying the love and admiration between us, the sort of thing any happy engaged couple might do on this day.

"Perhaps I should read to you for a while?" Gil asked finally—slowly, regretfully, pulling back to his corner of the settee.

"Much more appropriate," I agreed, my voice almost as cool as normal, though my heart was still racing.

"This may not be the occasion for a love sonnet, though, whatever the calendar may say." His blush was almost as impressive as mine. "Is that your latest book?"

"Yes." I had moved on from Anne of Cleves to something that might help with my next performance.

And so it was that when the ladies and Tommy returned, they found my beau reading from *Joan of Arc and Other Virgin Martyrs*.

Quite a happy, if unconventional, St. Valentine's Day.

Chapter 21

In Which Our Heroine Serves Tea and Comeuppance

On Thursday, Mrs. G's last day at the town house, she got one final opportunity for commentary in confectionery.

"Heller, did you invite Aline Corbyn to tea?" Tommy asked as I sat down at the studio piano, preparing for a little light vocalization.

"Of course not."

"Well, she is in the drawing room."

"What?" I hadn't seen Aline Corbyn since the previous spring, when she had thrown her unwilling and unappealing youngest daughter at Gil during our first misadventure, hoping to win a coronet and the considerable acclaim that came with it.

She was the society mama who had told the "Lorgnette" that Gil was courting her daughter, adding the extra little twist of the knife that as I was an old friend of his—exactly that description—I might well sing "Ave Maria" at the blissful occasion. Though I am indeed known for my moving version of the hymn, I hate singing it because it reminds me of my mother and my awkward place between faiths, something Mrs. Corbyn almost certainly knew.

In the event, none of her machinations much mattered, and I'd forgotten most of it.

Miss Pamela had since run off with a livery driver and was quite happy with her far less rarified life in the borough of Queens. As for me, I had assumed I was permanently persona non grata with Mama Corbyn and was not overly exercised in mind over the fact. I served on charity boards with many other society ladies, and there was a significant amount of strife amongst the matrons, so a coolness with Mrs. Corbyn did not pose any serious professional problem.

I thought for a moment as I rose from the piano and Montezuma flew back to his perch with an irritated squawk. "Today is not Tuesday or Wednesday, is it?"

"No, it's Thursday. No wonder you're having a hard time keeping track of days between all that sparking with your fiancé."

"Hush." I returned his grin with a glare. "I wonder why she thinks I'm at home."

"You *are* at home."

"No, Society ladies are 'at home' to visitors one day during the week, usually Tuesday or Wednesday. There's an insult in there somewhere. Perhaps I'm not important enough to have a particular day."

"Good gravy," sighed Tommy. "It's like the customs of some cannibal tribe."

"So true." I had no desire to spend any more time parsing Aline Corbyn's motives. "Nonetheless, we must provide tea for Mrs. Corbyn and find out what she wants."

He shook his head. "I bet I know what she wants."

"What?"

"To mend fences with a future duchess. Any number of people have seen you and the Barrister in recent days, including the 'Lorgnette,' and someone might even have been close enough to mark that little not-at-all an engagement ring."

"Yes, that dreadful item in the 'Lorgnette.'" I did not think the ring was large enough to occasion comment outside the family, which was one of the things I liked most about it.

"*'Could a true Cinderella love match be on the horizon?'*" Tommy quoted, ending in an unavoidable snicker.

"A truly justifiable homicide might be." I glared at him.

"Look at it this way, you'll get to serve her a little comeuppance after how awful she was to you last spring."

"I do not think this is worth it." I shook my head, and a piece of hair came out of my knot. "Oh, dear. I'm a mess. Tell Mrs. G to put on a very nice tea and stall her."

Tommy laughed. "Ask me, this one deserves plain bread and butter sandwiches."

"Bread and water, actually, but we must impress. I'll be down as soon as I put on something suitable. Where are the ladies?"

"I'm not sure. They went out in search of an apothecary a while ago—I know I don't want to know what for."

"Heavens, no." I gave him a little shove. "Go. Charm her. I'll be down as soon as I can."

It could not have taken me ten minutes to jump into a very nice violet cashmere dress with generous lace and ribbon trim. Rosa, though she was a bit annoyed at the interruption to her mending (and reading), was happy to help restore order and a little style to my hair and hand me the tin of rose petal lip salve on my way out of the bedroom.

She was also happy to observe that the "Lorgnette" might feel the need to acknowledge Mrs. Corbyn's visit. Please no. I muttered a small prayer to whatever God watches over gossips that something more intriguing would prevent at least that indignity.

Downstairs, the tea party had started without me. And

quite a party it was. The Highland ladies had returned from their pharmaceutical expedition and were ensconced in the drawing room with Mrs. Corbyn, all three observing her as if she were a new specimen of insect at the natural history museum.

The matron herself was in fine eau de nil wool, with creamy crocheted lace insets, and a truly impressive matching hat that combined plumes, pins and bows with considerable ostentation and little style. Her small, plump face lit up at the sight of me.

"Ella, dear, so nice to see you again!" She stood and we exchanged the standard loose embrace that is required at such times. "I've just been getting to know your lovely friends."

The countess flicked me a tiny glance and smiled at Mrs. Corbyn. "It's quite a pleasure to meet some of dear Ella's connections here."

"Of course." I bowed to the countess, glancing over the array of finely decorated cucumber sandwiches, tiny jam tarts and small meringues. Anyone who did not know Mrs. G would assume she had done her spectacular best, which indeed she had.

But a closer look at the jam tarts revealed that they were sour orange marmalade, and while delicious, they could also be read as a subtle and witty comment on the personality of our guest. Well done, Mrs. G, er—Greta!

The countess poured me a cup of tea, with a twinkle in her eye that told me she was greatly enjoying presiding over the parvenu, and I sat beside her on the settee, in what she clearly wanted me to pretend was my usual seat. The fact that she'd chosen the settee over her preferred spot in Tommy's wing chair told me that she was up to something, and I was happy to play along.

While the countess is delightfully free of aristocratic pretension, her gestures made it clear to me that she was about to teach a master class in the art of using politeness as a weapon. More, the tiny bat of one eye as I took my place told me she understood that I would be a willing, and skilled, assistant in the event.

Tea might just be enjoyable after all.

Conversation unfolded carefully and meaninglessly for what seemed an interminable time. We covered the weather, the fashions and the upcoming benefits, Mrs. Corbyn practically panting at the fact of being in a room with three actual titled British ladies.

The countess happily listened to her prattle, every so often dropping in an apposite reference to "dear Ella," a pat on my arm and a knowing smile to our guest about the delightful visit. Her sisters, also clearly in on the game, brought up occasional aristocratic arcana in tones carefully calibrated to make anyone who did not grow up in a Scottish keep feel insanely inadequate.

I was very happy indeed they were on my side. Which they made clear with comments like, "Of course, darling Ella's aware of this . . ."

Mrs. Corbyn had not been a polished and practicing snob for decades without understanding that she was the main dish in a particular sort of cannibal feast. And she was not going down without at least a little bit of a fight.

After yet another of the countess's comments on my skill as a hostess, my guest gave me a sweet and deadly smile, and threw her small squib. "So you do realize you have quite broken Mr. Duquesne's heart."

"I'm sorry?" I nearly dropped my cup.

"He was quite hoping to win you before the countess's charming son appeared."

Win was not the word for what Grover Duquesne had been hoping to do to me, but I could not, of course, point that out to her in any propriety with the ladies sitting there. And well she knew it.

I bit down a sharp retort and smiled. "I have truly been married to my work for most of my career. It is no insult to Mr. Duquesne that he could not compete."

"He's quite devastated."

He had seemed more angry and menacing than devastated in the dressing room, but I forced a light laugh. "I'm sure he'll find another soprano to divert him."

"Oh, quite likely."

The implication, naturally, that I am an easily replaced bit of fluff and not a respectable lady and accomplished artist.

"Well, Mrs. Corbyn," the countess cut in, with a tiny arctic flash in her eyes, "do you work with some of these charities for which dear Ella sings?"

She preened. "I organize many benefits over the course of a Season. We must of course help the deserving poor."

"Indeed."

It is said that there is no time in Hell. As the chatter wore on, I began to suspect that the tea was taking place in one of the better-upholstered circles of same. The game had been fun at the beginning, but now it was just wearing and depressing.

Finally, Mrs. Corbyn looked at the gold watch pinned to her bodice and sighed.

"I'm so sorry. I have a fitting for my gown for Mrs. Belmont's bal masqué."

An escape and a slap at once. Well played, if not overly well pronounced.

"Oh, of course you do, dear." The countess was sweet as the meringues, but with a great deal more steel.

"Thank you so much for coming." I rose first, as behooved the hostess, and the others followed.

"I am planning a visit to London this spring," Mrs. Corbyn said, her eyes gleaming with acquisitive hope. "Perhaps I will see you there, Dowager Countess?"

And there we have it. An invite from the Dowager Countess of Blyth would properly launch her into that new realm of aristocracy she had hoped a coroneted Miss Pamela might.

The countess cut her eyes to me and smiled coolly at Mrs. Corbyn. "I'm rather uncertain of my plans at the moment. We may have some family matters to settle in the spring."

"Oh. Of course." She turned to me, taking my hands with what she no doubt hoped was a friendly and encouraging face. "Well, Ella dear, if you should have happy news to share, don't hesitate."

"I shan't." I bowed. "So good to see you again."

"Indeed. Have a lovely afternoon."

"Yourself as well."

The door had barely closed when the countess and her sisters dissolved in laughter. "Well played, child. However do you deal with such people on a daily basis?"

I laughed, too. "I don't."

"Just so, my dear." Caledonia chuckled. "How I despise the robber barons and their pretensions."

"It was rather fun to toy with her, though," Charlotte observed. I glanced over at her and saw an edge of something frightening and feline in her aspect. The expression one sees when a cat is happily playing with a mouse before devouring it.

"I would far prefer a nice game of whist," the countess said decidedly, giving her sister a sharp glance. "Shall we?"

As I brought out the cards and took my place as a fourth hand, I reflected once again that I was very glad indeed these ladies were on my side.

Chapter 22

Honey to the Bees

While Friday brought no importuning matrons to our door, it did bring a good variety of interesting developments, on several fronts. The treat of the day was a late-morning visit with Cousin Rafe, and our surprising and amusing discovery of just how wide his appeal truly is.

Before we got that enjoyable moment, however, the day started early and with far less pleasant discoveries. Starting with how difficult it is to replace Mrs. G. On Hetty's advice, we had asked a reputable agency to send over a temporary cook. But while the agency was entirely above-board in its dealings with its workers, the cook herself turned out to be less than inspiring.

Mrs. Eliza McKinney brought a sheaf of good recommendations from society matrons and even the wife of a British Consulate official. Unfortunately, she immediately made it clear that we were beneath her, and our simple tastes unmistakable evidence of our inferiority.

However, she was the cook they had sent, and unless Tommy or I wished to essay a meal (a disaster to be avoided at all costs!), we were stuck with her for a while. I asked her to prepare some tea and treats midday for Rafe, and suggested a simple late luncheon of shepherd's pie and salad, a favorite of the house, and no more than anyone would want after a generous midmorning tea.

One would have thought I asked her to thump a few squirrels on the head and leave them on the table with the knives and forks.

"That's all? You have a countess, two ladies and a duke visiting and you want shepherd's pie?"

"Yes, Mrs. McKinney, I do. *They* do."

Her small nose wrinkled.

"They are Scots and Northerners and have little taste for preciousness."

"Well, if that's what *you* think."

"It is, thank you." I sailed right past that and offered her a small victory. "If you are feeling expressive, it's quite all right to be a bit fanciful with the cookies and canapés for Rafe."

She sniffed. "Even a family visit is a dignified occasion, Miss Shane."

"Well, dignify away, then." I shook my head. "No one but me will be about tonight, so you can go home early if you like."

"Perhaps," she sniffed.

Who was running this house? The person who was able to cook for everyone, unfortunately.

Thankful that I had a couple hours of vocalization and fencing before I had to confront my new employee's efforts, I swept out of the kitchen. On my way past the dining room, I saw Tommy sipping his coffee with a cautious expression, but the ladies seemed happy enough with their morning eggs at least.

They were also quite fascinated with the latest salvo in the newspaper war. While Congressman Chickering's bizarre end had taken up most of the front pages for the last few days, accidental though it apparently was, the *Republican*

Star had been waiting for its chance to fire back at the *Beacon* in the matter of Hetty vs. Eyckhouse.

They took their shot that morning, with a splashy banner story below the fold: DOES THE NYPD HAVE THE WAVERLY PLACE HOTEL MURDER ALL WRONG?

Quoting unnamed police sources and probably nonexistent experts, the paper suggested that Hetty, now by name and profession, was nothing but a sensation-seeker hoping to increase her employer's sales. The rival pointedly explained that they would never use a lady victim's name in such a case, except that she had publicly discussed the matter herself. And their "expert" cited Hetty's oddly cool account, suggesting that she was clearly making it up.

The *Republican Star's* in-house expert was of the opinion that a burglary gone wrong was a far more likely scenario.

So, too, were our in-house experts. The Highland ladies crowed about the "fact" that someone else was onto the correct theory of the case. And more, the countess advised me to give my dear friend a stern talking-to, because young ladies who lie about such things make it much harder for those who truly do suffer outrage.

I agreed wholeheartedly with that sentiment. The problem was, I strongly suspected that Hetty was protecting just such a victim. I could not tell the ladies that.

Instead, I pled a busy morning of work with my latest benefit coming up fast, and sped upstairs to the studio, hoping to drown my concerns in music and fencing. It worked fairly well, though I still found myself puzzling over what to do about Hetty at odd moments.

I cannot say I was at the top of my form.

I did try for a good session with Louis, who found a few moments for me in his own busy day, quickly running through the song for Preston's wedding, then moving less happily to my benefit piece. Louis gave me a searching look, even as he assured me that my Joan was all it should be: "There's nothing wrong with the performance, but you definitely seem uneasy."

"I really don't like Joan," I admitted. I had no intention of confessing that I'd remembered Aunt Ellen's disturbing vision of fire as I sang through the immolation aria. Perhaps, I told myself sternly, she had simply picked up on my dislike for this piece.

Louis gave me a sharp look over his glasses. "If you don't like her, why on earth are you giving this?"

I shrugged. "Someone at the organizing meeting allowed as how they'd never seen it, and I offered. I'm a fool."

"Not at all." He smiled. "Just kind as usual."

"Maybe."

"Kind, indeed. Anna's finished her work and the package is on its way."

His smile widened, and I joined the grin. "Excellent. I'm glad she had time to get it all done."

"For Preston and Greta, we find time."

"Absolutely."

The knowledge that our little surprise was on its way to the happy couple helped knock down my irritation and unease about giving Joan, and I was at least glad for that, if not fully concentrated, when I met a smirking Comte du Bois for an extra lesson, booked, of course, to keep me busy.

It was unclear if he was smirking about his St. Valentine's Day or mine, but we were both far too polite to discuss the question. Not to mention being determined to get in a really proper match after the previous interruptions. He won, but barely.

It was about eleven thirty when I finally came downstairs, having straightened myself up and changed into a lovely and warm lavender silk-and-wool jacquard day dress. Rafe was in the living room, with the countess and her sisters, as well as Sophia and Rosa, all happily hanging on his every word. Tommy and Gil sat at the checkerboard, absolutely unnoticed and utterly amused with that fact.

When Rafe Coyne's about, even august Highland ladies tend to forget the existence of other males.

The neglected ones looked up when I walked in, but Rafe, and his very peculiar harem, did not, even when Gil and Tommy stood to greet me.

"Is this usual?"

"When Rafe's around it is." Tommy chuckled. "There's just something about him. It's harmless enough."

Gil nodded. "He doesn't even seem aware of it."

"He isn't," I explained. "He firmly believes he's just having a nice talk."

"Does he have a young lady friend?"

"Not yet." Tommy chuckled. "He enjoys the company, but he's not in a position to marry—and he wouldn't court anyone until he is."

"So this happens when he is not trying?" Gil shook his head.

"Exactly." I stifled a giggle. "As if by magic."

Tommy watched the countess refill Rafe's cup and Sophia offer him more cookies, both basking in the same sunny grin. "He's something else."

The cookies, I noted, appeared to be standard sugar cookies, without so much as a whiff of cinnamon or lemon for flavor. Along with them were some cucumber sandwiches, composed with almost painful dignity on a flowered platter, and a batch of fairy cakes, which at least had pink-tinted icing. All was neat, well executed, and utterly boring.

I missed Mrs. G already.

Cousin Rafe was eating a cookie with a rather resigned

expression when he looked up and saw Tommy and me, his face immediately turning serious. "I meant to talk to you two."

"It's all right," Tommy said with a laugh. "You got a bit distracted."

"Quite all right, indeed," observed the countess. "Do you know that dear Rafael is an expert in woodwork?"

Rafael? Good heavens. His christening certificate probably said Ralph, not that anyone ever knew or cared.

"Especially antique fixtures like ladders and moldings," Caledonia added.

"And banisters, don't forget the banisters," finished Charlotte.

Gil, Tommy and I carefully swallowed our snickers.

"Been putting in some paneling in the hall at the Bridgewater place." Rafe put his cup down, the genial patter with the ladies forgotten for the moment.

"Cabot said he got some fifteenth-century pieces from a demolition in England," Tommy agreed. "It must be beautiful work."

"It is. What's not so beautiful is that family of his."

"Really?"

"The sister-in-law, the widow? You see her at shows sometimes, right?"

"Right," I said cautiously. "She's never actually spoken to me. Thinks I'm beneath her."

"That's about right, sorry, Ellen." Rafe winced a little, and the Highland ladies joined Gil and Tommy in scowls of varying depths. "I heard her and Teddy fighting, and it sounded like they were arguing about you. He's pretty taken with you, you know."

"Stage-door Lothario crush is all."

Rafe's eyes narrowed, and he looked to Gil and Tommy. "He seems a bit unbalanced, and if he's fixed on Ellen . . ."

My protectors nodded. The ladies shook their heads.

"We only have one benefit before the London run, and then we'll be out of the country for a few months," Tommy said. "That should cool young Teddy's ardor."

"At least discourage him for a time," agreed Gil.

"If not, one of the gentlemen might have a word," suggested Charlotte, only to be silenced with glares from her sisters, who likely wanted the matter left to the men.

"Anyhow, they're a pretty nasty lot, Tom. Your pal is nothing like 'em."

"He wouldn't be welcome here if he were," Tommy reminded him.

"They really don't like him, the other two. They're always glaring daggers at him."

"Probably a big enough house that they can just ignore each other," I pointed out.

"Probably. I'm likely just borrowing trouble."

"Such a lovely expression," the countess said. "I did not know the Irish used it, too."

"I believe it comes from an original Gaelic—" began Caledonia.

"It sounds rather better coming from him," pronounced Charlotte with a smile that suggested she'd once been quite the belle.

"In any case." Rafe was blushing as picked his teacup up again, glancing at another cookie and thinking better of it. "I thought you should know what those two think of you."

"I suspect any number of society types say awful things behind my back," I told him. "It doesn't mean anything."

"Except when it does." Tommy's voice was quiet. "We'll keep a good eye on her, Rafe."

The ladies nodded as one. I was reasonably certain I did not want them watching over me.

"You always do," I reminded Tommy, hoping, probably hopelessly, to discourage the ladies, then turned to Rafe. "Any further oddness related to Mr. Bridgewater?"

"None that I've seen. But the other two don't like him much, either."

Tommy's face clouded. "No?"

Rafe blushed a little. "They've said some horrid things about him when he's out of earshot. Nasty language you wouldn't think a society matron would even know."

Gil's eyes narrowed. Tommy and I exchanged glances. So did the ladies. We all knew exactly which horrid things, and Rafe knew we did. His middle brother Gerald is not the marrying kind, and Rafe had cracked a few heads on his behalf on the old street.

"People say all manner of awful things," Gil started carefully in his cool barrister tone, "but that doesn't mean they are actually up to no good."

Rafe nodded. "Very true. I just know that Mr. Bridgewater is a good sort, kind and hardworking even though he doesn't have to be—and those two are nothing but lazy and mean. They'd probably love for him to drop dead and get his money . . . but they likely don't have the energy to actually do him harm."

Tommy, Rafe and I exchanged grim little chuckles. To hardworking Lower East Side kids like us, laziness was the worst sin of all.

The ladies looked a bit puzzled.

Gil, who knew me well enough to understand, merely nodded. "Well, Mr. Coyne," he said, "we'll look to Miss Shane's safety and keep our eyes open."

Rafe burst out laughing. "Who's Mr. Coyne?"

Gil blushed and looked uncomfortable. "I merely—"

"Mr. Coyne was my da, now." Rafe patted his arm with that irresistible grin. "I'm teasing you. You're in the family, you know, you'd better call me Rafe."

Our aristocrat returned the smile, now clearly getting some inkling of Rafe's charm. "Then you'd best call me Barrister, as the rest of the cast around here seems to do."

They shared a laugh.

"You're all right, Barrister. Looks like Ellen chose well."

Tommy shot him a small glare.

"Well, when you two decide to make it official, that is," Rafe said quickly.

"At any rate, Rafe," I cut in for a desperate subject change, "hopefully you'll be done with the paneling soon, so you won't have to deal with the poisonous Bridge-waters."

He chuckled. "Mr. Cabot's already asked me to install another batch of paneling in the library next month. That should be safe. Those two wouldn't darken the door of a library if you paid 'em."

We all shared a laugh.

"You all right on books, Rafe?" I asked. With his classes and his work, he didn't always have time to run to a lending library, and of course, we were happy to share our stock.

"Now that you mention it, Ellen, perhaps I'll look at your shelves before I walk on."

"Good idea," Tommy agreed. "Once you finish enjoying the tea and company, we'll send you on your way with a bunch of books—and some sweets, too."

He was rarely so ready to give away treats from Mrs. G.

"Mother won't be happy to see the sweets—but she shouldn't complain. She can't bake to save her life."

Tommy, Rafe and I laughed. Everyone in our family had been the recipient of a very bad baked good from Aunt MaryKat as an expression of affection or sympathy in some time of trouble. Quite often her soda bread was really suitable only for use as a weapon. Depending on the particulars of the trouble, it could come in handy.

The British contingent merely shook their heads, probably assuming that we were unfairly insulting a relative. Sooner or later they would meet Aunt MaryKat—hopefully only once at the wedding, assuming there would be a wedding—and they would understand most of it. With any luck, she would not torment them with baked goods.

"Ah, well, Rafe," Tommy said, "we might as well enjoy our tea together now, since it sounds like we're all going to be fearfully busy."

"You've got the right of that, anyhow." Rafe picked up another cookie.

Chapter 23

In Which We Select Some Improving Books

Since Preston and Greta's wedding was on Saturday, the young ladies' book club had shifted to Friday afternoon. Rosa was at Greta's, helping Anna with the final fittings and preparations, with plans to slip back to the town house to spend the night before the wedding in the little sanctuary she'd created in the ladies' maid workroom. Especially during a run, when I had a very late show or some such, she would raid the linen closet and turn her large settee into a puffy bed, winkle some treats from the cookie jar and stay up into the wee hours reading.

Just as well she had her space, because the house was quite full. If anyone else came to stay, they would have to sleep on the couch in Toms's office . . . or the studio floor!

Rosa's stay stemmed not only from the practicalities of getting up early next day to help me with my very simple bridesmaid's dress but also from the desire for a quiet night away from her large and boisterous family, perhaps with a good book. I promised to keep an eye out for something to her liking, and considering that her tastes ran from sensational novels to the driest tomes on grammar, as long as she could learn something from the writing, I had a good chance.

No newspapers, though. She shared the opinion of the house that the print war over Hetty was getting quite silly, and was happy to leave the ink-stained wretches to it for a while.

It was one of those raw, nasty February afternoons, with no actual rain or snow falling, but a dampness in the air that strongly suggested unpleasant things might be on the way. Between the cold and the need to appear as respectable as possible while meeting Miss Mack at school, I bundled myself up in my heaviest and most boring midnight-blue wool coat and a simple matching hat. I did wear my black nutria fur stole and muff, but only as a matter of practicality.

Quite honestly, I don't especially like furs for any number of reasons, and the minute some brilliant inventor creates something that keeps one as warm as fur, I'll be wrapping myself in that instead. For now, though, I consoled myself with the fact that nutrias are unpleasant evil creatures and the hope that they'd been dispatched as humanely as possible.

It was probably better not to pursue that line of thought.

When classes were dismissed at St. Brigid's, I was waiting for Mary Grace, having introduced myself to the sister in charge, and spent a few minutes making polite conversation. Fortunately, I quickly discovered that Sister Francis was not only a cousin of Aunt MaryKat's late husband but also a rather modern-minded religious, despite her truly medieval black-and-white habit, complete with a wimple that looked like the only thing on earth more uncomfortable than stays.

A small, plump lady probably a few years older than I, with warm brown eyes, the good sister was not overly troubled by my profession, and entirely agreed with me that Mack was getting a bit lost in her busy family. She also shared my opinion that there is nothing better for young ladies than improving books.

I suspected we might not be in quite as much harmony on the definition of an improving book, since Mack's fondness for science and mechanical matters struck many people as less than ladylike. But Mack bounced up before we reached that sticky point in the conversation, so all ended well.

"Miss Ella!" Mack called, running up and favoring me with an almost tackle-like embrace.

"Mary Grace, dear, a little less enthusiasm." Sister Francis offered the reproof with a small, wise smile. "You wouldn't want to knock over Miss Shane."

"Um, sorry, S'ter. We're going to the lending library."

"I know. Miss Shane and I had a very nice conversation. Enjoy."

We made polite good-byes and walked off to hail our hansom and off to a wonderful interlude of books. Mack did very well: a new study of the elements and a history of Mr. Graham Bell's invention of the phone. Her mother we treated to a new work on Dolley Madison, continuing the First Ladies theme. For Rosa, I found both a thoroughly overwrought novel about the misadventures of a fair maiden and a Wicked Duke, knowing it would make her laugh, and a biography of Miss Bly. I suspect Rosa really wants to be a novelist, not a reporter, but it was in the right wheelhouse, considering.

For me? A new biography of Abigail Adams and an illustrated study of Holbein's portraits at the Court of Henry VIII. I would have appreciated something a bit lighter, but no such luck. It was not a great concern; I had picked up a fashion book at the stationer's when I bought Gil's Valentine, so I could turn to that if necessary.

After the lending library, we took a hansom back to the

McTeers' neighborhood, about ten blocks uptown from the town house, and ducked into a dear little candy and ice cream shop. Sweets, of course, were a dangerous temptation for me because of the impending London run, and ice cream was a poor idea for anyone on such a raw afternoon, but we spent some very happy time perusing the chocolates and candies before settling on a few choice treats to take home.

The point of the expedition, after all, was for Mack to just enjoy a little more time talking with someone who was entirely interested in her, without the distractions of siblings and bakery and domestic crises.

"I think you'll enjoy those books," I said, nodding to her bag.

"Oh, yes. I'll start the one on the phone after I help Mama with the dishes tonight." She grinned. "Andrew will be at dinner, of course."

"Really?"

"Well, of course. He's there most of the time now that he and Katie are engaged."

I smiled. "Couples do like to spend time together."

"You and that duke fella?"

"Well, sometimes." I managed a laugh with my blush. "We aren't formally engaged like your sister and her man, but we do like to be together when we can."

"What about your other men? Are they upset?"

"Other men?" I stared at her in shock. "Mack, I have never—"

"I don't mean you did, Miss Ella, but there were always men hanging around the theater, and I've seen some of them in your neighborhood."

"What?"

"Well, Katie and I saw that great fat man when we were walking near Waverly Place a couple weeks ago. I saw him heading off toward the hotel where the man got stabbed."

Grover Duquesne, Captain of Industry, and very poor loser, moving toward Gil's hotel. His mansion was one of the older Fifth Avenue places, not all that far from our neighborhood, and he might have been in the area on some innocent errand, but still.

"And there was somebody watching your house last week."

"Watching the house? Who?"

"I didn't get a good look at him, but he wasn't the fat man. Katie and I were taking coffee and cookies to Andrew at the precinct house. It was after dinner, so it was dark."

"What was he doing?"

"Just standing across the street and staring. We almost ran into him and he moved out of the way. He was gone when we came back through half an hour later." She shook her head. "You know, Katie and Andrew would just sit there and stare at each other all day if I let them."

Further interrogation would do no good, I knew, and might scare her. I managed a little chuckle. "Sometimes I want to just sit and stare at the duke, Mack."

She grinned. "Yes, Miss Ella, but he's worth staring at."

We laughed together. "Are you developing an appreciation of the male form, Miss Mary Grace?"

Mack managed a blush. "Well, Father Mike says God created us to love and appreciate each other. Nothing wrong with looking, right?"

I shook my head. I probably should have given her a stern lecture on the importance of feminine demeanor, but I knew that she was really far more interested in elements and engines than any male of the species. "Nothing at all."

Chapter 24

On the Wedding Eve

Of course the gents and the sports writers took Preston out to the watering holes the night before the wedding. Being Preston, though, he met Tommy and Gil at the house and arrived early enough to catch me alone in the parlor, preparing to light candles by myself.

I was more than slightly troubled by Mack's mention of men lurking in the neighborhood, but unless they showed up at the house with pikes, there was no way I would say a word to anyone before the wedding. Nor would I ask Preston if I should be worried that the *Beacon* vs. *Republican Star* war would really drag Hetty into a very serious donnybrook. Every trouble and danger that was here now would still be waiting for us after Preston and Greta were safely and happily wed.

They deserved their day.

"You're not actually getting a night alone, kid?" Preston asked as Sophia scurried off, still sulking a bit because Rosa was staying over and she wasn't. That was part of the treat for Rosa, after all, and the lady's maid always wins.

"Thankfully, I am." I took two candles from the whatnot. Normally, when I mark the Sabbath alone, it's a rather mournful thing, but this time, it was a relief after weeks of constant socialization. "The ladies are attending a chamber music concert, and of course, you gents have other things to do."

His smile hinted of things a lady had no need to know. "Nothing too bad. Sure, the writers may get a bit wild. But for me, it's just a way to kill the last night alone."

"You are very well matched." I put the candles in the little holders.

"We are. I never thought I would love again."

"None of us knows what life plans for us."

Preston shook his head as I picked up the matches. "That's true, but it's often a bad thing."

"Not this time."

"For either of us." He nodded to my hand. "I am not the only one who is well matched."

"Very true." I pulled a stick out of the box. "Forgive my terrible Hebrew."

"I wouldn't know the difference, kid."

After the candles were lit, we took our usual chairs, enjoying the light and each other's company.

"Are you ready for the wedding?" I asked. "I mean, the suit, the packing, all of that."

"Finished this afternoon." He grinned. "A sizeable parcel for Greta arrived this afternoon. I followed instructions in the letter."

I returned the smile. "Excellent. She—and likely you—will be very happy with the results."

"You and Miss Anna put your heads together, didn't you?"

"Well, if she's going to give up black, she should be able to do it right away." In our spare moments this week, Anna had whipped up a couple of day dresses and skirts, and I'd bought a few lacy shirtwaists and accessories, all in the creamy pale colors and soft fabrics that suited Greta. It would be a very good start, and he could help his wife choose the rest of her wardrobe later.

"Only you would think of that."

"No, any woman would. I hated the thought of her having to wear weeds on her honeymoon because she had nothing else. Just not right."

"It's not a very long honeymoon, kid. Too much going on at the paper at the moment, and the weather's horrid anyhow." He shrugged. "We'll be disappearing for a good long time in the summer."

"As you should."

Something absolutely magical flickered in his eyes as he smiled. "What matters is that we'll be married."

"And we will expect you for dinner as soon as you want to come."

"Well, we'll be back in town Tuesday night because Greta doesn't want to leave her son with her sister too long. I might make that children's hospital benefit of yours."

"Good. I'd like something happy after burning at the stake."

"You don't like singing Joan, do you?"

"I'm a terrible martyr." I managed a laugh. "It's silly."

"Not silly at all." He shook his head. "Most of your characters are heroes. You're happier fighting to victory."

"People will argue that Joan has her crown in heaven."

"Right. You're far too sensible for that."

"Exactly."

We nodded together. For a few moments, we were silent, just watching the candles. I refused to even allow the thought of Aunt Ellen's vision of fire into my mind.

"You know," Preston said finally, "even though I'll be married to Greta, and spending a lot more time with her, if you or Tommy ever need me, I will be right here."

"And if you, or she, ever need us, we will be right beside you."

"Good."

"We're just expanding the family a bit, after all," I offered.

"So are you. Maybe more than a bit one of these days."

I took a breath. I had, of course, never talked about motherhood with Preston, but he had seen me with Marie's and Anna's children enough times to know my feelings on the topic. "That's quite a ways away. First, we have to settle the marriage contract, and I'm not at all sure we can."

"Oh, you will." He grinned. "Sooner or later, love always wins."

"Exactly what I would hope a man would say on the eve of his wedding." Tommy stood in the doorway, smiling, too. "Ready for a taste of the creature?"

"Just please, choose a place with decent whisky."

"The Barrister is coming along, so we have to try for at least a bit of elegance."

"Not for my sake, please." Gil walked into the parlor. "When I was reading law, we drank things that were barely recognizable as spirits."

"Nor mine." Cabot followed, giving the company a sheepish glance. "At Harvard, we made our own."

All four laughed. I sighed. Boys were going to be boys tonight.

"What are the ladies doing this evening?" Tommy asked.

"Mother and her sisters are seeing a chamber music concert."

"Greta is spending the evening with her daughter, packing and prettying and primping."

I loved the almost-reverent way Preston said his fiancée's name. "And I, thank you very much, am going to my room early with a bowl of soup and a good book."

All four men laughed.

"The exciting life of a diva," Cabot teased.

"This house has become busier than Grand Central Station. I am going to take full advantage of the quiet."

"Quiet, gentlemen, is not in the plan for us." Tommy guided the others toward the door. "Though we will probably ask everyone to keep their voices low in the morning."

"And best of luck to yez!" I screeched the farewell at a volume and pitch deliberately far higher than my usual tone, getting more laughs and grins.

Before the door closed, Gil slipped back to me. "You know it's just drinking and foolishness. . . ."

"I have no cause for doubt with you. Ever."

"Nor I with you, *mo chridhe*."

He bent down and planted a quick kiss on my cheek, as Tommy called for him.

"Good night, boys!" I waved as the door closed.

Then I sent Sophia home in a hansom and went down to the kitchen to collect my dinner tray from dear Mrs. McKinney. She seemed to take the request for Rosa's and my simple meals of soup, bread, and a few cookies as an insult to her skills. She didn't even smile when I slipped a couple pieces of very good chocolate candy, bought at the sweet shop with Mack, onto Rosa's tray as a special treat.

I offered her some, too, of course, but she declined with a sniff. Finally, I just sent her home early, which had always been the plan. One might have thought that at least would have improved her humor, but one would have been wrong.

My humor was quite fine indeed as I spent the night before Preston's wedding alone in my happy bower. I knew we would have to deal with Mrs. McKinney soon enough, but we had far more important, and joyful, matters to consider at the moment.

I took my hair down into a loose sleeping braid, put on

a favorite warm flannel nightgown in a lovely purple rose print, and picked up that fascinating new book on Abigail Adams to enjoy with my dinner tray in bed. Really, as close to a perfect night as any maiden lady might hope for.

If I wondered what I might do the night before my own wedding, since it was starting to look like I might actually have one, well, that was none of anyone's business but mine.

Chapter 25

Before God and This Company

Experts in etiquette say that the remarriage of a widow is supposed to be a quiet and restrained affair, especially if the widow is a lady of years and discretion, marrying a gentleman of similar maturity. To which I, stealing a word from Miss Hetty, say: bosh!

The etiquette authorities, generally society matrons pontificating to revive fading family fortunes, also suggest that bridesmaids are not recommended, but if one must, they should be innocent young girls, and further, that everyone involved in such a ceremony should dress and behave with great seriousness. Apparently, according to these killjoys, one is no longer capable of happiness once one has any experience of life, or at the very least, one should be kind enough not to inflict one's happiness upon others if no longer in the first bloom of youth.

To that, I say things that are more appropriate for the sports writers.

In any case, neither Preston nor Greta nor any of us involved in the celebration were much troubled by such foolish advice. The plan was reasonably conventional, and entirely joyful. As is common for couples marrying without a High Mass, Preston and Greta's service was Saturday morning at Holy Innocents, with a wedding breakfast in the church hall.

Since Greta's son, Sam, a seventeen-year-old who'd already won a mathematics scholarship to a college in the City, was giving her away, Preston offended no one by asking Tommy to be best man. He also recruited Yardley and a few of the other sports writers to "stand up with him."

Greta's daughter, Alice, a nurse-in-training at Bellevue, served as maid of honor, and her sister Magda, who lived farther down on the East Side with her pipefitter husband, stood bridesmaid, along with me. Alice, chestnut-haired, with the promise of her mother's beauty, looked a bit uncomfortable in a pretty light pink dress, already clearly happier in uniform.

Magda, silver-blonde like her sister, and frankly matronly (in a good way) in what was likely her best dress of shimmery gray silk, and I, in a deliberately low-key grayish lavender shantung, may not have been the bridesmaids envisioned in one of Mr. Gibson's wedding sketches, but everyone's happiness for the couple outshone any possible deficiencies.

We carried small nosegays of light pink roses, with little sprigs of rosemary—for remembrance, as a reminder of the long and difficult road our beloved friends had taken to this altar. Greta's bouquet was a larger arrangement of the same, and Preston had a pink rose and a rosemary sprig in his lapel.

In one small concession to the maturity and seriousness suggested by the alleged experts, the bridal party decided against floral crowns. Alice had allowed as how she'd feel silly, and Magda and I, though sorely tempted by the fun of wearing one, decided we could not if she didn't.

Not that it mattered. The only female anyone was looking at was the bride: Greta positively glowed in that sea-green moire dress. Anna had fitted it perfectly and trimmed it extravagantly with creamy lace, echoed in the decorations on the matching hat. The hat had a tiny hint of a veil, a little sartorial wink at bridal tradition. All spectacular.

More spectacular was the shining happiness in her face.

Most spectacular of all, the expression on Preston's when he saw her walking to him at the altar. I am quite sure I was not the only member of the company who had to surreptitiously wipe away a tear.

The ceremony itself was brief and simple. There's not much to say, after all, once you've promised your whole self to another in front of God and this company, beyond asking for blessings and all the help, human and Divine, that you will need to carry out those vows.

I stepped away from my spot as bridesmaid after the first blessing to give the only musical selection of the ceremony, a setting from the Song of Solomon: "I Am My Beloved's and He Is Mine." A bit floridly romantic, but Greta asked me if I minded it, and of course for them, I would have happily sung Montezuma's favorite drinking song.

As I stepped back into the knot of bridesmaids, I glanced over at Gil, who gave me a naughty little-boy smile, leaving no doubt that he was well aware of the more colorful parts of the Song of Solomon that had been left out of the setting. Of course I was blushing as I took my bouquet back from Magda, who marked it with a small smile. So did Louis, who shot me a grin from the piano.

Father Michael gave a lovely homily on the miraculous way God brings people together, and the wonder of Preston and Greta finding each other after their losses and tragedies. That was when I noticed that Preston's eyes were damp, even though his voice had been clear and strong during the vows.

Greta, taking the bride's prerogative, had permitted herself a few tears as she made her promises, her voice wobbling a tiny bit on "till death us do part."

Near the end, Father Michael did what some—but not all—priests do, asking the entire congregation to vow to support the new couple in their marriage, and everyone joined in a hearty "We will!"

It was a true honor to be included in such joy, so dearly earned after hardship and tragedy. To surround our close friends with our love and good wishes, and send them into their new life.

As Father Michael gave the final blessings, I, of course, bowed my head, but my eyes strayed to the pews, where I saw Gil watching the scene with a bittersweet intensity that surprised me. He was far enough away that he did not realize I was looking at him, and I wondered if he was thinking of his wedding to his first wife.

If not for the Russian flu, he would be in London or Leith Castle with her right now, and I would still be very firmly married to my work. The Lord does work in mysterious ways.

"... and by the power vested in me by God and the State of New York, it is my great, great pleasure to pronounce you man and wife."

Cheers from the sports writers and applause from the congregation.

"Ladies and gentlemen, I present to you Mr. and Mrs. Preston Dare!"

Preston took Greta's hand, and they stood there for a moment, perhaps stunned and amazed by the realization that they had actually done it. Then Tommy gave Preston a joking shove, and they started down the aisle. The rest of the party followed, and we all joined in the cheers from the writers.

Father Michael caught up to Tommy and me as we

walked down to the church hall. "Please tell me the sports writers are going to show some minimal level of decorum?"

"Sports writers?" Tommy laughed.

The priest sighed. "Oh, well. I had to try."

"Of course you did." I patted his arm. "You're coming back to our house after, aren't you?"

"As long as the writers aren't."

Tommy shook his head at his friend. "I think most of them are going out drinking. One night out wasn't enough for them."

"It was for you," I teased.

"I'll be nursing this headache for days, thanks."

Headaches notwithstanding, everyone jumped wholeheartedly into the celebration, which was really quite sedate as these things go, just a very nice little reception with excellent baked goods and a gorgeous cake, all naturally created by the bride. The entertainment was the best possible kind: joyous circulating, visiting and talking. Dancing is not generally part of a wedding breakfast at a remarriage, which is just as well.

Tommy was far from the only guest with a headache. Many of the sports writers were moving slowly and eating little, but thankfully, Preston did not seem to be troubled by such problems. He and Greta sat at the head table, accepting good wishes and happily gazing into each other's eyes at every opportunity. If they ever stopped holding hands, I did not notice it.

I did notice Hetty and Yardley having what seemed like a rather sharp conversation at one moment, but didn't put much weight on it. Greta's son and daughter walked over to me just then, and I wanted to give them my full attention.

Both are sweet, with immaculate manners, as any child of Greta's would be. Sam is a bit awkward in that gangly way that older boys sometimes are, and he seemed to be happiest talking about numbers and machines. Alice, though, already had the wry, no-nonsense attitude of a good professional nurse, as well as a strong sense of humor. They were both happy for their mother and glad for Preston in their family.

Excellent.

"You make a lovely bridesmaid."

I turned to see Gil, who had been talking with Tommy and circulating with the sports writers in remarkably low-key fashion for a duke.

"Thank you. I hope that most eyes were on the bride."

"They were. You've done an admirable job of blending into the background." His eyes were close on my face. "Entirely deliberate on your part, I'm sure."

"It's their day, not mine."

He smiled. "The diva who is not a *diva*."

"There are many other days when I am the center of attention, after all." I returned the smile. "Have you congratulated the happy couple yet?"

"No, I was waiting until the family—"

"Come along." I waved him over with me, starting another happy session of handshakes and embraces and best wishes.

While Gil spent a few moments offering his compliments to the bride, Preston nodded to me. "Just marry him already."

"It's not so simple."

"At some point, you realize that nothing really matters but being with the person you love."

"I know, but—"

Preston's eyes suddenly turned very sharp. "We only have so much time, kid. Don't waste what you're given."

"What—"

The intense expression passed and he smiled again. "Weddings bring up things. I just want to make people as happy as I am, I guess."

"Understandable."

The best thing about wedding breakfasts, at least from a maiden lady's point of view, is that they are short. Soon enough, the cake was admired, and cut (and in the case of my piece, handed on to Tommy, who did not have to worry about fitting into a doublet in a few weeks), and the bride pointedly tossed the bouquet to her daughter with the admonition to wait a few years.

Everyone laughed, and the newlyweds ran out in a hail of rice and falling snow with resounding cheers in their ears.

"Always good to see a happy ending."

I hadn't seen Gil appear beside me, but I was not at all displeased by his presence. I took his hand. "Never a bad thing."

As Preston helped Greta up into their hansom, I noticed a large figure at the edge of our happy little crowd.

Grover Duquesne, Captain of Industry, in high top hat and heavy overcoat, gave the couple a jovial wave, wiggling his small fat fingers, his usual smile firmly in place over his eruption of whitish-brown whiskers. He might have been any kindly rich man wishing the lower orders well.

But then his eyes rested on Gil and me.

His aspect darkened, and the little eyes narrowed with malice, and quite possibly menace. Beside me, Gil tensed, but he composed his face into a carefully polite smile and nodded to the Captain of Industry.

Duquesne held the gaze for a moment, and if it were possible for one to shoot cold with a glance, everyone between them would have been covered in ice. Then he nodded to Gil and turned for the park.

"Well, if that wasn't the death's head at the feast," Gil observed wryly.

I remembered what Mack had told me, about seeing Duquesne lurking about, and could not stop a shiver. "Hopefully that's all."

"Cold?" Gil misread my distress for the start of an upset. "Come, sweetheart, let's get you home to the fire."

"I'm fine," I assured him.

"And I shall keep you that way."

I could not stop a smile at his sweet concern. Nor, though, could I stop the thought that Grover Duquesne would have no trouble affording a hired killer, and no compunction at all about finding one.

Chapter 26

After the Bouquet

Concerned about the cold, Gil insisted upon walking me right home and getting me settled in the warmest spot in the parlor, with a cup of barely adequate tea from the surly Mrs. McKinney. The ladies had stayed in with their books and cards, and when we arrived, they observed, but did not comment on, his careful treatment of me, saying only that it was indeed a terribly chilly day for a wedding. That meant they either knew something of what was in play or had chosen not to ask.

I doubted those ladies ever chose not to ask anything.

Either way, I was grateful that I did not have to delve into that particularly distressing area of my life as well, and just enjoyed Gil's solicitousness for the moment.

Soon, it became quite the convivial scene, as most of our friends returned to the town house to relax by the fire and watch the snow fall.

Hetty had muttered something about working on an article and walked away, and I assumed she had the same reaction I had always had to weddings until my own engagement: joy for the couple mixed with an unavoidable and nasty strain of self-pity and loneliness. Far better to keep busy.

Heaven knew I'd come home from enough weddings to spend the next several hours in the studio. It's actually a very good time to work on a new role, because the concentration required blots out all else.

We were certainly busy at our home. The ladies interrogated us about the wedding for a while, then started another spirited game of whist and the usual improbable argument over which of them would have won Lord Byron had he lived. I, naturally, swallowed both a giggle and the observation that the Regency rake would have had to live a long time indeed to court our belles.

Tommy, Yardley and Father Michael began a three-way checkers tournament that seemed to have few if any rules. On the bookshelf, Montezuma enjoyed some leftover carrots that hadn't made it into the new Mrs. Dare's aspic medallions.

Gil and I stayed on the settee near the fire, idly glancing through my postcard collection.

"A lovely ceremony," he observed. "I half expected it to be in Latin."

"Oh, if they'd had a Mass, it would have been." I smiled. Even my Northerner was unfamiliar with the ways of Popery. "But Preston is not especially religious, and Mrs.—Greta merely wanted the blessing, so they agreed on the simpler service."

"What about the Jewish service? I went to Joshua's reception, but not the wedding."

"I'm not sure. I know it ends with the groom stepping on a glass in memory of the destruction of the Temple, but that's all."

"Ah." He watched me for a moment. "Have you given any thought to our wedding?"

Our wedding. A lovely topic, if we could ever agree on matters. "I assumed a Protestant service."

"Really?"

"Well," I replied, as the blush crept up my cheeks, "a Catholic or Jewish rite might be problematic for you, and I'm not especially concerned with *how* we ask God's blessing on our marriage as long as we do."

For a measure or more, he just stared at me. "What an amazing woman you are."

"I'm merely trying to respect your conscience."

"I haven't got much of one, I'm afraid." He had a shy, almost embarrassed expression. "I know God is there, and I leave His ways to Him."

"So do I, mostly."

"We didn't put it in the contract, though of course we can. You'll want to keep your faith."

"I will always light candles on Fridays," I agreed. "But in England, I will also happily attend service with your vicar since Mass with Father Michael isn't available."

"I don't go very often anyway. But it might be good to share the family pew with my duchess."

"I would like that."

He took my hand and raised it to his lips, an entirely appropriate gesture for a courting couple, even if it did get me a wink from the countess. "*Bashert*, Shane."

"Just so."

Gil twined his fingers around mine. "And how do you intend to be called?"

"What do you mean?"

"Well, you have a few names to choose from, and a presence in your own right . . ."

"I assumed I would do what Marie does."

"Which is?"

"In the theater, she is Madame de l'Artois. In all other places, she is Mrs. Winslow. Simple, really."

"I rather like that." Gil smiled. "So you remain Miss Shane on the stage . . ."

"And your duchess at all other times."

"My duchess."

We were smiling foolishly at each other when a frantic knock came to the door, followed by a wild rush of Sophia and Rowan Alteiss.

"She's completely lost her mind, folks!"

The lawyer's shocking proclamation stopped everything, except little Sophia, who slid into the room behind him like a baseball player making for third. "Mr. Alteiss, miss."

A collective shaking of heads at Sophia was quickly followed by a move toward Alteiss.

"Who's lost her mind?"

"Hetty?"

"What has she done?"

"How—"

Alteiss, clearly much exercised in mind himself, waited for everyone to stop their questions before continuing. "Yes, it's Miss MacNaughten. She's decided to throw herself on the mercy of the court—hoping she'll be cleared on self-defense."

"Why?" I and at least two others asked, as Tommy guided Alteiss to a chair and poured him a sizeable whisky.

"I don't rightly know. She came by my office just now—apparently there was a wedding?—and said she wanted to finish it."

Yardley suddenly seemed to be trying to become shorter. "You don't suppose it was our argument?"

Tommy shot him a glare.

The countess shook her head. "Women do what they will and it generally has very little to do with men."

There was something odd in her aspect, and more so in

Charlotte's and Caledonia's. Moreover, those two were quiet, which was quite possibly a first.

Alteiss gave Yardley the sort of hard look I would not have thought he could manage. "I surely hope you had nothing to do with this, Mr. Stern."

"Perhaps I can talk her out of it," I said. "I will go see her."

"I'll walk you there," Yardley offered.

"Best not," Tommy told him, not unkindly. "Whether your argument is part of it or not, you won't help."

Yardley nodded sadly. "I shouldn't have said it at the wedding."

"What on earth did you say, young man?" the countess asked sharply.

"I told her I want a wife who will stay home and raise my children."

"*Your* children?" I gave him a pointed glare.

"My wife's and mine, of course. I know who I am, Ella. I'm not modern enough to accept the mother of my children doing exposé reporting."

Gil shook his head. "Mr. Stern, if you love a woman, you love all of her."

"I guess I don't, then." Yardley squirmed a little. "She's a good friend and colleague, and I enjoy working with her. But I'm not going to marry a colleague. I'm going to marry a woman."

Tommy shook his head. I rolled my eyes. We knew Yardley was a bit old-fashioned, but not like this.

Alteiss stared. "You cannot have said this to her."

"Not today, surely." Gil's expression mixed amazement and disgust.

"Close enough, I guess. Weddings bring up things, you know."

All of the other men, even Father Michael, exchanged glances, shaking their heads with varying degrees of annoyance and disbelief. The countess watched all of this with her own irritated expression and finally broke the silence.

"You've been very foolish, young man, and clearly you don't deserve Miss MacNaughten."

"That's as may be," I cut in, "but in the meantime, we have to find out what's going on here. I'll go to her house."

"I'll walk with you," Tommy offered.

"I should go to the hotel. I'll come with you part of the way," Gil added. In the midst of all the Sturm und Drang, I hadn't noticed until then that he was watching his uncharacteristically silent aunts with considerable intensity.

"Thank you." Alteiss nodded to us. "I will begin working on arguments for the hearing. The evidence is rather thin, but hopefully I can make a good case."

"You are a most persuasive advocate," Gil observed.

Alteiss looked closely at him. "You trained as a barrister, didn't you? And you have some criminology experience?"

A modest nod. "I do."

"After you see Miss Shane on her way, perhaps you'd be kind enough to come to my office for a bit of woolgathering?"

"It would be a pleasure."

I caught a glance between the three Highland ladies, and something that looked a bit like relief on their faces, which only increased my suspicions. There was no time to think about that, though. I took my coat off the rack, and Gil quickly helped me into it, as I smiled a little at his courtliness despite the exigencies of the situation.

"What should I do?" Yardley asked.

Father Michael said it for us all. "You've done quite enough already."

"I only thought it fair that she should know I would never marry a woman who—"

"Whatever the truth of the matter, Yards," Tommy cut

in, with a bit of an edge in his voice, "you couldn't have picked a worse time to tell her if you tried."

"I didn't want to lead her on, for God's sake. I'm not going to marry a woman who loves her work more than me."

"A woman, Mr. Stern, is quite capable of loving both her work and her man."

Gil's cool reproof stopped Yardley in his tracks and made me want to throw myself into my beloved's arms and show him what I think of the New Man. Or the improved one, or whatever he might be.

"Any man with sense knows never to talk to women about serious matters at a wedding," Father Michael, brother to five sisters, said quietly. "If there's anything left for you two to sort out, it can wait. Right now, we have to do our best to save Miss Hetty."

"Exactly right," Tommy agreed.

Father Michael shepherded Yardley out of the parlor, as I settled my hat in place and Gil, Tommy and Alteiss followed me to the door.

"Good luck, children," the countess said, with a light echo from her sisters.

Gil looked closely at them for a measure or so, but made no comment.

Outside, Father Michael firmly ordered Yardley to go to the news office and think about things, and took himself off to the rectory. Alteiss turned for his street and reminded Gil where to find him, just a block or so away.

Tommy, Gil and I started for nearby Washington Place and Hetty's family home. Her father, who taught composition at New York University, was not exactly pleased about his only daughter's occupation, but he was certainly not displeased at her proficiency and the good she accomplished by it. Her mother was quite proud of her girl and glad to still have one chick in the nest, but had been worrying at considerable length and volume for years that she might not be blessed with grandchildren, since Hetty's two older brothers were in no hurry to wed.

Hetty, however, was not the only female giving Gil cause for concern. "Did you notice that my aunts were silent?"

"Odd for them," Tommy agreed.

"Very odd." Gil shook his head.

"I wonder if perhaps they saw something at the hotel?" I suggested. "Perhaps they know something that might help Hetty?"

"Perhaps." Gil's jaw tightened. "They won't tell me a thing."

"Heller may be able to pry a bit of information out of them over tea."

"They'd be more likely to let something slip with you, Toms."

Gil shook his head, more than a little exasperated. "Please try, both of you, while I help Mr. Alteiss get his thoughts in order."

"I'm sure that lawyers are like any other professionals," Tommy said. "A second set of eyes and ears is invaluable at important times."

"Precisely. And your first duty, Shane, is to try to talk Miss Hetty out of this foolishness."

"I will do my best." I sighed. "I do not think this is just a reaction to Yardley's ill-timed comment."

"No?" Tommy asked.

"It's far too serious a reaction for the offense." I thought for a moment. "You know as well as I do that they fight and spar, but I honestly think there was no great attraction there. A true match looks and feels different."

Thankfully, neither of the gents could see my blush in the cold glow of the streetlamps. But Tommy grinned, and Gil casually, but not casually at all, took my hand as we stepped up on a curb.

"I believe we may be in a position to say on that matter," Gil observed carefully.

"Well, if Yards really thinks that way, they'd make each other miserable, so they're well out of it," Tommy said briskly. "Perhaps a little lesson for you two that you definitely do agree on all of the important things?"

Gil and I looked at each other for a moment. It was true. Three New York stands or two was far different from "I don't want a woman who loves her work more than me."

"Point taken, Toms," I said as we arrived at Hetty's corner.

"A good reminder, indeed."

We stopped, Hetty's house in sight, and I gave Gil a quick kiss on the cheek, admittedly a minor violation of protocol, whispering one word as I did: *Bashert.*

He nodded and squeezed my fingers. "Exactly. Good night . . . and good luck."

"You too."

Tommy shook his head. "We're all going to need it."

Hetty's father, a regal balding gentleman with half-glasses who looked exactly as you'd expect a composition professor to appear, let us in with an irritated shake of his head. "Perhaps you two can talk some sense into my daughter."

We couldn't, as we quickly discovered over rather weak, but at least warm, tea in the parlor.

Hetty's father was not the only one of her male protectors annoyed by her behavior. Alfred, Lord Tennyson, her elderly orange tabby, immediately jumped into my lap and sat there glaring at her. Lord Alfred, a large and cranky fellow, generally allows no one but Hetty to touch him, adding one more layer of inexplicable behavior to a day larded with it.

Certainly Hetty was not making a great deal of sense.

"It isn't about Yardley, though I could just shake him for saying such horrid things to me in the middle of Preston's beautiful day."

"No?"

"No." She shook her head decidedly. "Would you marry Cabot Bridgewater?"

Tommy coughed on his sip of tea, but I just shook my head. "Of course not. I take your meaning. No spark."

"Not enough to make it worth swallowing his nonsense about wanting an Angel in the House, for sure."

We nodded, just let her talk.

"It's hardly worth throwing away the life and career I've built for a middling sports writer, after all."

"You might consider a few changes if you love the middling sports writer," I offered quietly.

"I don't." She sighed. "I would know if I did, wouldn't I?"

At that, I could not stop a tiny smile. "Absolutely."

"Well, then if you're not upset over Yardley, why rush into anything?" Tommy asked, pulling the conversation back to practical matters.

"I want to settle this now. I'm still working on the idea, but I'm thinking of doing some kind of stunt like Nellie Bly, and I don't want to come running back for court dates every week."

"But you could do it after the case," I reminded her.

"I want this over. I want to move on with my career." She shook her head. "It's time for me to start making things happen instead of waiting for them to happen to me."

"Oh, Hetty . . ." I patted her hand.

"It's easy for you. Things just fall into your lap—the operas, the money, a duke, for God's sake. Ella, you don't know what it's like to wait for your life to get better."

For probably a full stanza, I stared at her in hurt silence.

I had never told Hetty all of the terrible details of my early life, only that Tommy's mother took me in after my own died. But still.

"I'm sorry," I said very quietly, putting my cup down and gently urging Lord Alfred to the floor, earning an irritated ruffle. "I think you are making a grave mistake."

She didn't know what she'd done, but she knew it was bad. "Ells—"

"I am going home now. I will come to your hearing Monday."

I did not look at her—or anyone else—as I walked out.

Chapter 27

A Buffet of New Questions

Outside, the air was cold enough to stop the tears before they overflowed. I knew I should not be walking home alone, but I did not want to wait for Tommy. In any case, I'm sure I moved quickly enough that any lurking miscreants would not have been able to catch me.

Thankfully, the ladies had returned to their whist and their old arguments, and I was able to run up to my room and cry in peace. Hetty had always been a good friend, and I knew she was better than this. But the idea that anyone who knew me at all could think that my life was easy and that it had all just fallen into my lap . . .

"Heller."

Tommy knocked on my door.

"I'm all right, Toms. Just need to be alone for a while."

"I set Hetty straight. She wanted to come apologize."

"Please no."

"She's waiting until after Mass tomorrow."

"All right."

"Open the door, silly."

I did. Tommy drew me in for a hug, and I rested my head on his shoulder for a moment.

"It's your own fault, at least a little," he said as I pulled back.

"What?"

"You're so good at making it all look easy, and so unwilling to let anyone know how awful it was that people just assume you've always been as you are."

"Not all people."

"Your man only found out because you were fool enough to pick up a needle in his presence."

"True," I admitted.

"So maybe don't be so hard on Hetty. She's just learned that a man she at least cared about wasn't what she thought he was. And you, having just added the love of a good man to all of the other wonderful things you have, are trying to tell her what to do?"

"Hard sledding for even a really good friend."

"Which she is." He shrugged. "I never thought they'd marry. She's smarter than he is, and though he's good company, he would never tolerate that in a wife. We'll just make sure they're never here at the same time."

"At least till she goes off on her big stunt, whatever it is."

Tommy smiled wryly. "It's as much getting away from Yardley as anything else."

"That will do."

We smiled together.

"Come downstairs, Heller. We still have to figure out what the ladies are up to."

"That's challenge enough."

In the event, we had another shock to deal with first. In the dining room, we found the ladies standing at the table staring at an impressively fancy evening meal. It was the sort of thing one might expect if one were attending a formal midnight supper at the Bridgewaters'. Croquettes and quenelles of varying descriptions, a mousse in the shape of a salmon, several platters of impressively overcooked vegetables and a confusing array of sauces, garnishes and assorted accoutrements greeted our horrified gaze.

It looked like one of the color plates from the latest edition of Mrs. Beeton's, and based on the cook's earlier efforts, I suspected the plates might taste better.

"Is this some kind of New York tradition, dear?" asked the countess.

"Are you entertaining the wedding party?" Charlotte inquired.

"Perhaps a late-evening celebration with the families once the happy couple leaves for their honeymoon?" Caledonia suggested.

Tommy and I exchanged glances, both of us doing our best to hang on to our tempers. Someone had decided it was time to show off her skills, needed or not.

"Not quite," I managed in a cool tone. "Our temporary cook apparently misunderstood my directions for the evening."

The ladies, no strangers to servant problems, I'm sure, gave me canny scowls.

"It hardly seemed consistent with the comfortable style of your home, dear," observed the countess, patting my arm as if she were trying to calm me, "but one never knows."

"I had planned a simple dinner of baked salmon . . ." I kept my voice quiet, but only barely.

"I prefer actual fish to fish in mousse form." Caledonia nodded to me, then gazed in irritation at the fancy molded offering. "Awfully precious nonsense and a waste of good salmon."

"Isn't that the truth." Tommy nodded to the ladies. "Well, help yourselves while we have a word with our employee."

Charlotte looked over the table. "At least there's bread and butter."

"Try a quenelle, dear," the countess suggested as we walked to the back stair. "They look rather bland, but they're terribly difficult to make and we should at least taste them . . ."

"I have never liked quenelles, and well you know it . . ."

From the tenor of the bickering, I had to gauge it highly unlikely that any food would be eaten for some time.

Mrs. McKinney was cleaning up the kitchen with help from Sophia, and the young girl saw us first. She nearly dropped the china platter she was drying, and let out a little squeak.

Sophia had worked for us long enough to know what it meant when Tommy and I had that expression.

"Um, Miss—Mr. Tommy!"

"Sophia, dear, we need to talk to Mrs. McKinney," I said, realizing that the countess's extravagant use of endearments was rubbing off on me. Good heavens.

"Why don't you see if the ladies would like some sparkling water?" Tommy suggested.

Mrs. McKinney turned as Sophia scuttled out, her mouth pursed in a self-satisfied smile that emphasized her jowls. "Are the ladies glad to finally have a proper meal?"

Tommy tensed beside me, and I shot him a quick glance. We could not throw her out because we would end up cooking for ourselves at least until the agency could help us, meaning Monday midday at best.

Unless he wanted me to make a large pot of oatmeal porridge for the next few meals, we had to keep this civil. No matter how much we wanted to throw her and her attitude into the street.

"We must have had a misunderstanding, Mrs. McKinney," I started carefully. "We wanted only a simple late supper tonight, because of the wedding and other events. I was rather looking forward to offering my Scottish guests a nicely baked American salmon."

"Well," she sniffed. "I know that's what you said, but you clearly do not realize what a simple late supper means for the Quality."

Tommy's ears turned pink. I reached up to smooth his lapel and whispered one word: "Oatmeal."

He took a breath.

"Mrs. McKinney, I'm sure you mean well," I said through clenched teeth, "but I am well aware of what is served at a late supper in a stately home, as are my guests, who are currently giggling over your quenelles."

She deflated a little.

"They find good food well and simply cooked much more satisfying than elaborate and often flavorless dishes."

"Well, if you wish to ruin the reputation of your household, I won't try to help you again."

At that, Tommy had reached his limit. "Our household had quite a fine reputation for hospitality until you started turning perfectly good salmon into nasty pink mousse."

The cook gaped at him. Men weren't supposed to comment on food beyond expressing appreciation, anyway, never mind correct the servants.

"Please keep things simple in the future," I said quickly, taking Tommy's arm as a reminder that he'd best behave if he hoped for breakfast. "If we are planning elaborate entertainments, we will let you know."

"Yes, miss."

Mrs. McKinney knew enough to know that was the only acceptable answer.

"And please send up more bread and butter. Thank heaven you were smart enough to get extra bread from McTeer's."

With that parting shot, I guided Tommy back up the stairs. As we went through the door, he started laughing.

"I'm sorry, Heller, she was just so damnably smug about her horrid food."

"And it *is* horrid."

"I haven't seen anything so awful since the Lincoln Dinner. She might as well have catered that."

"Really?"

"Oh, yes. You'd think a political dinner would be mostly raw oysters and manly joints of beef, right?"

"I hadn't thought about it, but yes."

"The oysters were sauced and Florentined and who knows what, not that I cared." He shook his head. "Thankfully, there *was* roast beef, but instead of decent mashed or baked potatoes, it was these silly little puff things. It would have taken about a million of them to get a decent meal—and they were so bland we just covered them in salt."

"Even Gil?"

"Especially him and Cabot. I gave up after a bite or two, figuring I'd find something in the kitchen when I got home. They had to have Cabot's awful nephew Teddy pass the salt, and the two of them might have used the whole shaker. It's the first time I've seen any sign of personality from Teddy—laughing as he kept passing the shaker."

I chuckled, too. "His mama probably doesn't let him have salt."

"Not on the nursery menu."

We shook our heads together, and just then came a musical laugh from the dining room.

"Oh, Caledonia, I haven't seen such an elaborate radish rosette since my debut!"

"Well, we'd best get back in there and eat our fancy dinner."

"I'm sticking with the bread and butter, thanks."

"It's McTeer's," I agreed.

"Katie's da is the next best thing to Mrs. G. But we can't get him to move in."

"And we're stuck with this hideous spread." But I had

an idea. "What do you say we send this on to people who need it more than we do? Is Father Michael sending the leftover baked goods from the wedding to the poor?"

"Excellent thought," Tommy nodded. "I think the cookies and treats already went to the orphanage."

"Good. Poor children never get sweets. . . ."

I trailed off and took a breath. It should have been a simple comment, but of course after the last harrowing hours it was anything but. I was too close to the memory of the day my teacher Miss Wolff scooped me up and took me to the school office after she found me with my mother. The hot sugared tea the nice ladies gave me was the first taste of sweet I'd had in months.

I still take black tea without sugar because I do not want to be reminded of that day.

"Are you quite all right, dear?"

The countess was standing at the dining room door, watching me closely.

"I'm . . . I'm fine," I said quickly, as Tommy put a reassuring hand on my back. "If you ladies won't feel slighted, I'm thinking of sending this elaborate buffet on to the rectory and putting out a feast of Mr. McTeer's good bread and butter."

"Splendid!" Caledonia exclaimed as the sisters materialized behind their sibling. "Can we help take the food to the unfortunates?"

"And we have not had a chance to talk to that dear young priest recently," Charlotte added. "Such lovely manners, and so widely read for a cleric."

So it was that the lot of us packed up Mrs. McKinney's fancy late supper and took it over to Holy Innocents, where Father Michael would make sure it got to people who truly needed it . . . even if they would be quite puzzled and probably no happier than the rest of us to see fish tortured into mousse. Tommy and the Father watched the

Highland ladies with admiration, mixed with a bit of be-musement, and we got a taste of the determination they bring to poor relief at home.

After all of the distaff drama of the day, Tommy decided to stay and help the Father, probably planning a good check-ers match after the food was given out. And after this day, who could blame him? I shepherded the ladies home.

Caledonia and Charlotte were behind the countess and me, and at first, conversation was neutral enough. I made a few attempts to bring things around to the murder at the Waverly Place Hotel, with Gil's mission in mind, but without success. They carefully and neatly deflected me each time, whether I pointed out Hetty's house, remarked on a young girl apparently scuttling home from work, or spec-ulated on what Gil and Mr. Alteiss might be doing.

It was not accidental. It was deliberate and coordinated. I had to agree with Gil. The ladies were indeed hiding something.

The problem was, I had no better idea than he what it might be.

As we walked on, the countess took my arm, giving me a sharp, assessing look. "What were you and Thomas dis-cussing in the hall?"

"Giving away the food."

Her eyes, so like her son's, held mine. I wondered how much he'd told her about my early life. I hoped not much.

"You said poor children don't get sweets, and the way you said it, dear, suggested you know."

"I do." I cleared my throat as it tightened a bit. "I'm sure your son told you I grew up poor on the Lower East Side."

She nodded. "I know it was rather more than that, but he wouldn't give me the exact details, and I won't ask you to."

"Thank you."

"Enough to say that I am more impressed with you every day, Ella dear. Such an early life could have broken anyone, and instead you've made yourself into the toast of the world."

"Thanks to the gift of a voice."

"And the determination to use it. Never forget that. A gift is only worth something if you can—and will—use it."

We smiled at each other in the light of the last street-lamp.

"You and my son are going to fight each other at every turn. But you are the only match for each other. And at the end of the day, he will do anything he has to do to keep you."

"Really?"

"Really. Don't abuse that knowledge, but don't forget it, either."

Another shared smile.

One of the aunts coughed.

"Come along, then," I said, "you're missing out on some most excellent bread . . ."

Chapter 28

We Know Our True Friends

"Ella, I didn't know." Hetty stood in the parlor door frame, her eyes sharp with concern, the deep purple smudges beneath them betraying a night of tears and no sleep. I should know—I had the same shadows myself, if for somewhat different reasons.

"I'm so sorry," she began.

"It's all—" I started. I had no more desire to talk about my past with her than with anyone else, and it was enough for me to accept the apology and walk on. Really.

"No," she said firmly, taking the chair by the chaise. "It's not all right at all. Even with the little you said, I should have known what it meant."

"I don't want to talk about it, Hets." I knew her journalist's need for detail would pull me back to that terrible morning in the tenement, and that was the absolute last thing I needed.

"I don't blame you. It's like Preston never talks about Gettysburg."

I was surprised that she even knew he had been there. All I knew was that he'd been a drummer boy and had seen terrible things. "You know?"

"Not much. I saw him at the memorial in the little park near the paper one day, and he mentioned it . . . in the tone that means don't ask."

"Right."

"And I imagine what happened to you was a lot like that, in its way. So I don't want you to tell me anything unless you want to talk about it."

My eyes filled, and I patted her arm. She was really trying to understand. "Thank you."

"No thanks required." She took my hand and squeezed it. "But can I just tell you that part of the reason I was so mad at you last night is that I wish I could be more like you?"

"What?"

"Nothing gets to you. Stage-door admirers, horrible society matrons, life, career, people trying to kill you, for God's sake—you just keep going as you've been. Usually with a smile. I wish I could do that."

"It's just the training." I shrugged. "Madame Lentini taught me how to behave."

"No, Ella. You're special. You always know who you are and what you do, and you don't rattle."

"I'm not the intrepid lady reporter. I don't go turning over rocks where angels fear to tread."

She blushed a bit. "I don't feel very intrepid right now."

"Don't make the plea tomorrow. Let Alteiss build a case—"

"I have to do this. I want to be free of this—"

"What if you lose?"

"Rowan Alteiss doesn't lose."

There was something in her voice and her eyes as she said it that made me mark the moment, but I knew it was the wrong time to explore what it might mean. "Well, Gil is working with him. I hope you are right."

"If I'm wrong, I'll write a bang-up exposé on conditions in prison."

Our eyes held for a measure or more. "Hetty, I think you're the brave one."

"I wouldn't mind if you'd lend me a bit of the good luck you've had lately."

Soon after Hetty left, Gil appeared, his aspect tired and troubled, with a small but angry-looking cut on his jaw. Surely not a shaving slip. Admittedly, even the exceedingly dapper Tommy has the occasional mishap, so perhaps Gil might as well. But still.

Our Barrister really was remarkably self-sufficient for a duke. Unlike men born closer to the title, he had grown up several critical removes away, only taking the coronet when a number of relatives died in assorted outbreaks and Imperial misadventures. With his sensible Northern up-bringing, he desired and required far less care and feeding than most aristocrats—and good thing.

"You don't seem to have slept well, either, my love," I observed as he took his usual spot by my chaise.

"I am very uneasy about Miss Hetty's hearing tomor-row. Mr. Alteiss has a fine mind for argument, but he has precious little to work with."

"And it would help if his client were entirely truthful."

"Undoubtedly."

"We tried." I did not want to tell him about my little unpleasantness with Hetty. "We could not move her."

He nodded, then just sat in contemplative silence for a moment before he spoke again. "I have to tell you, Shane, there is a very real possibility that the judge will not be-lieve her."

"Men have a particular idea of how women should be-have in the face of a threat, right or wrong."

"Most men." Gil watched me for a moment, then took a breath and continued. "My sister was briefly courted—if one can call it that—by a bounder with more money and title than morals."

I nodded, encouraging him to go on. The way the family had told it, his younger sister had been happily married to a Foreign Office diplomat for a good twenty years, posted to Australia for most of that time. But there'd never been any mention of her youth, and certainly nothing like this.

"If I had not happened to notice that they were absent from a supper party when I did, and gone looking for her, she might have been in fairly serious danger."

"A protective brother is a very good thing."

He nodded grimly. "I sent the *blaigeard* on his way with a bruised jaw and a clear understanding of why one does not mistreat Northern ladies. And Madeleine got in a good hard slap of her own."

"Good for both of you." I would have expected nothing less from a sister of his.

"I think so." He studied my face for a moment. "There is something in your aspect when we talk about this. You don't have to tell me more than you want to—"

"An art director cornered me, and Madame Lentini scared him off with a stiletto. Just like the one I gave Hetty, actually."

Gil waited.

"That's all, really. He never even got a kiss. But it was terrifying."

"I'm sure it was, *mo chridhe*." He took my hand and laced fingers with mine, his eyes warm and reassuring.

"Madame gave me my own stiletto and told me not to be afraid to use it, but I never forgot how trapped and scared I felt."

"Just as it was for my sister." Gil nodded, squeezing my hand, even as his face sharpened. "And as it was, I'm sure, for any number of women the judge might have seen."

"Which shows in ways that it simply does not with Hetty."

He nodded. "People handle shocks in many ways, of course, but as different as you and my sister are, the way you speak of the incidents is somehow similar."

I sighed. "Perhaps the judge will assume she is just being very factual because she is a journalist."

"We can hope."

For a moment, we just sat there together. I knew he was thinking about asking me more about that art director, and I had no desire to relive the experience any further.

And then there was the matter of that nasty slash on his jaw. An excellent change of subject, as it happened.

"I have no desire to transgress on our agreement to leave out things on occasion," I started, my gaze clearly on his jaw. "But . . ."

He gingerly touched the cut. "You noticed."

"I have eyes."

"And lovely ones at that."

Which I narrowed at him then, to discourage the sweet distraction.

"Fair enough. Mr. Alteiss and I both came out all right, but it was rather a close thing."

"*What* was rather a close thing?"

"We had spent a few hours talking out the arguments, and I decided I had best return to my hotel for some sleep, and he walked with me, to clear his head, since he had hours of work ahead of him."

"Understandable."

"Surely." He took a breath. "We had turned the corner and were crossing the street to the hotel side when we heard the motor."

"A motor?"

Gil shrugged. "If my younger son were here, he would

be very disappointed in me. All I can say is that it was some kind of small horseless carriage."

At any other time, I would have smiled at the mention of the junior Saint Aubyn and pursued the topic. Not now. "And . . ."

"Alteiss was closer to the curb than I. He just jumped up on the sidewalk and would have been entirely unhurt if he had not tripped."

"You?"

"I had a bit farther to get away from the motor, and dove for it. I still would have come out with no noticeable damage if not for a hedge."

"You will let me put some iodine on that." I stood, and Gil took my hand.

"It's not necessary."

"Perhaps to you. Your mother and aunts will cheerfully murder me if I don't patch you up . . . or they'll do it themselves."

Gil's face tightened a little. "They are not about?"

"Another museum."

"Thank heaven. All right, Dr. Shane, do your worst."

I grinned. "The medicine box is in the kitchen."

By the time I returned with my materials, having made a request for tea that drew a mumble and snarl from our very definitely temporary cook, Gil was on the settee, leafing through my most recent library book and doing his best to ignore Sophia, who was dusting the whatnot in between adoring glances. So much for her incipient crush on Connor.

The thought of Connor's last visit stopped me cold for a moment. I remembered the menace in Grover Duquesne's eyes yesterday afternoon. With his money, he might well be able to find someone outside the Five Points world. What if this were no mere mishap?

"Shane?" Gil's eyes were sharp on my face. He had arrived at the thought long before I had. "I am sure this was simply some young fool who couldn't find his brake."

I sat beside him and set the medicine box on the table. "I hope you are right."

"I am."

"We will discuss this again after Hetty's hearing tomorrow."

"You do realize Mr. Alteiss also has enemies?"

"Did he say so?"

"He did, and I reminded him that it was almost certainly a simple mishap."

"And?"

"He was unconvinced. I gather some people do not like defenders?"

"It has been noted." I picked up the iodine bottle and a bandage to absorb any excess. "You'd best loosen your collar so I don't ruin it."

He slipped the knot of his tie down a couple of inches and unbuttoned the collar and the first button of his shirt while I opened the bottle.

"All right, this will probably sting a bit." I carefully dabbed the antiseptic on the scratch, which really did not look too bad. But it is never safe to leave a cut untended. Infection is a real and terrible danger, and very hard to stop if allowed to take hold. Gil winced a little but said nothing. "Any other damage?"

"A few small bruises. Poor Alteiss scraped up one of his hands. It's going to show when he argues tomorrow."

I put another thin coat of iodine on the scratch, catching an excess drop with the bandage. It was a small enough cut that it would not leave a scar, and should heal well now that it was properly cleaned. "I think that will do."

As I tightened the top of the iodine bottle, I looked back at him, only then noticing how close we were, the pulse at his throat visible in the open collar of his shirt. I wondered what it would feel like, if the skin were warm from the blood so close to the surface. His eyes held mine, and he very carefully took the bottle out of my hand and placed it on the table.

"I think it shall," Gil said, with a trace of the naughty little-boy smile as he took my hand and gently turned it over. "Perhaps I should make sure my able physician is quite healthy."

He kissed my wrist then, his lips lingering at the pulse, as my heart raced from the touch. I caught my breath as our eyes locked, both of us stunned by the unexpected intensity of what had probably started out as a simple and playful gesture.

This was far more than play now.

If Sophia's giggle had not bubbled out at that exact moment, I cannot say with any certainty what might have happened.

As it was, Gil very quickly let go of my hand and started buttoning his collar, and I busied myself with restoring order to the medicine box. It was only after he'd righted his tie and moved far over to the other end of the settee that he spoke, a trace of huskiness in his voice betraying the fact that he'd felt everything I had.

"Right, then." He managed a neutral smile. "I'd much rather have you tend my wounds than my mother and aunts."

"Well, do try not to get hurt again in the near future."

From the safety of his end of the settee, he gave me another of those amazing, melting glances. "Next time, perhaps we shall go straight to the first aid."

Chapter 29

The Fatal Weapon

Hetty's hearing started almost dull for the high stakes. She stood beside a tense and quiet Rowan Alteiss, facing the judge, a tiny, cranky man who seemed so impossibly elderly that I was not entirely sure how he'd managed to climb up to his seat behind the bench. As Alteiss kept his eyes focused on the seal on the wall, she declared that she wished to admit she had killed Darren Eyckhouse, to prevent him from assaulting her, and throw herself on the mercy of the court.

And that it was against her attorney's advice.

The judge quickly riffled through the pleadings and might have been ready to pronounce sentence right then, except that the prosecutor clearly felt he had not had his star turn. So he demanded that she allocute, describe all of her actions on that fatal day.

Which is when matters started to go very wrong, and ultimately very right.

Not that I expected it to happen that way. I exchanged a nervous glance with Tommy, and he shook his head. I looked across to the Highland ladies, looking elegant and imposing in their perfectly fitted day dresses and coats in various shades of dark gray. They were carefully observing the scene and not looking at any of us, which was quite odd . . . and they were only here because Gil had specifically asked them to come, which was odder.

Admittedly our acquaintance was short, but I had yet to see them unwilling to turn down a sensation—or an improving scene—and it was still to be determined which this might be.

Hetty explained, in far too cool and professional a tone, that Mr. Eyckhouse had cornered her in the bathroom and pounced on her, forcing her to defend herself with her stiletto. I hoped the judge would see her calm as evidence either of shock or of a good woman who had no qualms of conscience . . . but I was not optimistic.

I reckoned without the Assistant District Attorney's need for a flourish. As Hetty took a few calming breaths, and I prayed she could at least summon a flush or a tear, the lawyer for the People of New York opened a box at his table, extracted an object I could not see, and walked over to within a few inches of her.

"And so, Miss MacNaughten, did you willfully, maliciously and with evil intent stab poor Mr. Eyckhouse in the eye with this knife?"

As Prosecutor Roland Johnrow roared the question, he brandished the weapon, still streaked with dried blood, and everyone stared.

Hetty's face went white to the lips, but she didn't waver or cry.

Tommy's eyes narrowed.

One of Gil's brows quirked.

Ladies Charlotte and Caledonia froze, and the countess suddenly seemed to be trying very hard to hold a neutral expression.

I just shook my head, because it had all become clear to me. I caught Gil's eye, and he blinked slowly, acknowledging that he had seen exactly what I (and Tommy) had. Gil stood and whispered in Alteiss's ear.

"Objection!" called the defender, clearly glad to have something to do.

"It's an allocution hearing. You can't object." The judge glared down at Alteiss.

"Fine. I'll just stand here and point out a serious problem with the evidence, then."

"What would that be?" As the judge snarled, the prosecutor turned the weapon in his hands.

"Miss MacNaughten said she stabbed the victim with her stiletto when he attempted to assault her."

"Exactly so," snapped the prosecutor. "And here's the stiletto."

Alteiss gave him a pointed look. "You may not be especially well traveled on the Continent, Prosecutor Johnrow, but anyone with even a passing acquaintance—"

"Stop showing off your culture, Alteiss, and get to it."

"That's not a stiletto. It's a dirk."

"Dirk, stiletto, what's the difference?"

Gil nodded to Alteiss and stepped out of his spot behind the defense table. "If I may, My Lord Prosecutor."

"This is America, John Bull," Johnrow snapped. "You call me Mr. District Attorney."

I knew from the flick of muscle in Gil's jaw that he was desperately tempted to inform the surly prosecutor that he could call *him* Your Grace, but bit it back because of the gravity of the matter.

"Mr. District Attorney, then. A dirk is a rather small dagger generally carried by Scotsmen. You may have seen a gentleman with one in his stocking when he wears the kilts."

"Gentlemen don't wear skirts over here."

"Indeed." Gil smiled tightly, a sign that he was truly reaching the edges of his forbearance. "In any case, that is absolutely, positively not a stiletto, which is a long, slim blade, originally used in Italy."

"And," Alteiss cut in smoothly, "I find it extremely unlikely, if not impossible, that Miss MacNaughten, a lady of Scottish descent and considerable familiarity with crime thanks to her profession, would not know the difference."

"Which means what?"

"I believe my client confessed to something she did not do in order to spare someone else."

I kept my eyes on Hetty. Surely she could not continue this charade any longer. And surely, even the ignoramus Johnrow could understand that a young woman, even one of those faceless little skivvies, had the basic human right to defend herself with the weapon at hand when a man was trying to assault her—without fear of losing her reputation and livelihood.

Hetty and I were apparently not the only women who felt that way. And she was not the only woman who had acted on it.

No wonder the Highland ladies had been so peculiarly quiet whenever Hetty was mentioned . . . and no wonder they plumped so determinedly for that balderdash burglary theory. They were trying to help the girl, too, and got their efforts all crossed up with Hetty's.

Good intentions and a terrible mess.

"Who was she protecting?" the judge cut in with a harsh tone, reminding us who was in charge.

"Us, among others." Charlotte's calm voice cut through the courtroom.

The entire ensemble turned as one to see the three Highland ladies standing in their row, all flashing a defiant expression that recalled generations of rebellious Scots. If he'd had them on his side, Bonnie Prince Charlie would surely have ended as King Charles III.

My first thought, and I'll warrant many others', too, was: *not another false confession.*

But then I caught the cold gleam in the ladies' aspect and knew it was likely what Darren Eyckhouse saw as he closed his remaining eye on the world. I had seen it once before. In Connor Coughlan's gaze.

"Aunt Charlotte, not another word," Gil ordered in his best command tone.

"Do hush, Gilbert." The countess shook her head. "I've read enough law myself to know that there is no crime in defending another person who is in imminent danger."

I strongly suspected three excellent ladies were in imminent danger at this exact second, and not from the long arm of the law.

Assistant District Attorney Johnrow's truculence was fading to amazement in the face of all of this. "Please explain, ladies."

"Thank you, dear man," the countess said, giving him a formal smile that would not have been out of place over a china cup. "It's really very simple. We were all coming back from tea at darling Ella's when we arrived rather unexpectedly in our suite."

Charlotte nodded to her sister and continued with a modest shrug. "I decided to run a hot bath as a bit of a treat, and instead I found that vile young man attempting to—well, assault—a poor little maid."

"She screamed, quite naturally," Caledonia cut in.

"I did not. I simply called for help, and you were right behind me," Charlotte reproved her sister. "Thankfully, Caledonia has never gotten out of the habit of carrying a dirk to protect her virtue."

Caledonia offered a deceptively harmless smile.

"You two stabbed him?" The judge stared at them, his eyes wider than they'd probably been in decades.

"Well, to be strictly accurate, as one must be in court," Charlotte continued coolly, "I did the actual stabbing."

A murmur in the gallery.

"We were not about to let that swine attack the poor girl," Caledonia added, her voice resolute and eyes steely. "Nor were we going to let her bear the consequences."

"Consequences?" Mr. District Attorney asked suspiciously.

"Come now, you're far smarter than that," Charlotte replied in the tone of a teacher with a student who wasn't performing to expectations. "You know she would have been dismissed without a character and ended up in the street or worse."

"It happens every day in Britain," Caledonia added.

"Indeed, it does," the countess continued, having been silent quite long enough. "Our newspaper in London says a good third of the unfortunate women on the street were maids who'd been dismissed. We at the Ladies' Charity Committee believe it may be far more."

"It happens every day here, too," Assistant District Attorney Johnrow admitted. The prosecutor, who had no doubt put away any number of just such unfortunates, softened a bit. "What did you do, then?"

"We sent her on her way," the countess explained, "and quite properly called the police. We had no idea Miss MacNaughten would also throw in to protect her."

"That was not our fault," Charlotte added, giving Hetty a mild glare.

"Noble though it was," Caledonia said, glaring at her sister.

The sisters would undoubtedly have started bickering if prosecutor Johnrow had not walked over to them, freezing them with his best inquisitor's gaze. "The two of you saw the victim assaulting a maid?"

"In the most vile and disgusting way," Charlotte confirmed.

"He would certainly have completed his evil act if we had not intervened." Caledonia met the prosecutor's pince-nez with her own calm eyes. "We are not sorry."

"Nor should you be, ladies," Alteiss said, trying to get back to arguments.

"I'll decide who should be sorry," snapped the judge.

Everyone was quiet for what seemed like a full stanza, the silence stretching out long and terrifying as the judge looked from Hetty, to the ladies, to the prosecutor with the bloodstained dirk still in his hand.

Then, finally, the little jurist shook his head. "Not guilty. Charges dismissed with prejudice."

"I'm sorry, what?" Alteiss gasped, speaking for everyone.

"Oh, I could accept Miss MacNaughten's ridiculous plea, and let you appeal while she sits in jail, which she richly deserves for lying about such things."

Hetty took a sharp breath but said nothing and kept her professionally calm face.

The judge gave her a long glare before shaking his head and continuing, a note of unmistakable irritation in his voice. "But we've had three suspects in the last ten minutes, two confessions, and at least one good case for self-defense. The appeals judges would laugh it out of the room."

Assistant District Attorney Johnrow, now merely exasperated, threw the dirk down on the prosecution table. "Get out of here. I never want to see any of you again. Go back to your needlework, women."

"And don't hurry back to the States!" added the judge, with an angry bang of his gavel for punctuation.

Hetty, still standing, if a little wobbly, put her head in her hands, her body shaking as she gave way to tears. I made a move in her direction, but the ladies quickly descended on her, pulling her away from the defense table and walking her out in a swarm, murmuring soothing, motherly things—even Charlotte, suggesting her disapproval had been somewhat limited. Rather aggravating, but still likely best to leave Gil, Tommy and me with the unenviable task of explaining all of this to Alteiss.

I was quite certain that although Hetty would no doubt get all the soothing and petting she needed right now, she was also a most useful diversion for her new protectors, who would have no desire to speak with their own nominal protector at the moment.

"Not your usual hearing, Miss Ella," Rowan Alteiss said with a wry smile.

"Not at all. Thank heaven we all know our weaponry."

Gil held out his hand to Alteiss. "I am terribly sorry about my mother and aunts."

Alteiss shook it and laughed. "Every family has the matriarchs. You can try to control them, but it's much easier to let them do as they will."

"Most matriarchs aren't quite as dangerous," I observed. "Thankfully."

"There's a girl somewhere who's very glad they are," Tommy put in.

"That's me."

We all turned in the direction of the high, almost childish voice, to see a slight, dark-haired girl in a plain black dress, with hollows in her cheeks and deep purple circles under her gray-green eyes. Though her hair was up and her skirt brushed the floor, suggesting she was in her late teens, she could have passed for a twelve-year-old.

"Mary O'Hanlon," she said, giving us a shy little bob of a curtsy. "I begged Miss Hetty to tell the truth. She gave me the knife after she saw Eyckhouse following me upstairs one day, but I couldn't get to it when he—"

"It's all right, child," said Alteiss.

She took a ragged breath but hung on to her composure. "I was going to confess—those sweet little old ladies wouldn't survive in jail."

"You know you did nothing wrong," the lawyer assured her, because he was the only one who wasn't struck speechless by the amazing description of Gil's relatives as sweet little old ladies.

"That's as may be, but it wasn't right for someone else to be locked up for me."

"No one should go to gaol for this," Gil averred, though it was clear from the set of his jaw that he had any number of non-penitentiary punishments planned for those "sweet little old ladies."

"Except Darren Eyckhouse, if the rat had lived," Tommy added. "Are you all right?"

Poor Mary O'Hanlon burst into tears then, undone as many others before her have been by Tommy's honest kindness. He put a gentle hand on her arm, and I patted her back, both of us murmuring reassurances and waiting for the storm to pass, as our two counselors watched uncomfortably.

Finally, she caught her breath, only to speak between more ragged sobs. "The ladies are right, you know. Now that it's all come out—they *will* dismiss me without a character. At least I'd have my keep in jail . . ."

Tommy and I exchanged glances over her head as she dissolved again. This was one matter we could fix easily, since we had an opening, after all. The poor little thing would be safe with us, even if we had to beg and bribe Greta Dare to train her.

Not to mention bringing a definite improvement in personality over Mrs. McKinney.

"Do you perhaps know how to cook?" I asked.

"Yes, and bake, too. Before Da died in the factory accident, I helped Mam all the time."

Tommy and I smiled together. She'd said the magic word—bake—without any prompting at all.

"Our cook has left to marry. If you'd like to try the position—"

"Yes! Yes, please."

Tommy patted her arm. "Excellent, Miss O'Hanlon. Why don't you come by this afternoon, and we'll work out arrangements?"

"Thank you! Oh, thank you."

"It's our pleasure." I shook her hand and smiled reassuringly, subtly guiding her toward a calmer demeanor. "You've suffered quite enough."

She smiled then, and even as tired and pinched as she was, Miss O'Hanlon became quite lovely. "I'll be glad to work for you."

"And we'll be glad to have you," Tommy assured her.

While it was a fairly simple matter to take care of Miss Mary O'Hanlon, several other females in the ensemble were going to require considerably more effort. Eventually, the ladies and Hetty would end up back at Washington Square, and we would have to deal with them.

From the set of Gil's jaw, I did not think it was going to be a happy family scene.

For my part, I had to get to the theater for my rehearsal, and family dramas would just have to wait.

Chapter 30

Love and Ethics

The rehearsal was uneventful, other than the rather odd fact of Teddy Bridgewater's presence at the theater. Apparently, he was considering sponsoring some sort of benefit himself and wished to see what went into mounting one. He seemed strangely fascinated with the sets; he kept returning backstage to walk around the stake and pile of wood that would be rolled out the next night for my immolation as Joan of Arc.

I had assured him that sets are not generally so elaborate for benefits, but still he returned to my fairly sizeable piece. I supposed I should care about this, because I would no doubt have to sing at any benefit he hosted, just for Cabot's sake—but I simply did not have the brain power to consider Teddy's activities at the moment.

Neither did Marie, who was giving her magnificent vengeance aria from the *Princes*, in her first performance since the family illness. She was the opening act on the bill, and leaving immediately after, because she did not wish to be away from home too long, but very glad to be returning to the stage.

She shook her head at Teddy as he watched the stagehands roll my stake away, and stepped into my dressing room, where Rosa was waiting to help me out of the white martyr's shift I wore as Joan. "What a strange, nasty little creature he is."

"I know."

"Paul thinks he's mad and dangerous, and told me to stay strictly away from him."

I could not help laughing. Neither could Marie.

"I know, but he says he reminds him of some hired boy who axe-murdered his employers in their beds."

"Paul is a bit overprotective."

Her smile was loving and indulgent. "All men have their little irrationalities. We tolerate it because we enjoy having them around."

"True."

"How are you and the Barrister doing on that contract?"

"Tabled for the moment. There's one major sticking point."

"Children?"

"What?" I gasped, stunned. I had no idea what she meant, considering she knew so well that I would not have been marrying at all if I did not hope for a wee one of my own.

She chuckled. "Not whether, dear, but when. Many women will tell you that a honeymoon baby is to be avoided at all costs."

"I see." I choked out the words through a truly volcanic blush. Rosa, thankfully, was busy fluffing up the dainty lace trim on my shirtwaist.

"Well, that's not it, then." Her eyes gleamed. "So what is it?"

"Still the New York stands. We haven't gone back to it . . ."

Marie gave me an irritated glare. "Really? Honestly, Ells, you are going to ruin this—"

"I can't give up everything for him."

"He's not asking you to, and you know it."

I sighed. "I do."

"Practice that." She looked at her little watch pin. "I need to go, but really—resolve it, Ells. You're going to have to learn how to fight to a draw once you're married, anyway."

"I suppose."

"Oh, you will." She patted my arm. "If you can do it with swords, you can do it without."

We laughed.

"See you tomorrow night," I said.

She grinned, knowing I was evading her, and allowing it—for now. "Yes, thank heaven. Back to the stage."

We embraced at the door, and I watched her go, shaking her head as she saw Teddy once again hovering near my stake. Paul, good protective man that he is, was no doubt seeing danger where none existed, but Teddy certainly was annoying.

I did not relish the idea of participating in any benefit he might engineer, even for Cabot's sake. But one does have to put up with a certain amount of annoyance for family and good friends.

In any case, I would not be giving Joan of Arc. Listening to Marie in rehearsal, I'd had the thought that I really should be emphasizing Louis's excellent new work in the *Princes*, and I decided I would offer one of his arias for the next several benefits. Magnificent music and far better than climbing up on a stake.

Teddy could have that ridiculous set piece if he liked.

Whatever the junior Mr. Bridgewater was planning, I had far more pressing matters to worry about at Washington Square. I had assumed Rosa and I would be walking into a whirlwind when we returned, but neither Tommy nor Gil, nor the Highland ladies, were in evidence. That was not soothing, since I had no idea what sort of trouble any or all of them might have found while I was at work.

The only member of the cast about was Father Michael, stopping by before the Monday evening printers' Mass to see how matters stood.

"I saw the special edition, of course, but I guessed there was far more to it."

"Oh, there is. You were absolutely right about Eyckhouse."

"Not just me." He shook his head. But his grim expression quickly gave way to wicked amusement. "And apparently we have all grievously underestimated the British ladies."

"Grievously, indeed." I returned the grin and turned the table to matters of interest to our cleric. "Also, we have acquired a new cook with baking expertise and a pleasant demeanor."

He beamed. "Really?"

"Really. You'll want to ask Tommy how he settled it all, but our table is about to become a happy place again."

"Delightful." His smile at that faded rather more quickly than I would have expected, though. "I hope we can look forward to rather calmer sailing for a while."

"You can at least put in a word with the Higher Powers," I pointed out.

"I always do. I'm still concerned about all the talk of mishaps and threats. I saw the look on that nasty Mr. Duquesne's face at the end of the wedding. He does not mean you well."

I shuddered a bit. "Still, we're all well protected."

"And Andrew may have a few minutes to have a word about that matter now that the Eyckhouse mess is over."

"Not the worst idea you've had," I agreed. I knew the

priest had to leave, and I did not want to leave him with such worrisome thoughts. "In the meantime, expect an invitation for a nice family dinner as soon as Miss O'Hanlon gets her balance."

"Family and friends."

"It's all the same here. Probably the whole cast, including the ladies, and the Barrister and Mr. Bridgewater."

Father Michael chuckled. "He's a fine man. I never expected a Knickerbocker to make a good friend."

"He is, though."

"Especially for Tom, which I like to see." The priest's smile turned a little rueful. "I don't always have time to run about and do things, and it's good for him to have another companion with shared interests."

"Particularly now that we likely won't be seeing nearly as much of Yardley."

At that, the priest just shook his head and took his leave. Least said, soonest mended, of course.

The house was still quiet when I closed the door. I knew this happy state would not last.

But when performing the next day, one must take rest where one can. I had just poured myself a medicinal sherry and settled onto the chaise with a book to divert my mind while I awaited further developments, when the house began to fill again. The first contender: Hetty's valiant defender.

I hid the sherry behind a vase and nodded to Rosa to take up her book and spot in the window seat, as forms required. Not to mention giving her a good view of the show.

"Miss Hetty is not at her home. I wondered if she might have come here." Outside of his natural element, Rowan Alteiss seemed a good bit younger, and far less sure of himself.

"I'm sorry, no. I've been at a benefit rehearsal for the

last few hours. All I know is that she was scooped up by the countess and her sisters, and I have no idea where those ladies would take her."

Alteiss looked downcast.

"Would you like some tea?" I asked, hoping refreshments might help.

"Please. That's very kind."

He was quiet for the few moments it took our soon-to-be former temporary cook to set out a tray with a handful of nearly stale wafers scraped from the bottom of a box of Greta's leftovers, the sparseness of the treats no doubt a comment on her impending replacement rather than on my visitor. Smiling at the resolution of that particular drama, I reflected that I would be very glad indeed to see Miss O'Hanlon in the morning.

Alteiss didn't want baked goods—or "bads"—anyway. He wrapped his long, bony hands around the teacup and looked down at the liquid rather than drinking it.

"It was a rather shocking day," I began. "It ended well, but what a way to get to safety."

"Miss MacNaughten did not confide in me."

"No. She was determined to take the blame."

"Noble, but misguided."

"Terribly misguided."

"But also terribly noble." He looked up from his tea, and I knew.

Why not? Hetty is a very intelligent and attractive woman, and Alteiss perhaps only ten years her senior, despite his illustrious career. Really, I thought, sipping my own tea, he's not at all unappealing, in a rawboned, Lincoln-ish way.

There is something about a barrister, after all.

"She is a woman of strong convictions," I agreed. "It is one of the things I admire most about her."

"As do I." He looked into his tea again, then back to me. "Understand, I would not be pursuing this conversation if she were still my client, and I will never allow her to retain my services again."

I suspected what was coming. "As a lawyer."

Rowan Alteiss, top defender, suddenly looked like a shy boy caught in the cookie jar. "Yes, as a lawyer, Miss Shane."

"I'm sorry," I said quickly. "I'm quite impressed by your ethics."

"We're bound to a code, after all. Our word and our principles are all we have."

"So true." I really liked this man, and strongly suspected Hetty might do the same. *If* he was not hoping for an Angel in the House.

"So about Miss MacNaughten," the lawyer said, putting down his tea, apparently unable to resist a bit of evidence gathering. "Was Mr. Stern a serious beau?"

"Not at all." Hetty's pride had been hurt far more than her heart, after all.

"Well, I am sure Miss MacNaughten has many other suitors."

"No one of any significance."

"How extraordinary. I would have assumed the gentlemen were lining up."

Time for *me* to do a little investigating. "The gentlemen might line up, Mr. Alteiss, but if they cannot respect her need to work, they'd best keep walking."

Alteiss smiled. "I have no more right to ask a lady to give up her life's work than she does to ask me to do the same."

"Quite modern of you."

"Well, I happen to believe that happy women make better wives and mothers, which for many likely means some kind of work."

I smiled. "I believe the same."

"I gather you and His Grace are working out arrangements?"

"As you will learn if you are fortunate, a woman who comes with a career requires a certain amount of accommodation."

"Just so. Any advice?"

"I would seek her out once she's had a chance to clean up and have a nice long rest, and perhaps offer to squire her for a walk."

"Something so simple?"

"You want to be able to talk, to assess each other as man and woman, not lawyer and client or reporter and subject."

"True."

"And approach carefully and gently."

He laughed, a wholehearted guffaw that warmed his severe features. Hopefully Hetty would see that early on. "Miss Shane, I'm hardly the sweep 'em off their feet man."

"You never know." I grinned back. "But all of that overwhelming the lady with adoration nonsense only works in sensational fiction. In real life, we like a man who wins us with respect and understanding."

Alteiss nodded.

"We don't need heroes. We need friends."

"I like that."

"You can use it without credit."

We shared a chuckle, and soon after, I saw him to the door, just as Sophia ran for the bell.

Hetty, her hair smooth and her eyes clear, now in her best hat and coat instead of the plainer things she'd worn to court in fear of being dragged off to jail, walked into the foyer.

Alteiss froze at the sight of her. Not unexpected. But she froze at the sight of him, with an expression I'd never seen when Yardley was about.

I let them just stand there for a while, gazing at each other as man and woman for the first time.

"Miss MacNaughten," Alteiss said finally, blushing as if he were Irish.

"Mr. Alteiss. So good to see you."

"Good to see you looking like yourself again," I offered.

"Oh, Ella." Hetty turned out a pretty good blush herself. "I thought you'd be done with the run-through by now."

"Yes." I smiled. "Mr. Alteiss has been looking for you."

"He has?"

"I just . . . I wanted to be sure you were all right."

Hetty smiled. He smiled.

"Hetty, I'm expecting the Highland ladies back any second. Perhaps you should let Mr. Alteiss walk you home, and we'll talk later?"

I kept down a giggle at the expressions of joy and relief on their faces at having someone settle matters for them.

"That's a lovely idea," Hetty said quickly, "if you don't mind . . ."

"I would be delighted." Delight was a pale word for the pleasure that warmed his spare face.

"Did you need something from me?" I asked quickly, as they turned for the door.

"Oh, yes." Hetty laughed. "I just wanted to thank you, and apologize to His Grace. I had no idea what his mother and aunts had done, and—"

"I'm quite sure he doesn't blame you. We'll make it up over tea later this week."

She nodded. "Thank you, Ells."

I smiled. "Have a good evening. You too, Mr. Alteiss."

"Thanks, Miss Shane."

He offered his arm to Hetty, and they walked out.

Back in the quiet parlor, I took up my sherry once more. It was dark outside, and it occurred to me that the ladies might be anywhere by now, never mind Tommy, and Gil might or might not come by. If I pleaded indisposition, topped off my glass, and asked our surly soon-to-be former cook to send a tray of soup and toast to my room, I could get a decent night's sleep and the drama would still be there in the morning.

Not to mention annoying her one more time by requesting a simple and spare meal.

It might well have been the best idea I had all day.

Chapter 31

An Evening of Drama and Danger

The old adage notwithstanding, there may or may not be rest for the wicked. I know there was little for me that evening.

I had no sooner arrived in my room, put my book and sherry on my vanity and taken my hair down from its heavy knot into a sleeping braid when there was a brisk knock at my door.

"I'm sure you're awake, dear. Please come out."

The countess, of course.

I opened the door, cautiously, to see the three ladies standing in a little cluster in the hall, their expressions like nothing so much as the misbehaving schoolgirls they probably were some threescore years before.

"Gilbert has ordered us to apologize," the countess said, managing a fairly credible contrite tone.

"We are not, of course, apologizing for saving that poor little girl," Caledonia continued.

"But we are naturally not in the habit of lying, and we shall endeavor to avoid it in the future," Charlotte finished, as they all nodded.

I swallowed a smile. I could not imagine what horrors Gil had threatened to get them to actually follow an order. "It's quite all right. I would have done the same. Well, except for the lying."

All three beamed, the sun returning.

"Of course you would, dear," said the countess.

Charlotte and Caledonia nodded, vindicated. Not for the first time, I reminded myself that it was a very good thing they were on my side.

"Are you really indisposed, or just in need of a quiet evening?"

The Barrister gets much of his perceptive skill from his mother, I suspect. I shrugged. "It has been an eventful day. I was hoping to make an early evening of it."

"So were we. We had a very generous and restorative tea at the Waldorf just now, so really, we require nothing more than a medicinal beverage to encourage sleep. Perhaps you would join us?"

I picked up my own sherry and a couple of hairpins to form my braid into a knot. In the interest of peace in the house, it was the right thing to do. "Lead on."

The four of us walked into the parlor, which was already occupied by our gentlemen, who seemed as exhausted and stunned as anyone else. Tommy and Gil rose when we came in, and the ladies tensed.

"I assume you've had an appropriate talk?" Gil said, his eyes sharp on his relatives.

"They've apologized, and all is forgiven," I put in quickly.

"But not forgotten." Gil kept his gaze on his mother, who nodded quite seriously. Once he'd seen the nod, he smiled. Slightly.

"Whisky, Barrister?" Tommy asked, moving to pour his own. "It's been quite a day."

"Thank you, yes."

"Ladies?" Tommy asked. "Perhaps a brandy?"

The three exchanged some sort of signal that I did not see, and demurred. Perhaps they simply wanted to escape Gil's gimlet glare in the hope that by morning his anger would have cooled further.

"We are quite exhausted," the countess began.

"Far too much excitement," agreed Charlotte.

"We must rest," Caledonia pronounced as the others nodded. They made quick, but not unfriendly, goodnights and swept upstairs.

Tommy topped off my sherry glass, then reclaimed his wing chair with a laugh. "Quite enough drama for one day."

"Enough for an entire opera." I raised my sherry to the gents as I took a small side chair.

"To a quieter tomorrow," Gil said from the settee, lifting his whisky.

"We can only hope." Tommy shook his head. "Is all prepared for the benefit?"

I nodded. "That big ugly stake is ready, and I'm as sharp on the aria as I need to be."

"Joan is a nice change of pace," Tommy reminded me.

"I hate martyrs."

Gil smiled. "You prefer the victors."

"What else? Martyr or no, with any luck this large gala will bring in enough money to keep the children's hospital in business for another year."

"Always a good thing," Tommy nodded.

"Is Cabot coming?" I asked him. "He said he was planning a generous donation, and I hope he's going to get something for his money."

His face clouded a little. "He's sick again."

"Again?" My voice betrayed the same concern as Gil's narrowed eyes.

"Another indisposition like he had after the Lincoln Dinner. Longest-running case of bad food I've ever heard of."

"I assumed I'd gotten a bad oyster somehow," Gil said thoughtfully. "But I recovered quite quickly."

"It could not have been an oyster for him, Barrister." Tommy shook his head. "Neither Cabot nor I eat them. Just find them rather nasty."

"And you say he's ill with the same symptoms as before?"

Tommy nodded grimly. "Without being too indelicate for Heller, let's just call it florid gastrointestinal distress."

"Dyspepsia from food isn't supposed to return like that," I said carefully, looking to Gil.

"With the exception of a few exotic parasites," he agreed slowly, "it really can't come back once the irritant is out of the victim's body."

Tommy glanced from Gil to me and back. "What are you suggesting?"

"I cannot be sure, but it sounds very much like some kind of poison, Tom."

"Good God." I shook my head as Gil's words made the possibility real.

"Arsenic, perhaps." Gil contemplated his whisky. "Though it could be any number of other things. . . ."

"Poison." Tommy shook his head, but I could see his wheels turning. "If someone had been trying to kill him . . . the ladder slat breaking . . ."

"The cracked stair that Cousin Rafe fixed," I reminded him.

"Perhaps even that silly mishap with a motor that night after the newsboys' reading group." Tommy looked to Gil. "But why? Who?"

"It must be someone in his house if he's taken sick again."

"Someone who would gain," I said.

"That narrows the list," Tommy nodded. "Rafe was right."

"Not just poisonous *thoughts* in that house," I agreed.

"Actual poison." Gil shook his head. "We may not have enough evidence to intervene, but—"

"I can surely go watch over Cabot until we do." Tommy nodded. "And if there's poison, they'll find it in the house. Heller, call Cousin Andrew and tell him to get someone up to the Bridgewaters'."

"Will do."

Tommy stood. So did Gil.

"You don't have to come, Barrister."

"I surely do."

A glance, a nod, an understanding. My men work well together.

They blew out without wasting time on a farewell as I headed for the telephone. Any other copper would not have entertained such a harebrained theory of crime, but Cousin Andrew knew us well enough to know we must have grave suspicions and would never invoke his help without very good reason, indeed. We also had considerable goodwill at the moment, since the Waverly Place Hotel matter was finally resolved without further work on his part.

He kindly promised to send on a colleague from the Bridgewaters' precinct, as well as a police chemist.

Despite the seriousness of the conversation, I could still hear a faint but unmistakable note of happiness in his voice. Engagement apparently agreed with our detective.

I could have run up to the Bridgewater manse, too, but my presence would have been no help. This one time, I decided the best thing I could do for my men was to play the conventional female role, and sit and wait at home. I took up my sherry once again, found my book, wrapped myself in an afghan and curled up on the settee near the fire. No reason I should not be comfortable while I waited.

Amazingly, I dozed off. Tommy found me asleep when he returned in the wee hours. The sound of the door woke me, and I watched him walk into the dim firelit room, looking weary and worried, silently pouring himself a whisky.

"So?" I asked finally.

"Arsenic in his bedside water bottle."

"Oh, dear." I sat up on the settee, making room for Toms.

"They've caught it in time. It will take him a while to recover, but he'll be all right."

"Thank God."

"Yes." Tommy sat down beside me. "We should have suspected sooner."

"Suspected who?"

"Teddy's mother, who else?"

"Really?" I supposed Teddy himself would have been an outside contender, but as Rafe had observed, murder would require effort.

"They found white arsenic in her planting shed. Her hobby is growing orchids, and she claimed it was an insecticide."

"Insecticides are usually colored." I thought for a moment. "It's indigo they use with arsenic, isn't it?"

"Yes. And arsenic isn't usually used to kill insects, anyway. Rodents." His jaw tightened as he remembered the scene. "They took her in, screaming all the way that it wasn't her."

"But of course it is."

"Of course. More for her little boy."

"Sick." I shook my head. "They've already got more money than they could ever spend."

"Ah, but if Cabot were gone, Teddy would be *the* Mr. Bridgewater, and she would have the prestige of being his mother."

"Yet more of this social status nonsense."

"Best get used to it now." He tapped the ring on my little finger.

"What are we doing in this world, Toms?" I sighed. "I'm looking at marrying a duke, and your good friend is above the Four Hundred. Totally out of our depth."

"The men themselves are worth having around."

"Very true."

"And we take what they bring with them because we must." Tommy gazed into the fire, his face sharp with concern. "I was more than a little worried about Cabot."

"Understandably. You two will be back to arguing about books and baseball before you know it."

He nodded, and just stared at the flames for a full stanza, his aspect clouded with some strong emotion.

"I wanted to hurt her, Heller." His voice was low, rough with revulsion at his own feelings. "I've never harmed a woman in my life, and I never would, but I wanted to."

Perhaps I should have been shocked, but I wanted to harm Lantana Bridgewater, too. "You wouldn't be human if you didn't."

"I suppose." He shook his head.

"Father Michael would have no trouble giving you absolution."

"True. He's glad Cabot and I are friends."

"Cabot is good for you. And the two of you are good for the newsboys and many others."

Tommy nodded and took my hand. "Count on you, Heller."

"Who's better than us?" I squeezed his fingers as I began our old childhood lines.

"Nobody."

"Nobody at all."

Chapter 32

In Which We Try Again to Fight to a Draw

It was probably a very bad idea to take another run at settling the contract after our late breakfast the next day, before I left for the children's hospital benefit. But everyone was in a relieved and relaxed mood with the resolution of the killing at the Waverly Place Hotel, and the rescue of Cabot Bridgewater, especially since the morning began with word that he was much improved and his evil sister-in-law was being held on an attempted murder charge. The display of cinnamon rolls, light biscuits, and winter fruit compote accompanying eggs perfectly cooked by our new treasure Miss O'Hanlon only added to the general happiness.

Not to mention the fact that Marie had urged me to resolve matters, and I would be seeing her in a few hours. Perhaps I might actually bring her happy news.

At least I was entertaining some hope as Tommy, Gil and I, with the addition of the dowager countess, adjourned to the drawing room together after our late and exceedingly tasty morning meal. Negotiations started rather well.

"All right, so where do matters stand?" the countess asked.

"We've settled everything regarding property," Tommy said, pulling his contract notes from his portfolio. "Heller maintains her share in the opera company and our buildings in New York, as well as recording rights and such."

Gil nodded. "Holdings in Britain remain in the Leith entail. Shane is, of course, entitled to some kind of jointure or marriage settlement."

"But I don't want or need one," I put in.

His mother smiled. "You should take it in any case. A woman should not sign away even one of her rights. Ever."

Gil nodded to her. "Perhaps she'll listen to you."

I shrugged. "If it matters to you."

"It does."

"All right. So why don't you do whatever is standard for a wife under British law?"

"One-third of the income, then, and naturally any jewelry acquired during the marriage is yours. Pieces that are specifically used by the Duchess of Leith, like the coronet, stay in the entail."

I grinned and held out my wrist. "Do I leave my charm bracelet to the entail?"

"That, you give to our daughter." Gil held my gaze for a moment, reminding us both what was really at stake here.

All proceeding nicely, really.

"Well done, children." The countess beamed. "So what's left?"

Gil and I both tensed. Tommy pulled out the Met contract proposal again.

"Performance schedules," Tommy said. "The Met has offered one production a year."

"Which we all agree is a good idea." I turned to the

countess. "Very prestigious, and logistically easy with all else that will be happening in our lives. We can just sail over and do the production."

"Quite sensible."

"As for large tours in the States," Tommy said, "we have been leaning toward one every other year."

"With the occasional out-of-town engagement in between." Gil nodded. "A full-scale tour is quite an undertaking, but I know you don't want to leave the road entirely."

"You don't have to come for the entire tour, of course," I reminded him.

"I also don't want to be apart for months on end."

"They'll be shorter tours, at least for now," Tommy pointed out. "We've done very well over the years, and the circuit is moving more toward vaudeville, anyway, so we'll just stay with the best venues in the largest cities. San Francisco, Chicago, Philadelphia. Boston too."

"San Francisco is glorious," I assured Gil. "You will want to come for that."

He smiled. "Perhaps a second honeymoon."

"I think I would like to see the Pacific as well, children."

"You are always welcome." I nodded to the countess.

"We will all enjoy San Francisco." Tommy grinned. He, too, loves the Paris of the West. Perhaps Cabot might even come as well, to look into the charity efforts there. "So we find ourselves back to the last remaining issue. How many New York stands in a year, besides the Met?"

"One."

"Two."

Gil and I spoke simultaneously, and our eyes locked, all of the warmth and happiness of planning our future life smashed in one syllable.

For a second, we stared at each other in shock. We had

not spoken of the disagreement since it first came up, but perhaps each of us had expected the other to soften, since everything else had been going so well.

How wrong we were.

"Why can't you understand—" I started.

"Can't you give at least—" he snapped.

"Children, I thought you had settled—"

"We haven't settled anything. If *he's* going to be so stubborn—"

"If *she* can't understand that I have duties and obligations—"

"And I don't?" I stood.

He stood, too. "I did not say that. I believe I am coming a very long way to meet you—"

"Reaching down?"

"I did not say that, either." He threw up his hands. "Why can't you bend a bit on this one thing? I need to be able to return to the estate—"

"I need to be able to maintain my career."

"You are absolutely irrational about this."

"No. *You* are absolutely irrational."

"You're both irrational," Tommy cut in, with a cool and deadly tone. "You are within one fairly minor issue of settling a marriage contract that allows you to be together and still maintain your own lives, which is no small thing in this world, and you're yelling at each other like schoolchildren."

"We are not!"

The unintentional unison just made both Gil and me angrier.

"I have a show to prepare for," I said in a steely tone. "If I'm still allowed to sing, that is."

"That was unworthy," Gil shot back. "I have never suggested you should give up singing."

Of course, he was right, but I was too angry to give him that. "No, just that I cut back my schedule enough that I may have no career left."

"Not fair, either." He held my gaze with a furious intensity. "I am not continuing this foolish argument. We will talk again when you are more rational."

"And when you're less autocratic."

He bowed. "Good day, Miss Shane."

So did I. "Good day, Your Grace."

If I could've managed to get that ring off my finger in time to throw it at him as he turned away, I would have. As it was, all I could do was flounce up the stairs as he marched out of the house.

When I reached the first landing, I heard voices.

"I'll talk to Heller."

"I'll talk to Gilbert." A sigh. "They really are a perfect pair."

"So perfect that they'll kill each other before giving in."

The countess chuckled, a small, musical sparkle. "Well, my friend, it's up to us to prevent that."

And good luck to you, I thought angrily, as I continued my furious progress up the stairs. I did not share the countess's optimism. If her son was really this impossibly stubborn, he was not going to bend, and I was just as well out of being married to him.

Horrible thought. But better to know now that he is not the man I hoped he was than to find out after I was his property. Run while I still can.

Did I really mean that? At that exact moment, it was entirely possible that I did.

As it was, I was more than a little distracted as we prepared for the benefit. If Gil and I could not resolve this, how could we resolve anything else? Surely, it would only be more difficult to manage my career and his obligations as we went on.

I was mostly alone with my thoughts. I took a good long vocalization session with Montezuma, who clearly sensed my unsettled mood, sitting on the piano's music stand and occasionally rubbing his head against mine, offering what reassurance he could. He is truly a dear creature.

The ladies had decided to go to a dinner at the British Consulate that evening, I suspected as much to remove themselves from the battle between Gil and me as to enjoy a visit with their countrymen. Preston phoned just before we left to let us know that he and Greta had returned, and he would see us at the benefit, though she was staying home to unpack.

That was encouraging; perhaps a little of his wise counsel might help. Or at least his warm presence might be soothing. Except that he would be wreathed in newlywed glow . . . something Gil and I might now never see.

Perhaps I didn't need Preston after all.

I was quiet and concentrated on the hansom ride with Tommy and Rosa, and both of them stayed well clear of me, settling into a desultory conversation on the shortcomings of the writing in yellow papers like the *Illustrated News*. As the cab passed the rows of houses and stores on the way uptown, a little stray snow spitting from the darkening iron sky, I wondered if I really *was* being irrational.

If I was, I wasn't the only one. Gil knew exactly what he was getting—that was clear from his inclusion of all three of my names in his proposal. It was surely unfair for him to demand I change now.

And men, of course, are always perfectly fair and sensible.

In any case, I was not going to resolve the matter in my head. Gil and I would have to try again. If we cared to.

No time to think about that now. First, I had to burn at the stake.

At the theater, Marie took one look at me and knew.

"You've had a terrible fight, haven't you?"

"Yes, I think we may break it off—"

She pulled me into her dressing room and practically threw me on the settee, amazing for someone so tiny, and glared at me like a fury. "The hell you will!"

"But he—"

"Are you still arguing about the New York runs?"

"It's about whether I can maintain my career—"

"Are you both really this stupid and stubborn?" Her eyes blazed blue fire. I had never seen her like this.

"Marie, he's not being rational."

"Neither are you."

"But I—"

"Damn it, Ells, do you really want to let the only man for you sail back to England?"

My eyes widened at her profanity, and the heat in her voice.

"You were there the night Paul nearly died. He's the other half of my soul, and at least I would have had my children to console me. What do you have if you send the Barrister away?"

The music. My career. Which was enough a year ago. I stared at her, silent for a moment, because I had no words.

"Half-hour call, Madame de l'Artois!"

The stage manager's knock broke the spell.

"All right. I have to get ready. Talk to your man tonight."

"I don't think he'll come."

"Then you go to him. Tonight, if you can. Don't let this rest."

"You may be right." We had fought to a draw before, after all.

Her sunny smile returned. "Of course I am. Come over

for tea tomorrow, play with the children and tell me how it goes."

"I'd like that."

She patted my arm. "He loves you, silly. It'll all wash out."

I hoped she was right. I almost walked into Teddy Bridgewater on my way back to my dressing room, and he backed away from me like I was on fire. Probably blaming me and Tommy for his mother's arrest.

Perhaps he'd stay away from my dressing room now. One less annoyance, anyhow.

Marie gave a magnificent rendition of "My Sons' Blood Cries Out," Elizabeth Woodville's vengeance aria from the *Princes*, and swept right out for home. I kept busy before my immolation with a few scales, as well as greeting the other singers on the bill and chatting with some of the organizers who filtered back. Anything to avoid thinking of Gil and what a hash I'd made of it all. *We'd* made of it all, thank you.

The night was starting to seem like the longest benefit in recorded history by the time it was my turn to give the grand finale.

It was actually a relief to climb up on my stake at long last, carefully tying the one loose knot of the ropes that appeared to hold me in place. I took my dramatic pose and signaled to the stagehand responsible for lifting the curtain.

It rose to enthusiastic applause, and the opening bars of my music began. But instead of the usual pleasure at performing, my only strong feeling was a desire to have this show successfully over. And no, that was not entirely because of what had happened with Gil.

No matter how good the cause, or how important to broaden the repertoire, I quite simply do not enjoy giving Joan of Arc. Admittedly, a lady in armor seems right in my wheelhouse, but while I admire Joan's bravery, I have little understanding of her fanatical faith and less of her conviction that the angels were speaking to her. Not to mention that ignominious end as a poor innocent tied to a stake in a white dress. Definitely not my style.

When I give Joan, I play her as realizing that there is no way the English will let her live, and very deliberately choosing martyrdom as a last spectacular act of defiance. Makes more sense to me.

That night, though, none of it mattered.

It was only as the opening bars sounded that I remembered Aunt Ellen's warning. "I'm seeing fire, child. No place or explanation. Just fire. And it feels very bad."

Chapter 33

Of Martyrs and Madmen

Even without Aunt Ellen's warning, I should have seen it much sooner. If I had not been distracted by everything that had happened in the last day, I would surely have seen it before I did, and every lost second brought me, and everyone else in that theater, closer to death.

As I sang my opening notes, I smelled it. The absolute last thing you ever want to smell inside a theater. Smoke—real smoke—not that of a cigar or pipe. I kept singing for a few bars, uncertain where it was coming from, and then, as I swept a dramatic glance across the theater, I saw the glow. Probably two yards or so from my feet in the wood piled beneath me, and not from the carefully arranged lights I'd seen at the run-through.

Dear God.

The wood pile Teddy Bridgewater had spent so much time studying yesterday. Teddy, who had been so excessively attached to me. Who reminded Marie's protective husband of a juvenile axe murderer. And who would have had all of the same opportunities to poison Cabot as his mother.

No time to think about that now. Every person in that

theater was in mortal danger. Nothing, nothing in our modern age is more dangerous than fire in a crowded building. I stopped singing immediately.

I had one chance to end this safely.

The orchestra screeched and was silent, the conductor staring at me in confusion as he motioned his musicians to wait.

"Ladies and gentlemen, I'm sorry." I spoke in my coolest and clearest tone. "We appear to have a small problem with the set. Let's all get out of the theater as quickly and calmly as we can."

For an instant, the ushers stared at me in shock, then quickly realized the gravity of the situation as they, too, smelled the smoke and immediately started moving people up the aisles. Below me, I saw the conductor urging orchestra members from the pit, and stagehands starting to fan out into the dress circle and help with the crowd.

As long as I did not say the dreaded word, hopefully people would not panic.

Panic was as deadly as flame.

"Yes, that's right," I called, using my own calm voice to maintain order. "We'll come back to Joan and her stake some other night. Just keep moving quickly now."

Thank God Marie had opened the show and should be safely alighting from her hansom in Brooklyn at this very moment. She had suffered enough.

The smoke was becoming heavier, and I took a moment to subtly clear my throat before continuing my encouraging patter. Only as I saw the crowd starting to move did I begin thinking about my own escape, unknotting my rope and looking around a bit. That was exactly when it became much more difficult.

Flames suddenly shot out from the base of the set piece.

Screams from the audience.

I kept talking, somehow finding a soothing tone. "Just a

pyrotechnic, now, nothing to worry about. Let's just keep moving. . . ."

I tried to remember what I knew of actual burnings at the stake and how long one had before complete conflagration. At least I wasn't tied down—

Shouts from the wings.

"Heller!"

"Shane!"

Gil was here.

No time to think about that, either, but it gladdened my heart.

"All fine," I called. I have no idea how I held my steady and cool tone, even as I looked for an escape. "Let's just keep calm. . . ."

For what seemed like an eternity but was probably just a second or two, I couldn't tell how I was going to get off that stake. The flames on the proscenium side were already so wide and heavy I knew I would not be able to jump over them.

I knew, too, as the screaming from the orchestra and balcony grew ever louder, and the shouts from the wings more anguished, that I had mere moments before everything else—including me—went up, the blaze helped along by the paint and treatments of the set.

"Fire," Aunt Ellen had said. "I'm seeing fire." I might have to give some credence to the second sight.

When—not if—I got out of this.

Joan may have been ready to choose martyrdom, but I surely was not.

As I cast about for an escape route, I decided that trying to jump over the flames was better than waiting for them to consume me. I might make it, which was surely better odds than just standing here. As I studied the fire on the stage side, I saw a small opening.

"Jump, Heller!"

"Now, for God's sake!"

For probably the only time in my life, I followed orders and leapt into the darkness.

I had enough time to wonder what awaited me at the end of the abyss. The smoke was blinding, and hot, and it seemed like I was falling forever, farther and longer than should have been possible. Over the screams and shouts, now, the fire was the loudest sound of all—roaring like some sort of angry mythical beast. I'd never heard anything like it.

Finally, I landed, hard, on the stage, off balance and out of breath.

There was more yelling, indistinct this time, and a pair of hands grabbed the back of my dress. Someone else took my hands and started dragging me away from the flames. Quickly enough, I realized I was between Tommy and Gil, working our way to the stage door.

As long as it had taken to get off that stake, it seemed only to take a blink to reach the outside.

The clean, cold night air hit like a slap across the face, but we all took deep gulps, relieved to be clear of the flames. We were far from the only ones. By then, there was a huge crowd, all milling about in varying states of distress. Patrons in evening dress were closest to the theater, but by the attire and aspect of those farther away, we had clearly become the City's spectacle for the night.

Just under a year since the Windsor Hotel fire. I hoped this night would not end that way.

Some people were just huddling together, others openly crying, still others watching the inferno as if it were part of the evening's entertainment. For some it probably was. Firemen were running in and out, still dragging a few patrons to safety.

They were not, though, trying to stop the blaze, which

appeared to be well out of control. It was an older theater, probably wood-framed, and just went up like a top.

As we reached the far side of the street, we saw Preston and Rosa standing and watching the conflagration. I did not need to ask to know that Preston had been heading back to the dressing room when it started and had brought Rosa right out. We walked up to them, and the lot of us just shook our heads together, too stunned to speak.

Gil put his arm around me, a bit of familiarity that would have been absolutely inappropriate at any other time. I rested my head on his shoulder for an instant, but just then, the first flames shot through the roof, and everyone jumped back.

"Good God," Gil breathed.

"Unbelievable, Heller." Tommy turned to me with a stern glance. "No more Joan of Arc."

"I'm done with stakes," I agreed. "Perhaps just a nice recital next time."

Preston gave me a wry smile. "Well, kid, you can't say you aren't leaving town with a bang."

We shook our heads together, relieved that we'd made it safely through. As terrifying as the raging flames were, as awful a disaster as it no doubt was—still, we were all outside the theater, without a scratch or a burn.

"We're safe, every one of us," I said. "That's all that matters."

"No truer words, *mo chridhe*." Gil pulled me closer again, his arm tightening around my waist, and for just a grace note, he rested his chin on the top of my head.

Propriety be damned, I could have happily stayed in his embrace forever.

I offered another prayer of thanks that Marie was well clear of the horror, and hoped she would not be too worried. We would have to invoke the phone for a few reassuring calls to family and friends.

Once we had soothed down the home crowd, that is; I was sure the ladies would fuss over us back at the house. But if aggressive tending was the worst of the night, we would accept that with thanks. All I wanted was my afghan and a very large sherry. I would be happy to curl up by the fire.

With Gil. I snuggled into his embrace a bit, drawing a kiss in my hair. We could fight it out in the morning. There had to be a way to reach a draw.

After all of this, we would surely find our way home.

Suddenly a ripple in the crowd, and new shouts and screams:

"Get out of the way!"

"He's got a knife!"

"Stop him!"

"Is he crazy?"

The terrified cries were all the warning we had, cutting through the roar of the fire and the murmurs of distress in the crowd. Gil and I pulled apart, and we all turned to see Teddy Bridgewater advancing on us, armed as advertised with a rather impressive knife.

The poison and the fire weren't enough for him.

I should have known.

"She was mine before you got here!" Teddy shouted, going straight for Gil.

Teddy was no nonentity now, his face sickly red in the fire glow, something demonic in his eyes that owed nothing to the conflagration.

I may have been dressed like a lady martyr, but I was still ready to fight like a man. Gil tried to pull me back, but I stepped into Teddy's path and grabbed for the knife with one hand, using the other to land a right cross on his jaw that would have made Tommy proud.

"Go back to your mama!" Not my best line ever, but it would do.

Teddy staggered but kept coming at me. I lost hold of the knife, and I didn't know where it was. For a measure or so, it seemed like I was tangled up with him, as he fought to get through me to Gil . . . and I stood my ground to protect my man.

Then Tommy thumped Teddy on the head, sending him to the pavement, insensible.

I turned back to Gil. "Well, that was an unpleasant surprise."

"Shane . . ." He was staring at me, his eyes wide in absolute horror.

"Oh, come now." I shook my head at him, surprised at this sudden delicacy. "It's not the first time you've seen me fight."

"Kid," Preston cut in with a strange note in his voice, "what happened?"

I followed his eyes to my waist and saw a spreading dark stain on the white dress. At first, I didn't even realize what it was. Without thinking, I touched the fabric, genuinely surprised by the wet, sticky feel of blood. When did Teddy stab me? Surely it should hurt more . . .

"It's not—" I started.

"Go call Dr. Silver," Preston ordered Rosa, in an absolutely cool tone of command. "There's a phone at the pub over there."

"Have her meet us at the house?"

"Right. Take a cab back after you make the call. Go." He gave her a little shove and waved to a nearby copper, who started running our way.

"Be safe, miss," Rosa said, briefly patting my arm as she ran off.

I nodded, some part of me amazed at my calm, though I've never been especially bothered by blood, even my own. It couldn't be very bad, anyway, if I was still standing here.

Probably just a scratch. Seemed like a good bit of blood for a scratch, though.

"Come on." Preston didn't bother waiting for the officer. He nodded to Tommy and then turned to me. "Let's get you home."

"I'm quite—" Still perfectly calm, and really in only a little pain, I started to argue.

Tommy scooped me up as if I were a child, and gave the transfixed Gil a push. "Get that cab, Barrister."

Gil broke out of his shock and flagged down the nearest one, climbing inside and helping pull me into the compartment, with Tommy and Preston climbing in just as the theater roof gave way with a deafening crash.

"Let's go!" Preston pounded on the partition and shouted at the driver, who was staring at the fire. "I'm not having her bleed to death while you watch the show."

"Sorry, sir!"

"Preston! I'm not bleeding to death. It's really not that bad."

"Shut up, kid," Preston said, his calm voice turning a little brittle as he unwound his scarf and looked at the other men. "I know more about this than you do, and a body wound is never a good thing."

Chapter 34

Just a Scratch, But Marry, 'Tis Enough

I wish I were the fainting sort. It would have been far better to daintily slip away and wake up all nicely patched up at home, to join my dear ones in a good laugh about our close escape.

Unfortunately, I remember every moment of that awful ride back to Washington Square. And none of us would ever laugh about that night. Preston took his scarf and the other men's handkerchiefs and used them to stem the bleeding as best he could, apologizing repeatedly for both the immodesty of having to put his hands on my waist and the pain it caused.

He kept saying: "You'll be fine, that's a brave girl, just hang on."

As if there were any question of that.

Whatever reassurance Preston offered, Gil and Tommy echoed it, mostly ineffectually, Tommy constantly reminding me that Preston knew what he was doing, and Gil practically counting the blocks, assuring me that we were almost home.

If I ever hear any of them tell me I'm going to be all right again, it will be too soon.

Despite the frantic, jolting ride, the pain became only a little worse, and the bleeding actually did slow rather quickly, as long as I didn't move. Unfortunately, we learned that the hard way, when Gil attempted to wrap me in his jacket, concerned that I was becoming dangerously chilled.

I knew he was also afraid of the terrible memories the cold would bring. But in all honesty, at that exact moment, I might have chosen my mother's tenement room over the scene in that cab.

As the wound started bleeding again, Preston snapped at Gil to stop trying to help, and Tommy snapped at Preston to be kinder to Gil, and I snapped at all of them to stop fighting. We all knew it wasn't really anger but fear driving all of this.

The physical pain was not the most awful part of that night. It was almost a minor consideration. Worse by far was having to watch my men suffer. Starting with the realization that Preston knew what to do because he'd been a drummer boy at Gettysburg, and this must be calling back those terrible days. Not to mention Gil's painful memories of his wife's deathbed. And most awful of all was the absolute terror in Tommy's eyes.

We could stand losing anyone, Toms and me. We could not stand losing each other.

I had never been so grateful in my life to see the house, and Dr. Silver, who was waiting for us with a small furrow in her brow. More, I was stupidly relieved when she bluntly ordered the men out of my bedroom so she could work.

I did not need to see their faces for a while.

"You are the luckiest person I have ever seen, Ella," she said sternly as she threaded a surgical needle a few minutes later.

"Oh?" Since I suspected what she was about to do with that needle, I didn't feel especially lucky.

"It's just a flesh wound—he got you on the outside of the rib cage. Nasty and bloody, and of course we'll have to stitch it up and keep it clean, but nothing serious." She looked up at me over the glasses she wore for reading—and, I now understood, fine work. "Another inch to the right and he'd have hit a lot of important real estate. That's why Mr. Dare is so worried. You might have lost your voice, or even your life."

I took a sharp breath and bit my lip as she painted the slash with more iodine, sending a white-hot burn through the whole center of my body, leaving me gasping as she poured another splash of alcohol on the needle and thread. How had I thought that the pain wasn't very bad?

"This is going to hurt something awful, but as long as it doesn't get infected, you'll be fine. And I'll give you some laudanum after so you can sleep off the worst."

"Thanks." I supposed the laudanum would not take effect before she got to work, anyway, and there was some reason she wanted me conscious for this.

Doctor and mind reader. "Since you lost a good bit of blood, I'd rather have you with me until I'm done so I can see that you're reacting normally."

"All right."

She managed a tight smile. "It's nothing compared to childbed."

"But you end up with a baby," I said through gritted teeth.

The doctor favored me with a small, knowing glance before she moved in with her needle. "Think of it as training."

"Right."

It was indeed awful, but over fairly quickly. Dr. Silver bandaged me up and handed me a little dose glass of laudanum.

"See? All done. You're a very good patient." Her face

relaxed into a genuine smile. "You'll be just fine. I'll check on you late tomorrow—you'll probably sleep 'til then, and I'll warn the boys. We don't want them to worry too much."

"Thank you."

"I wouldn't mind if they were a bit more protective of you." The doctor's smile faded. "I don't want to do this again, Ella. Please be more careful."

"I will."

"Good. Now drink up."

I'd never been sick or hurt enough to need laudanum before, and as Preston would say, it knocked me for a loop. I spent the night and most of the next day somewhere far from my usual sensible self.

What I have from that time is scraps of moments with everyone from my parents to Madame Lentini, to Joan of Arc, to my nearby family and friends. Some of it was real, and some of it was not, and I would never be entirely sure of the difference.

Just as I don't believe in Aunt Ellen's second sight, but I do believe that the brain can pick up things our science cannot yet understand, I cannot entirely discount the idea that there was some reality to my laudanum visions. Perhaps I don't want to believe I imagined all of it.

Logically, there was no way I could have been sitting in a warm, comfortable parlor with my parents, who seemed younger than me, and very happy together. Mama, who was in a pretty cornflower-blue dress like something Marie would wear, had lost her grayish bony look, replaced by a glow in her face that turned into a blush when my father smiled at her. Frank O'Shaughnessy looked remarkably like a redheaded Tommy, but with a wicked grin like Cousin Rafe's. And the same loving and protective gaze I'd come to prize from Tommy and Preston, only more so.

They hugged me, told me they loved me and looked me

over, then decided that I'd turned out rather well. After that, though, they lectured me sternly for scaring them and told me I would soon know how they had felt because I was going to have a couple of beautiful babies with my man. My father said, with just the grudging smile of every Irish da, "Your man's all right for a Briton."

Then I told Mama I didn't remember saying "I love you" that last night, and she told me she knew I did, and all three of us cried. After that, more hugs, before they started bickering cheerfully about how long they should let me stay, finally telling me I'd best go back now. I can tell myself that it was just the laudanum, but it felt real, and who's to say it wasn't?

Tommy and Father Michael were undoubtedly there, but I had no idea why they would have been arguing. It wasn't one of their amiable play fights. It was real and it was ugly. Tommy was angry and hurt, and the priest was trying to calm him down, telling him to forgive someone. Father Michael kept saying, "It's not his fault," but I couldn't figure out who.

Soon enough, it was back to the fanciful. Madame Lentini swept in, a whirlwind of towering fury and regal draperies, reading me the riot act in at least three, and possibly four, different languages. When she finally settled down into English, she folded her arms and scowled at me, reminding me that fighting is bad for the instrument, and stabbing worse. Warming to her topic, she snapped that she hadn't spent all that time training me to have me get myself killed playing the hero.

That's when I started crying, and of course, in classic colorful diva fashion, she burst into tears, too. Finally, she hugged me and told me that she would have done exactly the same thing for her manager and beloved, Mr. Fritzel. And shouldn't I just marry that poor duke already?

Joan of Arc took a much dimmer view of my behavior.

She stomped in, full armor clanking away, sword in hand, and coldly informed me that I was an absolute idiot to climb up on a stake without being forced to do so. And by the way, no matter how good a man is, he's not worth giving up your sword. Never mind dying for.

Preston might well have held my hand and glared down at me in quiet fury, saying with a complete lack of logic: "If you die, I'll kill you."

I know Gil was there. I'm fairly sure he stayed holding my hand for a long time, his thumb rubbing his mother's ring as if it were some kind of talisman. Whether he actually said, right out in the open court of the sickroom, that he loved me and could not endure losing me, I do not know. I doubt it, because I really was not that seriously hurt.

It sounds like I spent most of the time flitting from fancy to fancy, but there was really a lot of thick black nothing. At times, I remember trying to fight my way out of a fog, back to my life and my world, and losing strength before I reached the surface.

In the end, the fancies stopped, and the fog won, and it was almost a relief to fall into the deep, dark quiet.

Chapter 35

Sorting the Ashes

When I finally came back to myself, it wasn't a fight at all. I just woke up, a little sluggish, but otherwise like any normal morning at Washington Square.

It was quickly clear to me that it was neither normal nor morning. The oil lamps were going, and the fire strong, and I was not alone. Tommy was on one side of the bed, sprawled over a chair and snoring. Even asleep, he looked tired and troubled, deep shadows under his eyes, his hands formed into fists as if he were still ready to jump to my aid.

On my other side, Gil was also asleep, in a chair pulled close enough that he could hold my hand, fingers even now lightly twined with mine.

I took a deep breath and stretched a little, pleased to discover that while the wound still hurt a good bit, my body felt remarkably like it normally did. The movement was enough to wake Gil, who startled and turned.

"Shane."

For a second, we stared at each other. Whatever had been wrong before was gone, and all that was left was us. *Bashert*.

"Gil." My voice was thin and rusty, but recognizable.

"Thank God." He bent down and kissed my forehead. As he leaned close, I realized how tired he looked and how uncharacteristically disheveled, with mussed hair and open collar. As appealing as ever, though, despite the shadows under his eyes. "Shane, I—"

"Heller?" Tommy woke then and glared at me. "Don't you ever scare me like that again."

"It's not that bad." I moved a bit more, and my waist definitely did hurt, but not terribly.

"Bad enough." Gil shook his head. "The doctor had to stitch up the wound."

"And give you laudanum," Tommy added, with his own hard look. "You've been sleeping like the dead for most of a day."

From the set of both their jaws I knew the comparison was both deliberate and telling. Tommy wanted me to know how scared they'd been.

"She's awake?" Another vaguely familiar voice cut in.

The countess. I saw her now in the far corner of the room.

"Yes, Mother," Gil said wearily.

"Good. I told you she would be just fine." She, at least, looked like her normal self, smiling happily at me. "I'm sure she wants to straighten herself up a bit. And you should do the same, *mo laochain*. Perhaps even sleep for a while now that we know dear Ella is all right."

Gil's jaw tightened.

"Your mother is right," I told him, squeezing his hand. "You're both exhausted."

"If you insist."

"I do." I looked to Tommy, who nodded. His face was sharp and gray with fatigue, too, despite the relieved smile he couldn't quite hide.

"Come along, Barrister." He stood and patted Gil's arm. "Let's get something to eat and a bit of rest."

"Thank you, Toms." I held his hand—and gaze—for a second before he moved off.

"Go back to sleep, Heller, it's the best thing for you."

Gil pulled my other hand to his lips. "I love you."

"I love you."

"And that's all you need to say for now, children."

The countess gave that musical chuckle as she shooed the boys out. "Dear Thomas is right, of course, but if you'd like to change into fresh nightclothes first . . ."

I blushed. I was not going to let my soon-to-be mother-in-law dress me. "If you could call for Rosa?"

She nodded. "Nothing wrong with a little modesty, dear. I was the same way before I had my babies."

My blush deepened as she rang the bell. I did not need to think about babies just now. Especially after what my parents had said in that dream. If I was going to take the consolation that my mother knew I loved her, I also had to take the prediction of two beautiful babies. I was not certain I was ready to think that far forward.

The mind does do very strange things, after all.

But Aunt Ellen was right about fire.

As the countess turned away from the bell, she bent down and kissed my cheek. "Later, I am going to thank you extravagantly for saving my son, and lecture you extensively on your recklessness."

"Oh . . ." I knew I could not stand that at the moment.

"Don't worry. That can wait. Right now, just tell me one thing, dear. You two are going to settle this silly dispute over the contract?"

"Absolutely." I could not remember what had been so insanely important about three New York runs versus two. All that really mattered was that I keep singing, and Gil had promised he would not stand in the way of that.

"Excellent." She beamed at me, Gil's exact bad-child grin, as Rosa rushed in.

"Miss! You're awake!"

"Yes." I plucked at my crumpled nightgown. "Could you help me neaten up a bit?"

"Surely. I'm so glad you're all right."

"I'll leave you to it, dear." The countess kissed me on the cheek again and swept out, her eyes still sparkling.

Though not all that badly hurt, I was weak and wobbly, and it took far more time and energy than I'd ever imagined possible for the simple act of replacing one nightgown with another. Rosa, good dresser that she is, picked out a prettier one, with some very nice lace at the sleeves and neck, and added a little lilac-colored bed jacket. She also neatened my hair, which had been trying to escape the braid, tying it with a lavender ribbon, and handed me the tin of rose petal lip salve. "Just because your lips look a bit dry."

I added a swipe, surprised at how much I appreciated the floral scent. I wondered if I was going to be taking extra pleasure in many ordinary things in the wake of my brush with danger.

"Very pretty, miss," Rosa finally said with a smile, giving the bow on the bed jacket a little tweak.

"Thank you." As I gratefully, and gingerly, lay back against my pillows, I doubted I was anything resembling pretty, but I was certainly less of a mess than I'd been, and that would have to do. By then, I was ready to go back to sleep again, but there was a knock at the door, and Preston just barreled in.

"They said you were awake, kid."

He was dressed with his usual dapper care, but there

were deep shadows under his eyes. In one hand, he had a bouquet, much too large and showy to be anything he would bring, but I didn't care about flowers right now.

I nodded. "I'm all right."

"You came too damn close to not being all right," he said with a stern glare, sitting down on the chair Gil had occupied.

I smiled and reached for his free hand.

He squeezed my fingers. "If that knife had gone an inch to the right . . ."

"But it didn't. The laudanum was worse than the wound."

His eyes sharpened on mine. "You were reckless."

I just nodded, not agreeing with him, but letting him speak. He was wrong, and he knew it; when it happened, when Teddy lunged at Gil, there was nothing else I could have done. Except let him attack Gil. Not a possibility.

Preston's angry scowl didn't match his words: "We love you, kid. We didn't want to bury you."

His voice wobbled a little on the last two words, and I rubbed his hand. "I'm here."

"Good thing," he said after a moment. "You ever make me use my battlefield medicine again, I'll wring your neck."

"That's fair."

After a moment, the hard look faded a bit. "Good thing you're grounded for a while. You've got a bunch of messes to fix."

"What messes?"

"Let's start with these." He handed over the bouquet, a sizeable spray of large white roses tied with a blue ribbon. White roses usually mean innocent love or something in that direction, but there was nothing innocent about the card.

I am sorry I failed to protect you. You are safe now.

No signature, of course, and no need for any explanation of that second sentence. Connor.

Dear God.

"It's that gangster, isn't it? I saw how he looked at you last year." Preston shook his head. "The Bridgewater lawyers are already packing Teddy away to an expensive looney bin upstate. Even a Five Points kingpin probably can't reach him there."

"Probably." I couldn't stop the wobble in my voice. The last thing I wanted was a death on my behalf—even Teddy's.

"Well, kid, it's nothing we don't all want to do after what happened. But Connor Coughlan can, and maybe we let him."

I stared at him in shock.

"That crazy boy could have killed you—and hundreds of people in that theater. I don't have you and your duke's moral problems with hanging. Some men deserve it."

"But—"

"Leave Coughlan to his work. There's something to be said for having someone that bad on your side."

"True enough."

"Worry about what's happening in your own house first."

"Oh?" I did not like the sound of that.

"Well, Tom swears he won't speak to Cabot Bridgewater anymore because he blames him for not seeing how dangerous Teddy had become."

"I can fix that." That was fairly easy. I would ask him to make peace for my sake, and he would.

"And the Barrister's absolutely crushed. Were you still arguing about the marriage contract?"

"Yes."

"Is it really that important?" He gave me a searching look. "He loves you, he's willing to let you keep singing and spend part of the year here, how much more can you ask of a man?"

"Maybe I was asking too much." Lying there, slowly returning to awareness, I could not believe I had really been so close to sending Gil away over the question of one additional New York stand in a given year. "It doesn't matter now."

"Good. Don't let it matter." Preston patted my hand. "You're dropping off again, and the boys are probably already asleep. Talk to him when you wake again. Everything will make more sense then."

Again, I found myself staring dully at him, surprised that he knew how awful I felt.

"Laudanum's bad business, even when you have to have it, kid." He shrugged. "Couple months as an orderly in a battlefield hospital before they mustered me out. You're very glad for Dr. Silver, clean hands, and disinfectant."

"Speaking of which," said the doctor herself as she walked in, "I hear my patient is once again with us."

"No more laudanum," Preston told her with a sharp scowl.

"Of course not." She briskly brushed off the concern. "Now she just needs to rest and heal."

"Do what your doc tells you." Preston nodded to her as he stood.

"Of course." We shared a smile as he kissed my forehead, like the dear uncle he really is.

Dr. Silver took no time at all to check the wound, and once I was settled again, she gave me an approving nod. "Healing beautifully. Now you just keep it clean and you'll be fine, except for a scar no one will see."

I nodded. "No stays for a while."

"That's nothing to complain about. I suppose your

dresser will see the scar." She gave me a significant glance. "And perhaps one other person. . . ."

"I hope so."

"Now, *that* is good news." Her aspect moved from the polite and professional to the genuinely happy. "When you are healed, you should come see me about the things married women need to know."

"I suppose." Despite my weakened state, I felt a horrid blush creeping over my face.

"Dear, if your family is anything like the rest of the Lower East Side Irish, I can't in good conscience allow you to marry without a very frank talk."

"Probably so."

She nodded and patted my hand. "It'll wait till you get closer to the wedding. But you will get the information you need to be safe and happy."

"Thank you." I did not have the energy to contemplate that conversation at the moment. Or anything else, I realized as I drifted away again.

Chapter 36

In Which Preston Is Right: Love Always Wins

My sleep was normal, if heavy and mercifully dreamless. When I woke, it was still nighttime, and Tommy was sitting in his chair again, and Rosa reading by the fire. It must have been a good book.

Any book at all would have been far preferable to the fury in Tommy's eyes.

"Heller, if you ever step in front of a knife again, I'll kill you."

"Kill you!" Montezuma, perched on the bookshelf behind Toms, adding his own contribution.

"Fair enough."

"The three of us would have—"

I just looked at him. He knew as well as I did that this was a pointless conversation. "I'm fine, Toms. Let it go."

"As long as you give me your word that you will not be reckless again."

I wasn't reckless, of course, but it was the least I could do for him. "All right."

"Good." He held my gaze for a couple of measures before his voice came rough with emotion. "It's one thing to give you away at the altar, Heller, it's another entirely to watch them put you in the ground."

I took his hand then and dropped my gaze to our fingers twined together, so he wouldn't see me cry. Of course a couple of tears spilled over and fell on our hands, giving me away.

"Please don't cry, Heller. I can't stand that."

"I know." I took a breath. "I'm sorry I scared you all."

"Just don't do it again."

I nodded, acknowledging, not agreeing. I had promised not to be reckless, but I would not, and could not, promise not to risk my life for those I love.

"Love the birdie!"

Tommy and I laughed and took a few moments to pet and soothe Montezuma, who finally flitted over to sit on the back of Rosa's chair. He probably wasn't reading her book, but one can't ignore the possibility.

"All right. Now why don't I go get the Barrister so you two can make it up?"

"In a minute. Are you going to make up with Cabot?"

"What did Preston tell you?"

"Just that you're not speaking because of Teddy. You know that's completely illogical."

Tommy let out an irritated sigh. "Cabot is a very good friend. But he should have seen—"

"He could have died, too, for goodness' sakes." In the wake of the previous night's events, it did not take a course in criminology to realize that Teddy had been responsible for all of it, from the cut ladder to the attempt with the motor car—and, of course, the poisoning and leaving the arsenic in his mother's potting shed. Unnatural son, that one. "Teddy's been trying for a while, Toms."

"The ladder and the step . . ."

"The motor in Brooklyn." He nodded.

The motor that almost mowed down Gil and Alteiss,

too, I was certain. Teddy must have been the man Mack and Katie saw lurking outside the house. He was unremarkable enough that they wouldn't remember him. Didn't have much personality at all.

That made me think of something Tommy had told me—the one time Teddy had shown any flash of humor. "The salt at the Lincoln Dinner. It wasn't just salt."

Tommy stared at me for a moment, but then agreed. "You're right. He slipped arsenic in the shaker. That's why he was laughing as he passed it."

"Exactly. He figured he'd kill you all."

"We all did get sick."

"You less because you used less salt, but the other two used more and got sicker, right?"

"Right." He sat there for a moment, arms folded across his chest, eyes burning with fury. "That crazy little wretch. Right in front of all of us."

"*All* of us. Cabot was Teddy's first victim, Toms. Don't blame him."

"I know he's suffered, Heller, but he was the only one who could have figured out that it was Teddy. And because he missed it—you . . ."

"I'm going to be just fine. So is Cabot. Can't we all just thank God and be happy?"

"He was in the same house. He should have seen it."

"Right. Because we always know everything happening around us. For example, the fact that the three dear older ladies living under our roof had very coolly stabbed a man to death."

"That's different. Cabot put you in danger. I don't know that I can forgive that."

"Not deliberately. That should matter." I patted his hand. "Talk to him. See if you can still be friends."

Tommy's face softened a little as he shrugged.

"If only because I asked you to?"

He shook his head. "I hate when you do that."

"Why do you think I do it?"

We smiled together. At least all was right with us.

"Please tell me everyone's not downstairs, worrying," I said, knowing when to claim victory and move on.

"Mother's called practically every hour. I'm not sure why I ever thought she needed a phone. She, Kat and Suze will be over in the morning. Marie and Hetty were at least willing to wait for afternoon tea."

I sighed. I was clearly going to have a very busy social calendar despite my injury. "I suppose Dr. Silver will let me put on my wrapper and entertain on the chaise."

"And we'll make sure you move no further for a while."

"All right." I had no need or desire to fight Irish male protectiveness at the moment. In fact, I found it rather soothing. "Is all else well?"

"The countess and her sisters have been surprisingly useful, cataloging floral tributes, scaring off excess reporters and accepting calls of concern from just about every society matron in the City."

"Why, for heaven's sake?"

"You're a bit of a hero, you know. Nobody died in that fire because you started them for the egress. And, of course, the society types figure you're about to have some happy—and very prestigious—news."

"Right. Happy news."

"And you damn well are." His eyes held mine, loving and serious. "If you don't know by now that nothing is more important than being with the people you love, I can't help you."

"You're right."

"Of course I am." He grinned and kissed my forehead.

"Don't let it go to your head."

"Not even a little." Tommy chuckled as he stood.

"Right, then. You, young lady, need to sort things out with your Barrister."

"I do." Perhaps it was the aftereffects of the laudanum, or the disaster we'd just survived, but I could not remember why I had fought so hard for that extra New York run. I wondered if I had really been fighting the change in my happy and settled life.

Marie knew that was exactly what it was, and she had tried to tell me.

For months now, I had been afraid of what Gil and marriage would do to the home and world Tommy and I had built. Worried what Gil would do once I was in his power, perhaps, even with that contract. Promises and papers were all well and good, but in the end, I would still have to trust him to honor them.

An almost impossible leap of faith for a woman used to freedom and relying on herself, in a world where most men had no scruples about using the power that law and society gave them over their women.

Most frightening of all, though, were my feelings for him. I'd never been in love before, after all, never even thought that I would trouble with such messy things, and I was shocked by how much I wanted and needed him, and absolutely terrified by what that might lead me to do. Men often worry what women may do to them with their wiles, but I had nursed an entirely reasonable fear about what Gil might do with his.

Of course, none of my fretting mattered now. I had not realized until Teddy came at us with the knife that there were much more serious things to fear. Marie was right about that, too.

I would give up the second New York run and take Gil, and consider myself lucky. So incredibly lucky.

"I'll go get him." Tommy pulled his handkerchief from his pocket. "Here. You may need a surrender flag."

I threw it at him. "Draw, yes. Surrender, never."

"Surrender!" Montezuma crowed, as he flitted over to Tommy's hand.

"Not you too."

I'm reasonably sure they were both laughing as he walked out.

A few seconds later, Gil knocked on the door and walked in. Rosa looked up at him but quickly returned to her sensational romance. Dukes in books are far more interesting than real ones, after all.

This particular duke looked considerably better—freshly shaven, a clean shirt. But the dusky shadows under his eyes were still deep and his expression uncertain.

"Gil."

His face eased a little as our eyes held. "Feeling better?"

"Much."

"Good." He put a sheaf of papers on the nightstand and sat down beside me. I noticed the papers but cared much more about his eyes burning into mine and the gravelly note in his voice when he spoke. "I suppose I should thank you for my life. . . ."

"You would have done the same for me." I took his hand.

"But you—" His voice caught and he took a breath, his fingers tightening around mine. "I don't need a woman fighting for me. Or worse."

"I'll never fight for you again," I offered. "Alongside you, perhaps . . ."

A trace of a smile played at the corner of his mouth and he pulled my hand to his lips. "I love you, Shane."

"I love you." I squeezed his hand.

For a moment, we just gazed at each other. Safe and together . . . but now what?

Then he said it: "I was wrong and I'm sorry."

Father Michael's marital cure-all. Only one possible reply: "I was wrong, too, and *I'm* sorry."

His fingers tightened around mine. "And I won't leave your side if I can help it. Singing or no."

"I hope I can sing again soon." Only after the words were out did I realize it was probably precisely the worst thing I could say just then.

"You will." He gave me a reassuring smile, but his face clouded almost immediately.

Perhaps better just to jump in now. I started to speak, but he cut me off.

"About that. I had a fair amount of time to contemplate just now."

"One extra New York run is fine," I said quickly.

He shook his head with a sheepish little smile, picking up the papers on the nightstand and handing them to me. "I already signed for two."

"How?"

"I asked Tom and Alteiss to put it together from the notes of our last discussion."

"You did?"

Gil shrugged. "We were all grateful to have something to do while waiting for you to wake."

I nodded and looked at the document. It was indeed our marriage contract, with the Met production, plus two more New York runs a year, and his signature at the bottom. "Are you sure?"

"As sure as I am of air, or water or gravity." He took a breath, gave me a wry little smile. "Whither thou goest, *mo chridhe*."

My eyes filled. I couldn't speak.

"My eldest son can run the estate betweentimes. He'll have it all one day anyhow. I want to be with you."

I took a breath, managed to find a voice. "I want to be your wife. I can't stop singing, but—"

"I would never ask you to."

"I know. And I'm sorry I fought so hard over something so small."

"Not small to you. So not small to me." He picked up the little lap desk from my vanity and handed me the pen. "Sign it as it is."

I signed my name next to his.

Gil put the desk back on the vanity and sat there holding the contract for a moment. "So our engagement is now official."

"Yes."

He took my hand and ran his thumb over his mother's ring as he'd done while watching over me. So that part was real. "I will replace this with something more glittery if you like."

"No need. This is the ring you put on my finger."

Gil smiled and once again pulled my hand to his lips. "That will please Mother."

I glanced over to Rosa, who hadn't even looked up from her book, then gave my fiancé an encouraging grin. "Perhaps we should enjoy our first official kiss?"

"Is it quite safe?"

I leaned toward him. "Let's find out."

It was not, objectively, much of a kiss, considering exhaustion and injury and caution. But it was surely enough to seal the engagement and remind us that the attraction between us had survived all. And yet.

I sensed a new and concerning reserve from Gil as, far too soon, he slowly pulled away from me. I lay carefully back on my pillows, searching his face for some explanation.

He let go one of my hands and toyed with a curl that had come loose from my braid, his eyes holding mine with an adoring intensity I hadn't seen before. Perhaps I was imagining the excess of caution. Or perhaps he was just being careful of my injury.

"So when shall we marry?" he asked.

"Father Michael's been about." I was only half-teasing. Even with a signed contract, we probably couldn't make a legal marriage in a sickroom at night, but a good part of my soul wanted to settle this, to belong to each other formally and forever right now.

Gil smiled a little as he traced the line of my face. "*Mo chridhe*, I'd marry you right now, too. But I want to stand up with you in front of the world and make our vows."

As, of course, did I. He would know how much that meant to a Lower East Side girl made good. "Yes."

"That said, now that we've signed the contract, we're something more than engaged, if less than married."

"We are?"

His smile widened a fraction. "The ceremony is merely the acknowledgment and blessing of the legal agreement. Of course one would never take advantage of that fact, but it's a fact nonetheless."

"Thank you, Barrister." I was relieved to see his wicked grin and met it with my own. "Always good to know the facts in evidence."

Gil ran his fingers over mine. "In any case, I suppose it's unreasonable to organize a proper wedding before the London run, since we have only a few weeks and you'll be busy getting back into form."

"There's no time to put together a real wedding, with a white dress and orange blossoms and such, but—"

"You deserve nothing less, sweetheart." He thought for a moment, then shook his head with a wry chuckle. "Then it looks as if we're forced into the classical happy ending, the June wedding."

I shook my head. "Not especially original."

"But it will do nicely. We'll marry here?"

Once again, I was close to tears. "You would?"

"Of course I will. The bride has a right to be married from her own home."

"Then yes, here. In the parlor, probably."

"Now, children, you really must resolve matters." Countess Flora burst into the room, not even bothering to knock.

We turned to her as one.

"We have, Mother," Gil said, as I put a calming hand on his arm.

"A June wedding," I added.

She clapped her hands. "Oh, how lovely! Here?"

"Yes."

The countess beamed like a happy cupid. "Delightful. Now, my dears, we have much to do. . . ."

Gil and I exchanged glances, realizing that we were no longer in charge of our destiny.

Epilogue

When the Princes Come to London

As smashing a success as we had been in New York, so too were the Princes in London. A significant amount of the interest no doubt stemmed from the fact that one of the leading ladies was also the betrothed of the Duke of Leith. Much ink was spilt before we ever took the stage that first night, everything from silly fairy tales about the Lower East Side Cinderella in the yellow sheets to a stiff-necked jeremiad about what the world must be coming to if a duke feels the need to actually marry a singer in one of the fusty Tory dailies.

The company and friends quite properly ignored all of it and concentrated on the show, which was every drop as good as the New York production. Perhaps better, since most of the cast and crew had been working together so long, and we were all so close as colleagues and friends now. After the curtain, we received congratulations from a much smaller and more carefully screened group of well-wishers than would have been welcome before the disaster at the children's hospital benefit.

Had there been any stage-door Lotharios about, they

would have been firmly banned, with Gil exercising the prerogative I'd happily granted. But there *were* a goodly number of society matrons who felt the need to come back and have a look at—and down on—me and appeared to leave quite disappointed after I offered polite and cultured conversation instead of the gin-soaked profanities they no doubt expected.

On the good side of the ledger, the dowager countess and her sisters and a few of their friends came by, and Tommy and I quickly realized, much to our amusement, that she'd informed the excellent ladies that I am Jewish, but not Irish as well. They assumed the same of Toms (Was the name originally Hurwitz, dear?), and we had a truly hilarious and entirely well-intentioned discussion of religious and cultural differences while the countess turned pinker with every passing second.

She, of course, was terrified that we would be offended, but we understood that it was her misguided effort to present us in the best possible light, and we laughed it off.

Other family members were not in evidence: Gil's sister was of course in Australia, where her Foreign Office husband was posted. She had sent a friendly and welcoming letter, and I looked forward to meeting her, whenever she next returned from the Antipodes. As for his sons, the younger was still on his Grand Tour and had sent a note making clear that his absence meant no slight—but the elder was on the estate in the North and very pointedly made no offer to come down.

Disappointing perhaps, but not surprising. There would be a certain number of people who would share that Tory newspaper's opinions about our marriage. I had hoped any son of Gil's would at least meet me before judging me, but apparently not *that* one.

No judgment and indeed a warm welcome from another quarter: Uncle James and Sir Ralph were planning an appearance in the second week, and I was very much looking forward to it.

At any rate, our London first night ended much as any other, with flowers and visitors and glowing reviews. The only difference came just before the end of the evening, when Gil and I had a brief moment alone in my dressing room while Tommy called the hansom and Rosa slipped out to flirt with a charming Cornish stagehand.

It was still a new and delicious pleasure to be an officially engaged couple, with all the public approval and private privileges that implied. Not that we'd had time to take much advantage of the privileges, since he'd come to London a few weeks ahead of me, and I'd been busy recovering and rehearsing.

Gil helped me into my coat, running his hands lightly down my arms to lace fingers with mine. "A sensation as always, Shane."

"The reviews should be good, I think."

"And your review of the London audience?"

"I have no complaints."

For a measure or more, we simply stood there watching each other. Since the theater fire, there had been a strange little step of distance between us at private moments. He was as loving and kind and solicitous as always, and of course absolutely determined to marry me in June. But there was an undeniable and worrisome reserve in his embrace.

"Excellent."

I considered, for one insane moment, simply throwing myself into his arms and forcing the issue. Surely he was not going to treat me like a piece of china in the vitrine forever. But finally, I just got on tiptoe and gave him a very light kiss, drawing the now-usual restrained response. "Good night, my love."

"Good night, *mo chridhe*."

And for the rest, we would have to figure it out as man and wife in New York. I hoped.